Bang

ADDICTED TO YOU
BOOK TWO

LYDIA MICHAELS

EDITED BY
TRUDY L. KOZAK

Dedication

For Trudy

Listen to the Addicted to You Playlist!
Click Here to Listen!

One

Cord

CORD AWOKE AND STRETCHED, reaching out for the warm body that had been beside him during the night, his thoughts—and unrepentant dick—focused on having her once more before starting the day. *December.*

Her taste still lingering on his lips, the corners of his mouth pulled into a smile. It was as if his entire life had just begun, his heart fuller than ever before. He reached for her, stretching a greedy hand across sheets drenched in her delicious scent, ignoring the cold tingle of guilt.

When he came up empty, he blinked his eyes open and took inventory of his surroundings. His little escape artist was already up and moving, but he'd lure her back. The fireplace was going and the scent of coffee filled the house.

He flopped onto his back, his body languid and sated from a strenuous night. His blood thickened, and his cock elongated, as his aching hunger for her stirred once more.

Shoving away any untoward thoughts that threatened to encroach on this beautiful morning, he cleared his throat and called out, "Where'd you go?"

She was such a morning person. He thought she was grumpy before coffee, but turned out, December was an up and at 'em sort of girl. Once that coffee started brewing she never stopped. He liked that about her, loved her indomitable spirit hidden behind all her sweet submissive softness. Her living in his house and working beside him at the store exposed sides of her he treasured.

His mind, determined to prick his happy bubble, imagined what she looked like in her own house. Making coffee for Austin.

Austin.

Too many emotions to combat before his brain was fully awake and while his body still held the scent of his best friend's wife. How was he going to tell Austin?

December proclaimed she wanted *him*. She'd come to him willingly, released from her marriage —and all implied obligations—by her husband.

Her body sang under his touch and he'd pleasured her last night with no time for regrets.

It was more than desperation for human contact between them. He knew there was something deeper going on, whether or not she was prepared to face it. As far as *his* feelings, they were solid—a brick fucking wall that would surely protect against his sense of betrayal of his friendship with Austin.

Don't think about that now. You did as he asked. Begged him not to put this on you.

But you took what you wanted anyway, didn't you, you greedy bastard?

Fuck. His conscience was not his friend right now.

Cord had intended to take it slow with December, avoid Austin's asinine wishes despite his own growing desires. Lord knew he was well practiced at denying his lust. But by no means was he backing away from the responsibility—no, the *honor*—of taking care of a woman like December. He intended to be the friend she needed, a comfort to her emotionally neglected heart. But then, last night...

He sighed, letting his head sink back into the pillows enveloped in her soft scent. Who was he kidding? He tried his best to resist the temptation, when paradise had been offered. But when that temptation was standing naked in front of him, begging to be touched, his will was as breakable as glass.

There was no going back now. What they'd shared wasn't a one-off. All his pent up need and love for her had poured through his touch. And he knew she'd felt it, too.

He didn't want her feeling guilt or regret. Austin had been the one to suggest this path, after all. Cord cautioned him about the consequences, but his warnings had fallen on deaf ears. Why should either he or December stress over what they'd shared? What was done was done and they had only the future consequences. The future and Austin.

You can think about him later.

"Ember?"

He was tired and too lazy to get up just yet. He'd persuade her back to bed and snuggle her for a while. They didn't have to rush. Sometimes a day full of stolen kisses, meaningful glances, and secret smiles made for the best foreplay.

He was down with teasing her with gentle touches and suggestive glances that turned her skin pink. Actually, he found the idea of knocking her off balance sort of arousing, the anticipation building while he helped customers and she managed the register at the store all day.

He'd never dated an employee or lived with anyone. Too much expectation and messy aftermath. The old Cord avoided lovers outside of the bedroom, but not with Ember. She was different. He'd waited a long time for her, his dream come true—mostly.

Where the hell was she? "Hey, kiddo, what are you doing out there?"

Silence.

Cord frowned. Shutting his eyes he listened closely. No television rumbles, but December wasn't much of a couch potato. And other than occasional music, he didn't think she required background noise. The other day she'd stayed pretty quiet, allowing him to sleep while she prepared breakfast. She was sweet like that.

He didn't smell bacon or eggs or even pancakes. Just the aroma of the fireplace mixing with freshly brewed coffee. Maybe she was gathering wood.

"December?"

A sense of disquiet slowly flooded him. Rising from the bed, he found his pants folded neatly on the dresser—*so thoughtful*. When he used the bathroom, the sink was wet, but spotless. He walked past her room and noted her bed was made. She was a tidy person without a doubt.

"Ember?"

He entered the den and saw the fire could use another log. A mug sat by the coffee pot, waiting for him, but no December. Then he spotted the paper folded on the kitchen table, his name scribbled across the front, and his stomach locked.

Worry twisted sharply in his gut, but he forced the anxiety back. Maybe she ran out to get something she needed for breakfast. That was likely it. His lips twitched as he tried to smile at the thought, but his grin fell short.

The throb of his heart blocked out all other sound as he reached for the note. He cautiously unfolded the note.

Cord,

I'm sorry. I can't. Please forgive me.
~December

His nostrils flared as his fist closed around the small sheet of paper. A sense of betrayal assaulted him, cut short by every acknowledged instinct warning him this sort of outcome was inevitable. She went back to *him*. Her fucking husband who treated her like shit and would rather drown in his own self-pity than face his devoted wife and address the needs he'd neglected.

His knees buckled and his ass landed in a vacant chair as he stared stupidly at the blank walls of his empty fucking home. This was exactly what *he* deserved. She was exactly where she belonged.

His jaw locked as his mind unleashed a barrage

of *I told you so* insults on his once honorable heart. Fuck *him* for playing into this whacked plan. Fuck Austin for dangling something no man could resist in front of Cord's face. But most of all... Fuck, he couldn't blame December for any of it, because he'd known it would come to this in the end. It was his own damn fault for even thinking anything would change after one night together.

"Fuck me." His arms folded on the table as his shoulders collapsed.

She loved Austin. She'd *always* loved Austin. And he couldn't blame her, because despite his friend's recent struggles, Austin was an amazing guy. Cord knew that better than anyone.

"Fuck!" He shoved back from the table and threw the crumpled note at the wall.

Adrenaline spiked as he paced in the small kitchen. "Goddamn it!"

His hand shot out and shoved a chair, sending it toppling on its side. Here he was, exactly where he knew he'd be. Alone.

Grinding his molars until his jaw popped, he glared at the ceiling. Too many contradicting emotions raced through him to catalogue a single one. He laughed gruffly and without humor.

A vivid image of his friend flashed in his mind, an arrogant, self-satisfied glint in Austin's eyes as December fell back into his arms.

"Well, you got what you wanted, asshole." He shook his head, certain whatever friendship they shared had been tested and lost at the gamble they'd taken.

"She wants you. Check all your fucking reservations about *that* off your list."

He marched back to his room and slammed the door, needing some time alone before he could face what would likely be one shitty fucking day. Throwing himself face down on the rumpled bed, now tortured by Ember's scent, he made a monumental effort to rein in his rage.

Breathing through his careening emotions, he sat upright, wincing. How would Austin react when Ember went home? And told him? Or confronted him? Whatever shit storm blew up, she shouldn't have to face it on her own.

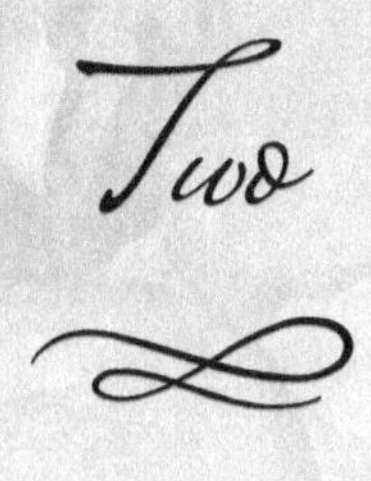

Austin

THE TREMORS WERE GETTING WORSE. Austin had lurched, crawled, and stumbled his way from one end of his house to the other, but December wasn't there. He thought she was, his mind playing tricks on him, shimmers of her standing in his peripheral in that cute little dress she wore the day he'd met her drawing him from one room to the next.

Collapsing on the carpet, he caught his breath, giving his screaming muscles a break. She was taunting him. Rage and frustration had him breathing hard through his nose. Slowly, his volatile emotions weakened into hopeless self-hate.

Weak. He was so fucking weak.

His head was swimming, his pores sweating out his poor choices as his gut rolled with an agonizing sense of disquiet. There was no undoing what he had done.

His vision jerked, tormented by only a shadow of light and the hope that she'd returned. Another fucking mistake.

At first he thought it was really her, come back to save him. But then he tried to see her bare feet and every time he focused too hard on the flickering image she disappeared.

His mind jerked, randomly pulling in a different direction as a nerve twitched under his eye and he shivered. "Pull it together, you fuck."

Licking the sweat off his upper lip, he tried to stand and gave up, already losing interest. He was so fucked. She was gone and she was never coming back. Why would she?

The mere thought of her being gone forever sent his heart thrumming into rapid vibrations that staggered his breath. His hand pressed into his chest. "Fuck!"

Grasping for calm, he breathed through the vise crushing his ribs, crawled to the bed, and collapsed. The cramping—no, fuck cramps—this was death. Even lifting his goddamn arm was too much work, so he lay there and sweated, letting his heart pound itself down and then sweating some more. All the while his brain shit on everything he was and tried to be.

Anxiety clawed at him, so deep it seemed to scrape at his bones. He was too tired to go to the sink and drink. Nothing would stay down anyway. No appetite. No strength. His body trembled hard enough to shake his organs, but he needed to win this fucking war, needed his demons to stand the fuck down. And as his brain sloshed from one random, delusional thought to the next, he was completely aware that the battle he was fighting was against himself.

He could drink. Ease some of the pain. If he wasn't afraid he'd die from being upright, he'd have gone to the liquor store hours ago. What time *was* it?

No. Fuck that. He shoved the doubt away, his mind desperately seeking out any hint of hope. But the lack of trust—in himself—was a brutal enemy to face down. He was a worthless piece of shit and wanted nothing more than to prove to everyone he could be a success again. So tired of feeling hopeless. So tired of proving them right each and every fucking time he failed. Whoever they were. Not December. She believed he could get through this, didn't she?

Maybe. Maybe not anymore. *She's gone...*

He rolled to his side and looked for his phone. Shit. He'd left it in the living room. Or maybe in the kitchen. Downstairs was too far. His gaze traveled to the alarm clock perched on the nightstand beside their bed, but it was facing the wrong direction. His vision seemed out of focus anyway.

It felt like days since he'd woken up, but he wasn't certain. It was either incredibly dreary out or still fairly early in the morning judging by the bleak haze outside the window.

No wonder some people didn't make it through the first few hours of detox. But only alcoholics detoxed. Normal people just put down their beer. Fuck. Reality dropped on him like an anvil and he was too damn weak to save himself from the assault.

"You're sick, Austin." The words whispered in his ear, so soft and subtle he wasn't sure if they were spoken at all.

He turned his head toward the ghostly voice, his vision wavering as one headache layered on top of another, delivering agonizing spikes of pain to his temples. She sounded so far away, but she was standing right there.

"Ember?" Calm took hold of him as he breathed through the churning of his stomach. The skin on his back rippled with shivers. He was so cold.

"You need help, Austin."

She was beautiful in her little dress, bare shoulders showing under the thin straps and her breasts teasing at the low cut neckline. "I know."

"Call someone."

"I can't... I left my phone downstairs."

"We can go get it. Together. I'll go with you."

She was always there with him when he needed her. He pushed himself up and caught his breath as he leaned against the wall. Progress. "I'm—"

Frowning, he looked around the room. She was gone. Shit. The hallucinations were getting worse.

His head tipped back, contact with the wall delivering a painful thud to the back of his skull. "Fuck."

He should know better. It was freezing outside and yet, every time he imagined her, she was in a summer dress. But the visions seemed so real. And why the hell would she be there anyhow after he'd chased her away, broken countless promises, and shoved her into the arms of his best friend?

His face contorted as the severity of his stupidity slammed into him like an ax. He couldn't go there right now. Couldn't.

The crunch of snow under tires caught his ears and childlike panic set in. His heart kicked against his ribs as he listened, fearful anyone might see him in this state. Eyes wide, he breathed heavily as the clear sound of a car door slamming drifted from just outside.

No one could see him like this.

Sliding closer to the bedroom door, he quietly locked it and leaned his dead weight against the wood. His ears strained to track any sound, but all he could hear was his rapid breathing and the echo of his pounding heart reverberating in his skull.

Under his breath, he pleaded, "Go away."

The click of the front door locked up his throat. A cold sweat gathered on his already clammy skin as feet shuffled through his house.

Go away...

Footsteps made slow progress as whoever it was searched his home. Maybe they'd assume no one was there and leave. His fingers curled into the fibers of carpet under his sweaty palms as he pressed his weight into the door.

The slow thud of boots grew louder as the intruder took the stairs. His chest tightened. The familiar creak of the top step sent shards of ice splintering through his veins and his breathing stopped, a deathly silence stealing the air from his lungs.

"Austin?"

Ember.

Maybe it was just another hallucination. It sounded different from the others. The other times she'd sounded ghost-like. Her breathing hadn't been audible, nor had her clothing rustled. Now, there was something uncertain in her tone, something too raw to be a dream.

Her steps approached the other side of the door and he continued to hold his breath as a tiny scratch sounded on the other side.

"Austin, are you in there?"

Her voice was low, the way it usually sounded after she cried. He couldn't face her. Where the fuck was Cord? He'd told him to keep her away. It was Cord's job to spare her from any more heartache.

That used to be your job.

He was suddenly panting, his shallow lungs stretching painfully with each swallow of air. She deserved better and he'd done what he had to do to see she found better—away from him. No more maltreatment by a drunken asshole. Although he was stone fucking sober now, which did shit for making him more stable.

The knob jiggled. "Austin, please open the door."

His eyes shut, he remained silent.

"I know you're in there."

Fearing she'd find the skeleton key for the house, he did what he had to do and begged, "Please go away, Ember."

A long silence held them suspended in time as he anxiously awaited the sound of her retreating steps. No matter how much he wanted her to help him through this, he couldn't make her suffer another minute of the mess he'd let spill into their once happy life. Best she go.

Muffled by the door, the unmistakable press of fabric slipped lower down the hard surface. He imagined her dropping to the carpet and mimicking his position on the other side of the door. Except she'd have her head tilted the way she did when focused on him, her long hair spilling around her beautiful face.

"I need to talk to you, Austin."

He waited. She could talk, but he was only capable of listening at this point. Speaking required thinking and if he thought too much the pain overtook him and he couldn't deal. He waited for her to continue, worried she might have left without him knowing, as his mind jerked about like a pinball in an ever-churning maze.

He was so confused. His skin was damp and hot in some places, cold in others. Maybe he had the flu.

The slow drag of fingers beneath the door crack sent a dry reverberation up the wood. "Touch me, Austin, so I know you're there."

Blinking the sweat out of his eyes, he glanced down and struggled to focus his vision. Three little fingertips peeked out from under the door. Something about touching those fingers seemed so daunting and finite. Business was often concluded with a handshake. Was that what this was? *Their* conclusion?

He didn't want to touch her if that were the case. This was far from over. He just needed more time. He'd get there.

Yet, the idea of her leaving and him missing the chance to feel her one last time would haunt him forever. No longer driven by courage, he allowed the fear of losing her to take hold. His motive was desperate and pathetic, but he couldn't turn down the chance to feel the warmth of her skin one last time.

His hand dragged along the carpet and slowly reached for those little fingers. Fingertips could be so sensitive. His calloused thumb buffered the first caress, but then her soft tips brushed over his digits and tickled every microscopic groove. Air choked him as he gasped roughly on what seemed dangerously close to a sob.

"December," he wheezed, as two fingers curled against his as best they could with the hard barrier of the door between them.

"I'm furious with you, Austin."

"I'm sorry." He was losing it. He wasn't one to cry, but left alone to his own devices, that threshold was quickly crumbling.

"You crossed a line."

Which one? He crossed so many it was amazing anyone could keep count. He wanted to ask her what happened with Cord, but he was too much of a coward. Fear had never controlled him like this, but recently it was all he knew.

He used to be an admirable man, courageous, and brave. Sometimes he tried *too* hard, took on the persona of an even better man, but part of him believed in that guy too. Now he was sitting on their floor, crying, afraid of his own shadow.

"I came to say goodbye."

Her words cut through him, slicing open the wall of pain so efficiently a new agony bloomed, spreading aggressively like a lethal cancer. His heart bled for her, for him, for Cord, for all he'd destroyed. There were no words powerful enough to reverse his actions, no promise worth trusting when he'd shown her how untrustworthy he truly was.

She needed to go, before he started spewing bullshit he was too weak to back up. Sucking in a deep breath, he forced the words out. "He'll take care of you, Ember. The way I hoped to. I did the right thing. I just want you to be happy."

Her words didn't come immediately, but when they did he wasn't certain of their implication. "I don't need someone to take care of me. I need you to get better. That's all I want. The rest... it's too late now."

If he got better, would she come back? Was it too late because of Cord? Was she walking away for good? Picking *Cord*? Maybe nothing happened. Maybe she was back and planned to stay, but telling him—

"I wrote you a letter. I'll leave it for you."

Her hand withdrew, severing that fragile connection, like air pulled from the lungs of a drowning man.

"Ember—" A cough crippled the last syllable of her name.

As the sharp corner of an envelope came into view, he shut his eyes, unable to face the paper sword that would cut him down to nothing—destroy everything he lived for. The note slid over the carpet, catching on each little thread as she gave it a delivering push.

They'd chosen this carpet together. That should mean something. Their deep connection deserved more than a letter, but that was all he'd offered her...

"I love you, Austin. Always. Never forget that."

Fabric again slithered over the wooden panels and his head lifted, his stare tracking the sound. She was leaving? The room got suddenly colder. The stair creaked and her steps retreated. *Fuck, fuck, fuck!*

Too weak and fearful to go after her, he transferred his gaze to the envelope, stark and mocking him, with his name scribbled across the front.

In the distance a car door opened and shut, and an engine hummed to life. She *was* leaving. He panted, anxiety crowding him like a strangling fist he was powerless to escape.

He should stop her. He should go after her, but he couldn't move. Weak. That's what he was, weak. No, he was strong. It was the fight to do right by her—finally—that depleted his strength.

She was wrong. The best thing he could do for her was let her go—for now—until he got better

—*if* he got better. She needed someone to take care of her and that man was Cord. Right now, he wasn't even a man.

Fuck, he couldn't bear the fucking uncertainty. The sound of her car backing down the drive filled his soul with a hollow ache. His chest shook as raw sobs ripped from his throat, belying his tumultuous thoughts. Brave, weak, courageous, afraid. The truth was, without her he was nothing. Just...nothing.

Time passed and he shut his eyes, waiting for some sense of purpose to return. Drifting on what seemed an eternal sea of pain, when he opened them again the sky wasn't as dull. He grabbed for the letter, resenting its heaviness yet finding it too light at the same time, tearing it open.

> Austin,
>
> If reading this will make you want to drink, please put it away until you're stronger.
>
> I haven't always been a trusting person, and you are perhaps the most challenging person I've ever put my faith in. But every word from your mouth, every opinion, mirrored my own and I trusted you.
>
> You earned every bit of my trust by

proving to be a man of great determination and kindness. Perhaps it's because my trust was so hard earned that it became the most fundamental part of who we were. You were always dependable. I never believed you could be anything else.

We had a beautiful life. Our love is one for storybooks, filled with secret promises, and wild romance. You made me believe I was strong enough to be the woman I wanted to be and have the life I so desired—with you. It wasn't about the money that funded our dreams, but about the love and encouragement we steadily provided one another. Our home was made of love. That love and trust was the foundation of everything we created together.

I knew you were changing and I couldn't accept it. Perhaps I should have been more patient, more understanding. I thought we could overcome any obstacle, but I was wrong.

When I read your letter, I experienced an agony too great to put into words. My hurt over the past year had been slowly chipping away at every absolute I'd come to depend on. Whatever was left turned into dust, your letter delivering the last blow my battered heart could take.

You see, you are strong, but I'm not. The person I was, the woman you married, I think she died. I don't know what's happening to me. I can't think straight and I'm so confused. You thought you were doing the right thing, but you asked me for something unspeakable.

I did what you asked.

It solved nothing, but I think it broke me once and for all—broke us. It made me feel something I have no right to feel.

Your best intentions and my capitulation have broken something sacred, done something that can never be reversed. Do you feel better now that I can take the blame for destroying our marriage?

I want to hate myself for what I've done. I've destroyed not only my marriage, *but a lifelong friendship between you and Cord, between me and Cord. Everything is ruined.*

What's done is done. I can't undo the past any more than you can. I never thought a life like ours was possible until you showed me it could be, and now it's over. I wish I had been thinking more clearly last night, but I wasn't. I don't think I'll ever think clearly again.

Call Cord. He's your friend and he loves you to a fault. He'll get you through this. You need someone strong by your side. Sadly, that isn't me.

But I will always love you,
Ember

He struggled to comprehend the disjointed sentences, breathe through the roar of denial building in his chest. The throbbing in his head on top of the sour stench of whatever liquid he'd sucked back after Cord left...whenever the fuck that was... There were no pieces of clarity shaking around in his rattled brain, but so much had happened since. So much.

It wasn't any use. All he could do was feel—feel and accept he'd fucked up monumentally and driven—*given*—away the best thing in his life. Her pain eclipsed his and he crushed the note against his chest in a futile effort to soothe her.

"Ember. Please. I'm so fucking sorry. Please."

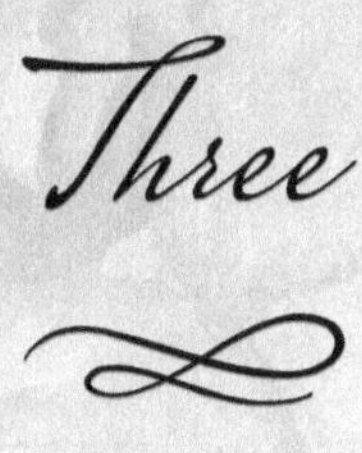

Three

Cord

CORD SPED up the drive over what appeared to be fresh tire tracks and prayed she was there. When the house came into view his worry doubled. Austin's truck still sat beside the house, but December's Jeep wasn't anywhere in sight.

He had to find her, but first he had to find his balls and walk into that house. Traces, clues as to where she might have gone could be on the other side of the door. She was bound to be upset and he didn't want her driving around in the snow with nowhere to go.

And fuck...if Austin hurt her again... No. He couldn't go there. Breathing raggedly, he forced himself to move before his mind spun into a nightmare of assumptions.

He rushed out of his truck, hoping Austin knew where she was—or was at least sober enough to help him find her. They had to make her see there was a way to fix this even if it meant him bowing out.

Fuck that. His good intentions wavered. He wasn't bowing out.

The door was unlocked, a good thing, because he didn't have the patience to grab the hidden key.

"Austin?"

He stilled and listened. The house was too quiet. When he heard the rattle of something upstairs he took the steps two at a time. "Austin?"

He checked every empty room as he stalked down the hall. The door to the master bedroom was locked. "Austin." He pounded on the wood and jiggled the handle. "Open the door, Austin."

More noise came from inside. The distinct sound of him shuffling—no, banging—around. Something heavy hit a wall. A moan. What the hell was he doing in there? "Open the fucking door or I'm breaking it down."

Something substantial hit the other side and Cord jerked back, frowning. He didn't have time for this. How much could a man handle at once? He needed to find December. She could have stayed with him. He would have given her her own space if she didn't want to...be with him.

Regret surged, making him nauseous. The blame no longer belonged solely to Austin. This was his fault too. He never should've touched her. They shouldn't have done something irreversible when he knew—fucking knew—she wasn't thinking clearly, despite her pleading that she wanted it. Wanted him.

"Austin, open the goddamn door! I'm counting to three."

He waited, praying for patience. Rage replaced regret, focused on the man on the other side of the door.

He jerked the knob. "One." He waited. "Two. I'm not kidding. I'll break it down." Silence. *Fuck.* "Three."

When nothing happened he stepped back, ground his molars, and kicked at the knob. The door shook, but didn't budge. *Fucking old houses.* He kicked again and the lock splintered as the trim snapped. *Third kick's the charm.* He aimed his boot at the crack and the door burst open.

"Austin?"

The room was a disaster. The blankets were ripped off the bed and the frame of the broken mirror lay on the floor.

Cord stepped over papers scattered along the carpet and headed toward the bathroom where he could hear Austin shuffling around. Cord shook his head in disgust, seeing him huddled over the sink, gulping water from the faucet.

"Didn't you hear me knocking? I broke your fucking door."

Something dropped by Austin's bare feet and skittered across the tile floor. Tilting his head, Cord waited for whatever it was to stop rolling. The object stilled and he realized it was a pill bottle.

"Shit!" Cord shoved Austin away from the sink just as he shoved a fistful of pills in his mouth and went for another mouthful of water.

Cord plowed into him. Their bodies dropped to the tile with a hard thud and Austin's shoulder slammed into the tub making a hollow, resonating whack that amplified Cord's fear. They struggled as he grabbed his friend's jaw, the skin clammy and cold.

"Get the fuck off!" Austin garbled, shoving Cord's hands away from his face.

Cord slapped him roughly, knocking a few pills loose. Austin sealed his mouth shut. Cord tried to pry it open, working his thumb into the corner of his lips, as Austin snarled behind his teeth.

Frantically glancing around the room as they wrestled, struggling to block Austin's aggressive hands, Cord's foot shot out. The nondescript plastic bottle soundlessly rolled with the impact of an avalanche. His gut fell a mile as he registered it was completely empty.

How much time did they have? He needed to call 9-1-1. "Spit them out!"

"Fuck you!" Saliva bubbled, awash with flecks of white.

He couldn't lose him. Dear God, he couldn't. Not both of them. "Goddamn it, Austin!"

Cord grabbed his face again, slapping the damp flesh repeatedly as his friend sealed his lips shut. "Goddamn you!" His fingers shook as they pried Austin's mouth open, scraping over his tongue and teeth, pulling out whatever he could reach before the pills went down and dissolved. *"Do you want to fucking die?"*

A punch landed on his ear and a sharp hum whistled through his brain as he lost his grip and Austin went sprawling across the floor.

Fear raced through him along with a million flashbacks of their friendship. Such potential, such a great man, and such hopelessness. His heart shredded as nearly three decades rolled through his mind in the blink of an eye.

Him and Austin scheming against the class bully. Riding their bikes—no hands. Sneaking out to see a concert on a school night. Discovering girls as girls. Taking their first, underage drink together. Fuck. He couldn't lose him.

Crawling over him, Cord gripped his best friend's jaw and pinched his nose, taking charge and all Austin's choices away.

"Fuck off," Austin choked, as Cord's knuckles scraped along his teeth. A fist lodged into his side.

Heaving his friend's weight off the floor, he thrust his fingers deep. Fuck, he'd swallowed them. He wedged his fingers over his tongue, pressing against the spongy tissue. Teeth cut into his skin as he jammed two digits down Austin's gagging throat. With Austin's struggling body up against the tub, he leaned in hard to keep him still, using the angle to put pressure under his ribs. Cord's desperation and determination to see his friend live overwhelmed Austin's waning strength.

Retching sounds filled the room as Austin choked and jerked.

"Puke, damn you." Removing his hand so Austin could pull in a breath, he waited as he coughed in some air, then again jammed his fingers down his throat. "You don't get to die. I won't let you do that to her—or me—you fucking coward. Now, puke!"

With one final shove of Cord's fingers, Austin's face flushed red and his shoulders locked. Yanking his hand back, Cord turned his friend's body over the edge of the tub as he vomited violently. A stinking, liquid mess erupted into the tub, littered with intact—and partially dissolved— little white capsules. Austin moaned and heaved.

"Do it again," Cord commanded, as his friend shook forcefully and spat.

"Get. Out." Austin's gruff voice was ravaged, as though he'd swallowed a thousand razor blades.

"You don't get a say." Cord wrestled him back from the tub, holding his friend in a near choke-hold, and gagged him again.

Struggling, Austin's flailing hands scratched down Cord's face, and then instinct kicked in, Austin's reflexes taking over in order to expel every toxin from his system. He collapsed over the edge of the tub, gasping, and emptied whatever was left in his stomach.

Cord panted as he waited for the spastic vomiting to end, trying not to breathe in the stench. He'd never heard someone throw up so viciously. When it seemed to be over, Austin dry heaving and dripping with sweat, his skin pasty white, Austin collapsed. The fight was out of him and he weakly deflated over the porcelain wall of the tub.

Cord was ready to collapse as well, but needed to get his best friend to a hospital. Who knew what else he'd done to himself? Any hope of finding December vanished as he came to terms with taking care of Austin first.

Reaching in his pocket, his hands shook violently as he pulled out his phone and dialed 9-1-1. "I need an ambulance." He rattled off their address and gave a quick explanation of what just happened. And then he waited.

So many words plowed through his mind. *Why? How could you? Don't you love her? Us?*

What would we do without you? But he bit the words back as they both panted through the stretching silence.

Five minutes later sirens blared in the distance. Austin's body sagged, a mockery of the man he once was. He sputtered through soughing breaths and groaned feebly, resting his cheek on the porcelain. Defeated. He looked so damn defeated.

Cord shifted from the wall and rose on shaky legs. Easing Austin's limp body to the tile floor, taking care that his mouth was unobstructed, he turned on the bath faucet, flushing away the remnants of his best friend's attempted suicide. Methodically, he collected a bottle of over the counter pain reliever, stuffed it in his pocket, and flushed a few dropped pills down the sink as he washed his hands.

The wail of sirens grew closer. "We have to go downstairs. You're going to the hospital."

"Fuck. You." Austin's words were weak, but laced with venom.

Yeah, he hated himself too. Everything he'd felt a few hours ago disintegrated in the light of how badly he'd fucked up—how badly they *all* fucked up.

Vehicles chugged up the long drive. He glanced out the window. A police cruiser followed the paramedic's van. "Come on. They're here."

"I'm not moving. Tell them to go."

Cord looked at the medicine cabinet. Making

a quick decision, he swiped all the products from the shelves into the improvised apron of his shirt and carried them to the bedroom. Opening a drawer, void of contents, he dumped his findings where Austin hopefully wouldn't see and went to let the specialists inside.

The officer and paramedics followed him upstairs as he spoke and he led them to the bathroom. Austin hadn't moved. They crowded into the master bath and one paramedic opened up a first aid bag.

Scrambled words came from the walkie-talkie on the police officer's jacket as the cop mumbled something that Cord didn't catch. Austin stared listlessly into space, ignoring every question thrown his way.

A female medic kneeled alongside Austin's legs. "Sir, can you tell me your name?"

Austin remained mute.

"His name's Austin Garret," Cord supplied.

"Mr. Garret, do you mind if I take your pulse and blood pressure?" When he didn't voice an objection, the medic obviously took that as consent. She checked Austin's vitals and asked, "Can you tell me what you took?" Nothing. "Why did you try to hurt yourself, Mr. Garret?"

Austin showed no interest in getting help or communicating. The medic glanced at him. "You're the person who called?"

"Yes. I'm his friend." *Was.* "I got here maybe twenty minutes ago."

"What's your name?"

"Cordovan Bay."

"Do you know what your friend took and how much, Mr. Bay?"

Cord removed the bottle from his pocket and the officer took it, reading the label off to the medic as she continued taking Austin's vitals. "How long ago do you think he took it?"

Cord shifted uncomfortably, shoving back the strange sense of guilt as if these people could detect the role he'd played in his friend's desperate misery. Imagined blame or not, he couldn't shake the sense this was his fault.

"He was still trying to take them when I walked in. I broke down the door, wrestled him over the tub, and tried to get him to spit them out."

"So you made him vomit?"

By the smell in the room it should've been obvious. "Yes."

"And did the stomach contents contain pills?"

"Yes, but I'm not sure everything came back up."

Say it. He tried to kill himself. He wanted to fucking die.

The medic removed the contraption she was using to check Austin's blood pressure. "Mr. Garret, we're going to take you to the hospital now. Can you come with me to the ambulance?"

Austin didn't move so Cord stepped forward. "Austin. Come on, buddy, it's time to take a ride."

The officer moved closer. "Mr. Garret, it will make life easier for everyone if you could willingly come with us. There's procedure to follow in cases such as yours and I don't want to have to cuff you."

Austin's jaw, shadowed with hair beneath a sheen of sweat, twitched. His head rotated slowly as his eyes narrowed a hateful stare in Cord's direction.

Fine. Whatever. He could take it. Austin could direct all his rage at him if that made this easier. He was going to the fucking hospital.

Four

Cord

THE ENFORCED seventy-two hour observation period for psychiatric evaluation was a blessing. It gave Cord a chance to process what had happened and formulate a plan.

Once Austin was secure and safe, under the watchful eye of the hospital staff, Cord returned to his friend's house. He'd called December numerous times, left her several messages, each one voicing his concern for her wellbeing, but never mentioning what Austin had done. She never picked up and never called back...

Pretending to be her husband, he'd called the surrounding hospitals, setting his mind at ease when she wasn't listed as a patient. And then he didn't know where else to look. He consoled himself with the fact the authorities would come to the house if anything bad happened to her, though the very thought had him cramping up with terror. No, she'd simply put distance between them.

He knew she had a little money, and prayed she'd found an okay place to hole up, because it was still fucking cold. Ember was resourceful, and she'd figure it out. He had to believe that—for the next while.

Tidying the bedroom, he found her letter to Austin on the floor. It wasn't his to read, but they were all in this together. Lost together. Too many emotions were stirred by her words of regret. She loved Austin. She loved him in a way she could never love Cord and why wouldn't she? She was Austin's wife after all, and Cord was just a friend. A friend who'd crossed a line.

Her feelings were obviously a mess, splattered all over the crumpled pages, but her regret was clear. It hurt. And things were only going to get worse. His part in all of this contributed to Austin's attempt to die. When Ember discovered how close they'd come to losing Austin, she'd hate Cord for sure.

Everything was fucked. He'd been weak to agree with his best friend's wishes—and too selfish. A part of him greedily treasured the memory of December in his arms, so he couldn't muster the remorse a decent man might suffer. But he did regret the consequences. He needed to make amends, with Ember and with Austin.

The first day Austin was in the hospital, Cord cleaned the house. It was obscene how many bottles of alcohol still existed, hidden in places he wondered if his friend would recall hiding them. Could it be they had been deliberately overlooked the last time he vowed to get sober? The tank of the toilet, the washer, the tool shed. Denial had let things go this far—too far. And they all were guilty of denying how deep in the shit Austin really was. All of them.

On the second day, Cord contacted his parents. He'd already given them a watered down and highly edited version of what was going on, and they volunteered to take care of the store for a bit. It gave him the freedom to plan.

He'd researched methods of dealing with alcoholism and found the entire search disappointing. There were as many posts praising Alcoholics Anonymous as there were discrediting it, tales of success and failure. But Cord couldn't decipher the variables that made the program work for one and not another. Perhaps the program was the crutch and the success depended on the person embarking on the long journey.

Austin had once been the most determined man he knew. Now... He wasn't sure how to describe him. Maybe that determination would work against him, if he was intent on not giving up the booze—intent on dying.

He didn't know what to believe and only wanted to offer his friend the most helpful solutions. He bought books on the subject and pored over them, searching for an answer. But there were no guarantees. These were only tools. The solution lay with Austin. If he didn't want this, Cord was certain it would never happen. And where did that leave everyone?

One thing was for sure, Austin had a long journey ahead and Cord would be lying if he said he was certain Austin could recover. His friend was hurting and wasn't the same person he'd once been. Their easy friendship was no more, and not only because of what had transpired with December.

December. His mind snagged on her name every few minutes, a constant distraction and debate of which friend was in more desperate need. Definitely Austin. He had to keep telling himself that so he didn't abandon his friend to go find her like he badly wanted.

She was still out of touch and he was torn with worry pulling him in two different directions, which seemed to be driving all of them further and further apart by the second. Rubbing his palms against his eye sockets, he increased the pressure as if it would somehow force out his stress. He was only one person!

In the last twenty-four hours of Austin's confinement, Cord made a decision. He moved some personal belongings into Austin and December's spare bedroom and set up camp for a long winter stay. He would get Austin through this. His friend needed someone who wouldn't back down when he yelled, someone who wouldn't fear him if he lashed out.

As far as family went, Austin was fucked. Since his mom passed, Austin's dad became even more useless than before—if that was possible. Plus, with the way his father drank, he wouldn't be the sort to bring around Austin right now. Not to mention one minute with Mr. Garret always landed Austin in a shit mood. But he had Cord, who would do everything in his power to save his friend. He owed him that much—now more than ever.

Cord had one last thing to do. Driving back to his house he taped a note to the door. Leaving his house open for her seemed too little too late, but it was the most he could offer at the moment. He hid a key and drove where he was needed most. As he idled outside of the hospital, he called her again.

"Hey, kiddo... I'm not going to be home for a while. I'm keeping an eye on Austin and doing my best to get him better. I, uh, just wanted to let you know my house is empty and if you need a place to stay, you can go there. It's yours. I won't bother you and you can stay as long as you like. The spare key's hidden behind the woodpile. Please... go there if you don't have anywhere else. I'll fix this, Ember."

His mouth tightened. That might be a lie. "I'm doing my best to fix this. Call me if you need *anything.*" He ended the call and stared at the phone until the screen went black. "I love you."

Heading in to get Austin from the hospital felt like the start of a scary journey with no end in sight. Austin wore the clothes Cord had brought him, the material hanging loosely on his frame. Shaven, his friend's face was markedly pale, his eyes showing as dark smudges above gaunt cheekbones. Even Austin's hair looked defeated, lying flat against his scalp.

The paperwork already done, all it took was a signature and Austin was free to leave. The heavy door locked behind them and Austin shuffled along beside him, silent, his stare on the floor. In the truck, Cord didn't offer small talk, figuring everything that needed saying would eventually be said.

When he pulled up at Austin's house, he handed over the keys and his friend climbed out without a word, dragging his ass up the steps to enter his home. Cord followed, hesitant to predict what would go down.

Austin stilled in the foyer and Cord gave him a minute to process. There were no telltale signs of Cord's presence in the house. His personal belongings were all tucked out of sight, but he didn't doubt Austin could sense something had changed, maybe the smell of bleach replacing the scent of dust.

"Was she here?" he asked.

Cord's heart pinched at the depleted hope in his friend's voice. It killed him too. "No. Sorry, man."

Austin's hands remained in his pockets as he faced the staircase. "Have you talked to her?"

"No. I've called, but she's not answering. She doesn't know...what happened."

"Good."

Austin's foot lifted to the first step and Cord announced, "I'm moving in with you for a while. Go take a shower and I'll make something to eat. Then we'll talk."

It had to happen. Enough dancing around the issues. But he braced, holding his breath, for Austin to lash out.

Austin merely nodded, levering his weight on the first step as if a million mile trek was ahead of him. "Good."

Cord expelled a relieved breath. Finally, some common ground they could agree on.

When he disappeared at the top of the second floor, Cord went to the kitchen and dumped a few cans of beef stew in a pot. He stared at the mixture with resignation—he wasn't a cook.

His nerves were shot, frayed to nothing. When the water upstairs shut off, his anxiety grew. Austin would likely see the safe upstairs where Cord had moved all the medications. Any firearms his friend owned were now locked in the gun cabinet at Cord's house. He'd been on the lookout for sharp objects and such, but there was only so much a man could do.

Ladling out two large bowls of stew, he set a loaf of bread in the middle of the table, then took a seat as he heard Austin coming down the steps. His friend kept his gaze averted, but maintained an unshakable presence. It gave Cord hope.

Austin had always been an incredibly strong-willed guy, always in control of himself and those around him. Cord liked that a hint of that arrogance simmered beneath the surface even now.

They ate in silence. Cord continuously drew in breath to say something, but his words fled before they took form. Austin was the first to break the silence.

"Thanks."

Cord swallowed the last bite and pushed his bowl aside. "You're welcome, though I'm not sure what you're thanking me for."

"You know."

He didn't. He hoped Austin would do the same for him if he was in the same boat. More importantly, he'd slept with December—Austin's *wife*. It didn't matter that his buddy had pretty much orchestrated it. Cord wasn't a puppet to dangle on someone else's string. In any event, there was no call for gratitude. He wouldn't blame Austin if he knocked his teeth out, though he might punch him back.

Sighing, he said, "I picked up some things at the bookstore." Reaching to the counter he grabbed *The Big Book* and slid it in front of Austin.

His friend laughed derisively. "Alcoholics Anonymous."

"I've read it. There's some good stuff in there." Austin didn't move to touch the book so Cord went on. "You need this."

"A book won't get her back."

Cord wasn't sure if that was true. "You need to do this for yourself, Austin. Get control of your life again and then we can worry about putting it back together."

His eyes closed and Cord waited as his friend worked through whatever torture he was facing on the inside. Austin cleared his throat. "It's getting easier. I no longer feel like my insides are shutting down and I've finally stopped sweating."

"Good."

"Not really. If you gave me a drink right now I'd take it. I'd do it all over again because I don't know how to stop myself and the craving's consuming me. My keys are already in my pocket because no matter how much I know I can't, and tell myself not to, part of me still plans on ditching you and walking out that door to go find what I need."

"Give me the keys."

"No."

"Austin."

His stare lifted and narrowed, slicing through their tentative banter and delivering a jab of unwanted challenge. "You think you can stop me if I make up my mind?"

No, he didn't think that, but he was also tired of being the fucking enemy. "I'm here to help you, Austin."

His smile twisted into an insincere sneer that told Cord he'd rather spit in his face than take his help at the moment. "I have to be in control. I have to make the decision not to leave. You can't do it for me. No one can. I know that much."

The tension in the room was climbing and he needed to drop it back down to the polite place it was a second ago if they were going to even tolerate each other for the next few weeks.

"How about this? We hang the keys up and they're there for you if you want to be weak. But so long as we both see them there I'll know that you're still strong." He let that sink in for a beat. "Hang up the keys."

Austin didn't give up the keys, but he did

flip open the book. "You think reading a *book* will help me?" His tone was laced with skepticism.

"I think there's a valid program there and if you approach it with the right attitude, with the same determination and the need for perfection that's driven you for the past twenty-nine years. I think you stand a chance of beating this."

"Those meetings are for losers."

"How would you classify yourself at the moment? Think about the last fight you had, with December." Austin blanched and Cord hurt for him, but he pushed on. "I've seen you tear into other men for disrespecting their women only a fraction of the way you've disrespected her. That's not you."

"No shit. It's the *new* me," he said with disparaging accuracy.

"No, it's not. Those meetings may have their fair share of losers, but they've also turned people who've lost everything into winners. It takes dedication to try something like that, real courage. That's not being a loser, Austin. That's the exact opposite of losing. You've already lost. Might as well try to win it all back. What more have you got to lose?"

Austin sneered. "Certainly not my dignity."

"Then try. They say by the end of step five you'll feel like the problem's gone. It won't be, but I imagine getting to that point will give you back some hope. At least try to get *there*. If you can't do it for yourself, do it for her."

"She's not here."

"Well, this is your best shot at getting her back here. Give it ninety days."

Austin fanned the pages of the massive text. "What happens in ninety days?"

"You attend ninety meetings. I read about it online. It's called the 90-90. How far you get in that ninety is up to you."

"You actually believe in this?"

Cord wished he could proclaim absolute faith in the program, but he'd read too much about those it failed. "I believe in *you*."

Austin met his gaze, transparent fear in his eyes, but he nodded. "Ninety days."

Five

Austin

"THERE'S A MEETING TONIGHT."

Austin stiffened and shoved the intimidating book aside. Everything in his body tensed as the elephant in the room anchored its ass on his shoulders.

He'd agreed to go to the stupid meetings. Wasn't that enough? Did they have to keep talking about it?

When he didn't reply, Cord said, "They're in the basement of the Catholic Church on Willow Street. I can drive you."

Resentment boiled in his blood. "I don't need a fucking babysitter."

"How about a friend? Do you need a friend?"

His molars locked as another headache came on. Cord wasn't his friend. Well, sometimes he was. He saved his life, but look what else he'd done, although that was Austin's own doing.

Fuck, he missed her, and the not knowing... If ever he needed an excuse to drink...

"I said I'd go to the meetings and I'll go." He stood and carried his bowl to the sink, not like he had an appetite anyway.

He and Cord would be sharing the domestic drudgery that Ember made seem so effortless, and eating take-out or crap from cans for God knew how long. He wanted his wife back—wanted his life back. He scoffed at himself. As if having his precious wife back so he could avoid housework and eat better was the real reason he wanted her in his life. He simply *needed* her. Maybe if he learned to cook or something it would give him a smaller goal to focus on.

"Will you go to the meeting tonight?"

"Jesus, Cord, back off!" Fuck, the guy wouldn't leave it alone.

"What's the point of avoiding it? The Austin I know says he's gonna do something and does it."

His bowl clattered into the sink. "I said I'd go!"

"Well, the first one's in an hour."

He was going to break something. His fists

tightened as he leaned all of his weight into the counter on his knuckles. "How long is it?"

And why was it in a church? He didn't need the Bible crammed down his throat along with that other big ass book. Fuck! He was holding on by a thread.

"Does it matter? It'll take as long as it takes."

He was so fucking tired of everyone else acting like they had all the answers, acting as if they had a fucking clue what this felt like. He hadn't even started and he already wanted to quit trying. He wanted a fucking drink. He went to the fridge. Juice. Milk. Soda. *Goddamn it.*

Pressing his lips tight and breathing through his frustration, he slammed the fridge. The urge to move ate at him. Something fierce crouched inside of him, prepared to attack.

What was he supposed to do, roll up to some church with his big book, and smile?

Hi. I'm here because my friend made me go. How did he manage that? Well, he fucked my wife —at my request—and walked in on me attempting to end my life, choked me into survival, threw away all my booze, and now he's living in my goddamn house. Babysitting me. Where do pussies sign in?

"Austin?"

He spun and roared, *"What?"*

"You need this." Cord's calm mocked his own fraying composure.

"I know what I fucking need!"

"Are you scared? I'll go with you."

Scared? No he wasn't fucking scared. "I'll go to the stupid fucking meeting. Now shut up about it."

Cord stood. "You should probably get there early since it's your first one. If you want me to drive you I will."

He didn't need a fucking chauffeur or some flannel covered jerkoff acting like his mother. "I'll drive myself."

Cord hesitated by the door to the kitchen, likely weighing every possibility of Austin bailing on the meeting and hitting a bar. Finally, he sighed, like he'd resigned himself that Austin wouldn't be led by a fucking leash. "Okay. I'll see what you want to do in a little bit."

Cord's steps echoed through the empty house and Austin didn't exhale until he heard the guest room door quietly close.

What he wanted to do was throw Cord's smug, self-righteous ass out of his home. The only reason he didn't was because he kind of needed him there at the moment, not really trusting himself. He didn't trust anyone.

When had he become so cynical of everything and everyone around him? It was like he couldn't separate the truth from the bullshit. It was all suspect.

The house was too damn quiet. He turned on the faucet and did the dishes just to make some noise. There, he was making progress. The frothing water suddenly irritated him and he tossed the dishrag over the edge of the sink.

He missed his wife. It had been so long since she'd come up from behind and wrapped her arms around him, giving him that unshakable boost of confidence she never let flag.

He'd been giving her space, respecting her edict, and the fact she hadn't responded to Cord either told him space was exactly what she wanted right now. But maybe he should drive over to Cord's and have it out with her. Maybe take that letter so he'd know what to talk about. Right. And she'd throw herself into his arms and forgive him, considering how he looked. And felt. It would be another fight none of them needed right now. She needed time and he needed to make sure he was past whatever this was before he started spouting promises again.

When he finished the dishes he looked for something else to do. Everything was too peaceful, too fucking quiet. His house smelled different when she wasn't there. December usually had music playing and was always making noise working on something or other. She'd been nagging him to fix something in the laundry room over the past month, but he couldn't remember what.

What the hell was it? She never shut up about it. Shelves...or something. He'd give anything to hear her nagging him now. He'd fix anything just to have her back.

Needing to keep busy—hopefully he'd get so wrapped up Cord would see he didn't need a meeting to distract him—he went to the laundry room. The second he opened the door he was bombarded with sensory overload.

Everything reminded him of December. She was there, in the scent of the detergent, the forgotten pile of linen napkins left folded on the dryer, the little floral mat she bought to keep her feet warm while she stood sorting clothes.

He eyeballed the shelf and immediately saw the problem. The thing had pulled from the wall and needed a new molly bolt to anchor it back in place. Such a simple fix, a two-minute job and he'd neglected it for almost a year.

How many minutes had she wasted, caring for him, taking extra time to grab the fabric softeners, bleach, detergent and other shit from the table across the room over the last few months because the shelf usually housing that stuff was broken?

He was an asshole.

Moving to examine the wall closer, he took note of the screw, wondered where he left his drill, and before he knew it, he was sliding the washer away from the wall...

"It's gone."

Mother. Fucker.

Austin unfolded his body and turned slowly, seething behind gritted teeth. "What's gone?"

"The bottle you're looking for. They're all gone."

"I wasn't looking for shit." Lie. He'd lied to himself. He *was* looking for that bottle. Already concocted a subconscious excuse of fixing the molly bolt, worked a nice image into his head, sipping on the sly, while he fixed December's shelf. Jesus. What was wrong with him? He couldn't even trust himself.

In thirty seconds he'd devised an entire scheme to deceive everyone and disguise his actions with good intentions. He'd fix the shelf, replace all her supplies, have a few sips, face Cord as though deserving of some sort of praise for doing something normal, stash the bottle back behind the washer for later, and roll into the meeting with a mouth full of lies and whiskey on his breath.

Goddamn, he was sabotaging himself, and couldn't stop.

Rather than thank his friend, he lashed out. "What, did you search my whole fucking home? I wasn't looking to do anything more than fix the shelf."

The lies wouldn't stop. It was as though he'd lost total control of the part of his brain that formed the truth.

"Yes, I searched the house. They're all gone." There was no remorse in the reply.

"I'm not a fucking child!"

"I know. You're an alcoholic."

He was going to crack a molar if he didn't relax. He wasn't a fucking alcoholic. Alcoholics were drunks, failures, people who had nothing to live for.

His mind flashed to the memory just before he swallowed a fistful of pills. Sweat beaded on his skin at the familiar rush of urgency he'd experienced in that moment, wanting the pain to end. He *never* suspected he'd be capable of killing himself, yet in that moment it was the only goal he had, the one thing he assumed he could succeed in doing. But he'd failed at even that.

He couldn't even successfully kill himself. Fucking Cord interfered in that too.

He glared at the crooked shelf to hide the rage seeping from his pores. His tattered pride forbade him from saying so, but he needed Cord. That broken shelf represented everything his life had become...weak, unstable, one knock away from landing in the garbage.

How many other things around the house needed repair? If he was dead, who would fix them for December? *He* wanted to fix them. He wanted her gratitude, her warm smiles saved for heroes who captured spiders and opened the tight lids of olive jars. God, it was so easy and he'd somehow fucked it all up. And for what?

His hands reached into his pocket and closed over his keys. "I'm going."

Cord stepped in his way. "Where?"

Where the hell did he think? "To the fucking meeting."

His friend didn't move. "Do you want me to drive you?"

Austin's tongue pressed hard to the back of his front teeth. Without unclenching his jaw, he breathed, "No."

It was obvious Cord didn't trust him. And why would he? Austin didn't trust himself. It had been just over three full days since he'd taken a drink and he had absolutely no clue if he'd make it to four.

A sick and twisted part of him took pleasure in his friend's apprehension. It didn't seem possible to appreciate someone and resent them so much at the same time. Hugs or murder... It was a toss-up, but either way he was glad the guy was sticking around to find out.

He stomped past him and grumbled. "You're just gonna have to trust me. I wonder if you'll have more luck at that than I will—we'll see how the night plays out."

Six

Austin

"EMBER... IT'S ME."

Austin let out a long sigh and pressed the back of his head into the headrest of his truck.

"I'm sorry. I know I've said it a million times and you have no reason to believe me, but I'll say it every day if I have to. I love you."

He stared through the dark parking lot at the church. He'd never been inside that particular church before.

"I'm parked outside of that church you always said was so pretty, the one at the top of the hill in town. I'm supposed to be inside sitting through my first AA meeting, but I can't seem to get myself

65

out of the car." He laughed sadly. "At least I'm not driving to a bar, right?"

Sighing again, he tapped his fingers on the steering wheel. "I know you hate me. I hate me too. I'm trying to get through this. If I do, I have to believe you'll at least hear me out eventually. I haven't had a drink in three days." *Three days, ten hours and counting...* "That's the truth."

He checked out the cars in the lot again. There were nine including his. He wasn't sure what was worse, the idea of only nine people witnessing his shame or the hope that there would be more so he could blend in. How the hell was this anonymous?

He let out a hard breath. "I should probably go in. I've been sitting here for twenty minutes. Wouldn't want them to start without me. I...I love you, baby. If you believe anything, please believe that."

He ended the call and shut his eyes. *Open the door. Just open the door and then worry about what comes next.*

He hadn't been expecting this paralysis. Fear of the unknown had him on lockdown. He should just go to Cord's and tell her all this in person. Better than a stupid meeting.

Scrubbing his hands roughly over his face he groaned. "Fuck."

His fingers finally closed on the latch of the door, but didn't pull. Tiny clips of preconceived images filled with strangers scrutinizing him bombarded his mind. Would it be mostly men in there? What if he recognized someone? What if someone recognized *him*?

If they're there, they're drunks too. Misery loves company.

Maybe he should just leave. He could go home. Go to Cord's. Or he could take off and go wherever he wanted. He didn't have to answer to anyone. Who was Cord to tell him what to do? Austin already had a wife, and damned if he didn't want her there, telling him, pushing him...

His bravado lasted only a second. His wife didn't want to see him. Cord was the only person left who cared whether he sobered up or died. Okay, Ember cared, but he couldn't expect her to prop him up, not after what he'd done.

He wished he could get rid of the resentment he'd been carrying toward his friend, but it was so deep and so toxic. It had been there, under wraps, before everything happened with Ember and he wasn't even sure what triggered it.

He could go to a bar. The liquor store would be closed by now, but The Bucket was open until two. The scent of vodka could be covered. He could hit a bar outside of town where no one would recognize him and have a few shots and be back home within an hour. Or not. He'd likely start drinking and not care whether he got home in time to lie to Cord.

But he'd told Ember he was going in. Shit.

Who knew if she'd listen to her messages? It was a hell of a lot harder to lie to her sober than it was drunk. And she might drive by...

Forcing his legs to move, he climbed out and shut the truck door before he could climb back in. *Just walk to the door. Get to the door and then worry about opening it.*

It took another five minutes to coax his feet to the entrance of the church. When he pulled the handle he came up short. It was locked. Something inside of him bloomed and celebrated. *Time to go home.*

"You looking for the meeting?"

Austin turned abruptly. "Uh..."

The girl was young, maybe twenty. She was bundled up to her neck and smoking a cigarette, shivering. She couldn't be an alcoholic. She barely looked old enough to drink.

Angling the cherry red tip of her cigarette toward the church, she pointed. "It's through those doors over there. You new?"

He had to get out of there. "I think I'm in the wrong place—"

"It's pretty common to be scared for your first meeting. I was. I didn't convince myself to go inside until the last fifteen minutes. Then I left five minutes early. That worked for a while. Then it didn't. There's still about forty minutes left. You should go in. No one will bother you."

Yeah, right. He'd walk in and be forced to say

the whole spiel he'd seen a hundred times on television. *Hello, my name is Austin and I'm an alcoholic. Hello, Austin!*

Fuck my life.

She ditched her cigarette in the receptacle and moved toward the other entrance. When she yanked on the handle he was relieved she was leaving. He couldn't do this.

"You coming?" She held open the door.

Fuck. Austin slowly followed her, fearing she'd talk to him and draw unwanted attention. She didn't. Rather, she disappeared down a long corridor and left him to his own devices.

The scent of stale coffee assaulted his cold nose as he shuffled a step closer to the table outside of the doors at the end of the hall. A male voice spoke in the distance, too far away for Austin to make out the words. It was surprisingly quiet. No one made a sound except for the person talking.

A table was filled with pamphlets on addiction, and prayer cards. He wasn't too keen on being cornered into some religion he had no interest in. AA was appearing more and more like a cult.

Pocketing a sheet of paper with the words *Alcoholics Anonymous* emblazoned on the front, he, again, subconsciously devised an alibi. Proof he'd gone. But what was he proving, that he could lie? There was no dignity in artificial victory. He had to stop sabotaging himself.

He stepped quietly through the door. Holy shit, there were a lot of people there. They weren't sitting in a circle like he'd dreaded, but rather, in a sort of assembled order, all facing the man who spoke behind the podium. Was that the instructor? He didn't look like a drunk.

Austin sat in the very last row, closest to the door. He barely breathed for fear his metal chair would make a sound and alert the others to his presence. Appraising the backs of everyone's head, he did a slow scan, judging every last one of them the way he feared he'd be judged. What was wrong with him?

No one really looked familiar. Tickles of recognition teased, but there was no one there that immediately popped out. He'd leave before everyone turned around, he decided.

He glanced at the man talking. His eyes took in every last detail of the room before his ears opened to what was being said.

"...I remember rushing around the school, praying with everything I had that Billy would be waiting at the swings. When he wasn't on the playground I didn't know what to do. If I called my wife she'd never forgive me. It didn't help that I was so drunk I could barely stay on the road.

"I drove around for an hour looking for him. A lot of that time I spent mentally berating Sheryl for making a hair appointment and dumping her responsibilities on me. I did that a lot, assumed *our* responsibilities were hers because I wasn't responsible enough to handle them.

"After I'd looked everywhere, I gave up. I pulled into the driveway and just sat there. Parked. Frustrated and tired of searching, no clue what to do. I don't know how long I sat, but it was a while. To this day I can't fathom just giving up while my eight year old son was missing, but that's what I did."

Austin's brow tightened as he scowled at the man telling the story. What a horrible fucking story. What happened to his son? What sort of twisted dad gives up on his child like that? He ignored the flare of painful memories from his own jacked up past with practiced ease.

"My neighbor eventually saw me and knocked on my window. She'd told me Billy had come to her door when he walked home because no one picked him up from school and the house was locked. I should have been grateful for having such a good neighbor, but all I recall is aggravation. I was so threatened that she might tell Sheryl I lost our son.

"That was six years ago and I still can't seem to forgive myself. Maybe I could if that was the only situation like that I'd caused, but it wasn't. There've been hundreds...."

Austin didn't want to hear any more. This guy wasn't the instructor. He was an alcoholic, or at least used to be. Six years? Six fucking years since that happened and he was still attending meetings? This was never going to work.

Sucking in a breath, he prepared to stand, but stilled as he caught someone looking directly at him. Not casually glancing around the room and looking away when there was that uncomfortable moment of eye contact. No. This guy's stare was drilling into Austin's eye sockets.

Austin narrowed his gaze. *Turn around, asshole.*

He didn't recognize him, but worried the man might know him somehow. Why else would he be eye fucking him? Searching his memory, he tried to place the stranger. He was a big guy, dark skin, bald head, older than him. Austin didn't know anyone who came close to looking like that.

The group said something and started clapping, distracting him. His breathing labored, pumping rapidly from his lungs, as he feared the meeting was over. He had to get out of there before people started talking to him and asking questions.

He looked at the guy staring one last time. He was no longer rubbernecking. *Time to go.* People started moving and Austin quickly stood and slipped out the door. He stilled in the hall when everything again got quiet. Glancing back into the room, he saw a woman approach the podium.

"Hello. I'm Julie and I've been sober for seven hundred twenty-one days."

"Hello, Julie," the group chorused.

Is this what they did? Shared story after story? How the hell did that make a person sober? If he wanted to lose weight he wouldn't join a club that discussed cake. He'd seen enough.

Pushing through the exterior doors, he sucked in a deep inhalation of cold air as though he were breaking the surface of a bottomless lake and breathing for the first time. He wasn't cut out for AA. It wouldn't work for him. He'd just have to do it on his own. He could do it.

"Right about now you're convincing yourself you can handle it on your own and don't need any of this."

What the fuck was it with people sneaking up on him in this place? He pivoted and found the tall black guy that had been studying him from a few feet away. "Do I know you?"

"Maybe. There's a good part of my life I don't remember. Met a lot of different people during those years. Name's Harley."

He held out a hand and Austin automatically reached for it. "I'm..." He hesitated.

Harley laughed. "Anonymous? No sweat. We know each other. The anonymous is for the outside world. It doesn't work unless we can trust those who understand."

Austin cut contact and stepped back. He could do small talk for a few seconds, get a feel for what the others got out of the meetings. Harley gave off an air of confidence Austin wanted to match. He wouldn't show fear to this man. "I'm Austin."

"I'm assuming this is your first meeting, Austin?"

No fear. No fear. "Yeah."

Harley nodded. "You want to grab a cup of coffee? I've been at it a long time. Might be able to answer some of your questions. The anonymous goes beyond those doors."

Did Austin have questions? A few. Probably a thousand. "You're an alcoholic?"

"Recovering. Haven't had a drink in sixteen years."

Holy shit. Austin needed to get his shit under control, but the idea of not making even a toast in almost two decades? No way. He wanted to *manage* it, not completely give it up.

"I think we should talk, Austin. I can see you're still grappling with the truth. How about I head over to Debbie's Diner and if you want to join me, I'll be at the table in the back. If not..." he shrugged.

Austin watched as the man walked away and climbed into a black Escalade. The headlights crawled over the quiet lot and then he was gone.

Did he want to have coffee with some big, leather-wearing Wesley Snipes type guy? Not really. Was he curious about what he had to tell him? Hell, yes. Curious for the first time in a long time.

"Damn it."

He walked to his truck and drove to the diner. When he pulled up he spotted the Escalade. His eyes scanned the windows and he saw a waitress delivering a pot of coffee to the back where Harley sat.

Austin glanced at the clock on the dash. Cord would start to worry if he wasn't home soon. Some diners had liquor licenses. He wasn't sure if this one did. Strangely, the idea of worrying Cord motivated Austin to go inside.

The bell tied to the hinge of the door jingled and Austin's eyes took immediate inventory of his surroundings. As if it called to him, there, right beside the towering display filled with pies was a fridge filled to the top with six packs for takeout. His hand was in his pocket before he even formulated a plan, withdrawing his wallet.

Where the fuck *was* his wallet?

Cord.

"Can I help you?"

Austin looked at the waitress but said nothing. He didn't have any fucking money.

"He's with me," Harley called from the back. His voice was so deep he didn't need to do more than speak above a whisper.

The waitress smiled. "I'll grab another place setting."

As she walked away Austin just stood there.

Harley waved him over and his feet slowly shuffled toward the table.

"Have a seat," Harley invited with a wave.

Austin kept his expression blank and lowered himself into the booth.

"So...how long have you been an alcoholic?"

I'm not an alcoholic. "I just like to drink. I don't think I'm where the others are."

"Oh. Good." Harley smiled. "So you're happy."

No. "I'm not *un*happy."

"Really? Huh. I remember when I first admitted I had a problem I couldn't control. It made me fucking miserable."

The waitress approached and a paper placemat drifted in front of Austin. She flipped over a mug on a saucer and filled it.

"Thanks, darling," Harley said. "We'll call you if we need anything else."

"You got it, Harley."

Did this guy live around here? He seemed pretty familiar with the people, yet Austin was certain he'd never seen him before.

"I'm guessing right about now you're convinced AA doesn't work and you have no place in the room you just left."

Correct. "I'm not like them."

"Everyone's different. I'm not like a lot of them either, but we do have one thing in common. We're all drunks."

"I'm not a drunk."

"No? Good. This should be easy then. Do you know the difference between an alcoholic and a person who isn't?"

Austin remembered learning in high school that anyone who could drink more than a few beers in one sitting was an "alcoholic". If that were true, every guy he knew was one. "They can't stop drinking. I stopped."

"How long ago?"

Fuck. He had no reason to lie to a stranger. "Three days." No need to be exact, although those additional hours and minutes were starting to mean something. No need to tell him he was locked up for most of that time.

"That's a start. Stick with it and I can honestly tell you some of the hardest days are behind you."

It was more than a start. It was an end, an end to giving in, an end to feeling out of control, and an end to fucking up. He wouldn't have really tested that bottle behind the washer—if fucking Cord hadn't found it.

"So you're all good now."

"Yeah. I'm good."

"Good." Harley sipped his coffee.

The silence got to Austin. "Are you one of those sponsor people?"

Harley shrugged. "That's all part of it. It's a pay it forward sort of thing. I've sponsored others.

It isn't a job you apply for. It's one you're elected to."

"Elected by who?"

Harley's head lifted as his dark eyes angled to the ceiling. "Whomever. When it's a good match, you know. So does the person looking for you." He eyed him critically for a moment. "You strike me as the kind of guy who's a good leader."

Austin liked to think so, but his track record of late spoke to the contrary. "I've been known to take control of situations when life called for it."

Harley chuckled, his face set in a friendly grin. "Bet it pisses you off you can't control this."

Yes. "I'm managing."

"I can tell you how to make it easier. If you're interested, that is."

No meetings? Could this guy give him some pointers so he could avoid all the uncomfortable bullshit in between? "How?" Austin took a sip of his coffee to avoid looking too eager.

Harley eased back in his seat, dominating a good part of the booth with his broad shoulders. "You allergic to anything, Austin?"

"Penicillin."

"You ever accidently take it and have a reaction?"

He didn't remember ever having a reaction to the medicine. He'd just always been told he couldn't take it. "Maybe when I was young. I don't remember."

"My sister, she's allergic to strawberries. Gets hives and all sorts of shit. Can't touch them, 'cause her airway might close up."

Wonderful story. He had visions of some woman clasping her throat. *What am I doing here?* He waited for the other man to divulge the information he needed.

"She doesn't eat strawberries now. It's the strangest thing. You know why?"

Austin was growing impatient. If Harley didn't start telling him what he wanted to hear, he was gone as soon as he finished his coffee. Sooner. "Uh, they'll kill her."

He aimed his dark finger at Austin like a gun and made a clicking sound from the side of his mouth.

"You got it. And you know what, she's okay with that. Crazy, she thinks living is worth more than strawberries."

"Good for her." He knew he sounded like an asshole, but this guy was pushing. He slurped at his coffee, each gulp getting him closer to his escape. Bailing early on the meeting meant he had to kill a little time before going home where his babysitter waited to quiz him.

Harley smiled and another minute ticked by. "So, I'm guessing something you didn't like happened three days ago, had yourself a bad experience. Alcohol likely played a hand in whatever happened and, like my sister, you decided to cut it out. I guess since you're not an alcoholic and you know booze makes bad things happen to you, you'll have no problem giving it up. Like Tanya and her strawberries. She never thinks about strawberries anymore."

He hadn't thought about drinking since he picked up his coffee cup. And now, as he considered the other man's words. And then about thirty seconds before that and less than a minute before that.

"You look like you don't agree."

"I think about it, but that doesn't mean I'll drink."

"Good." Harley flicked his finger casually in the air. "You know what has me wondering though? How much easier would your life be if you *didn't* think about it, say, every few seconds? How peaceful would it be if you could go a minute or an hour or even a day?"

That would be pretty damn nice. He shrugged. "I guess that would be easier."

"It's a shame that group down the road ain't for you. There's some good people there. People who need support and to know it's okay to be like them because they're not the only ones." He waved his hand. "Ahh, those meetings don't work anyway."

"Then why were you there?"

"Because I'm part of the solution. The program's a bit broken right now, but if someone got down to the basics, understood the bare bones of the solution, they'd succeed."

"Seems to me, all they do is reminisce about getting drunk when they should be talking about how to get sober."

A black brow lifted, wrinkling Harley's smooth forehead. "But they are sober. The trick is *staying* that way. You see, the program's been watered down over the years. You ever get drunk on watered down booze, Austin?"

"No." He'd quit mixing soda or water with the hard stuff because it didn't do the job as fast as he'd liked.

"So, you see, what you have there is a watered down program. Ain't gonna get well on that any more than you'll get drunk from watered down booze."

Exactly. He'd already decided those meetings were an utter waste of time. "So, why go?"

"If you were starving and someone threw you a bucket of scraps, mostly fat and gristle, but you knew there were some prime cuts of edible steak in there somewhere, would you sift through the slop to find the good stuff to ease your hunger?"

"Sure."

Harley nodded. "There's still some good stuff in there. It's just been butchered over time with people's opinions and theories. What works for Chuck, Bob, and Mary, might not work for the Connies, Harleys, and...Austins."

"So there's no guarantee."

The other man lifted his cup and saluted with it. "Life doesn't come with guarantees, Austin. You know that. AA, however, comes with a book. That book has the facts. It helps separate the bullshit from the cure. I can't promise you'll stay sober. It all depends on the person. You're the guarantee it comes with."

"I think I have that book. My friend bought it for me."

"Interesting. Why would a friend buy a book like that for someone who isn't an alcoholic? Pretty presumptuous."

He thought so. Kind of. "I drink a lot. Used to."

"I see. That book can save lives. I hope you read it—with an open mind of course."

He might breeze through it. At the moment—meaning this present *second*—he felt pretty confident about the road ahead. And just like that the 'seek and find' urge to reach for a beer or a shot returned. *Fuck.*

"What is it you like to drink?"

Everything inside of him went on high alert. He shrugged. Not sharing. *Nothing to see here.*

"I was a vodka man. Loved my vodka. There really is nothing like a nice glass of top shelf, smooth premium vodka on the rocks. I used to love coming home from a hard day's work and sitting down with my glass. It was a ritual of mine."

Austin didn't add to the conversation because his instincts told him it was a trap.

Harley sighed. "So long as I had my vodka at the end of the day, everything was just fine. Some days that was all it took. One glass to take the edge off." His shoulder lifted in an *aww shucks* movement. "Then there were the days it took a little more. Those sorts of days were rare during the first half of my life. But after a while it was the days I stopped at one that became unusual. Not sure when the shift actually happened." He laughed. "It's sort of a blur."

"How'd you stop?" He told himself he didn't really care, but the guy bought him coffee.

"Once I stopped lying to myself it didn't seem so bad to stop drinking. Sucked. Hurt like a mother-fucker, but once I started opening my eyes and honestly appraising the man I truly was, I figured out how to change the stuff I didn't so much care for. That's where AA comes in."

Austin frowned. "But you said it didn't work."

"I said the meetings *alone* don't work, and they don't. Anyone can give an hour. To succeed you got to be willing to give the rest of your life—to the cause. The cause is you, my friend. Alcoholism isn't a team sport. It's solitary, terrifying, and can only be beaten by incredible determination and strong will. No one can give those qualities to someone else. We got to build them on our own and it literally takes a lifetime."

Austin's shoulders knotted with tension as he processed Harley's words. His clothes suddenly felt restrictive and his throat swollen and achy like just before a cold.

Harley finished his cup of coffee. "Tell you what, Austin. You seem like a pretty good guy. I come here for coffee every night around this time. I'd like to talk with you tomorrow if you're up for it. I'm thinking you might be over this way same time tomorrow too."

"I'm not sure." No way was he committing to anything. This guy obviously had a problem some years back, and now was trolling to lord it over others. Right?

"Well," the other man checked his watch. "The invitation still stands. I gotta get going before my woman starts to worry. You got a woman?"

"I'm married." Estranged from his wife, but he was still married.

Harley smiled and stood. "I bet she's worried about you too. It's getting late. See you tomorrow?"

Austin still wasn't sure. "Maybe." He shook Harley's proffered hand.

"Good enough. Oh, and Austin..." Austin turned and Harley grinned. "The veil, that invisibility cloak that booze provides, the one that lets you hide from all the discontent you don't want to see... It'll betray you. Somehow, what once saved us from our problems starts to magnify them. It'll be a weight off your shoulders to take that cloak off for good. I can help you hang it up."

With a nod, he left and Austin glanced at the table. The things he wanted to happen weren't happening and the things he didn't want to happen, were. At one time, drinking made him...pleasant. A fun guy to be around. When had that changed?

His entire world became unmanageable. That was the hardest part. Not only had everything fallen apart, he'd lost the control to stop and say when. Earlier, when Cord had been trying to dictate his every move, he'd felt like a puppet, resenting his strings.

It wasn't Cord telling him he had to stop, or December begging him not to drink that challenged his control. It was his own will—just as Harley said.

He stared at the money on the table that Harley left. The man had dropped a generous tip for their waitress. As Austin ogled the cash, he contemplated swiping a few bucks to buy a six pack. He looked at the waitress. She was young. It seemed odd she'd be working alone with just the cook at a diner this late on a weeknight.

He thought of Ember. He'd hate to see her

have to work late at a place only truckers and recovering alcoholics visited at this hour. Chances were, it wasn't an ideal situation for this waitress either.

He could take her money. No one would know. But what if she needed it? And *he* would know. He used to be the sort of guy to throw another few bucks on a tip just to be a gentleman and help a person out. Of course, that was when he had a job and money and wasn't walking around without a wallet.

He wasn't a thief. He stared at that money, knowing it could get him what he craved, but decided he wanted his life back more... It was the first time he'd sensed the return of any control.

He made the decision to walk away, not someone else. *He* had to decide this path and he had to walk it, even when no one was there to guide him.

He stepped back from the table. Rather than focus on how easy it would be to skim the tip, he focused on how difficult it seemed to walk away, and mentally celebrated the private reward of achieving that little victory. December used to always tell him the difficult choice was usually the right one.

He said goodnight and walked out to his truck, pockets empty, chest full of personal pride. Once he started the truck, he paused. The last five minutes had been concentrated on integrity. Occupying his thoughts with honorable objectives seemed to quell his obsession with finding his next drink.

He should celebrate.

A sudden need for a drink frayed his revelation around the edges and he shook with the effort to retain the lesson, the understanding.

It hit him. This really was a one-man show. The audience was there, watching, critiquing, but they'd never understand the full story. They'd never see close enough to feel all the little thorns that pricked along the way.

He somehow drove straight home without detouring past Cord's. No way would he be able to stay away from Ember if he got that close. As he drove he kept replaying the event in his head. The moment he walked into the house the television shut off and Cord looked anxiously at him.

Austin blanked his expression, already irritated by his friend's relentless presence.

"So?" Cord asked.

"I went."

His friend let out a huge sigh of relief. "Thank God. How was it?"

"Sucked." He was coming to terms with the idea that this solo act would read like German subtitles to those who weren't privy to the script.

"Are you smiling?"

Huh. Maybe that's why his face felt odd. Yeah. He was definitely smiling. He gave into it, let it take over his face as he met Cord's confused stare. "I didn't steal the waitress's tip."

"What?"

"You had to be there."

Cord frowned. "Where? You were supposed to be at the church."

"I told you, I went. Me and a guy from the meeting grabbed some coffee after and got to talking. I think he's nuts, but he's sober."

"Should you be hanging out with someone like that?"

Austin laughed. There was always a critic. "Newsflash, Cord. You sent me to a place where every alcoholic in town congregates. Who did you expect me to meet?"

"How long has this guy been sober?"

Austin's smile faded. Couldn't his character assessment be enough? What made Cord the better judge of a person? Austin could have easily told him the guy had been sober for almost twenty years, but that shouldn't matter. His friend should trust his judgment. No one wanted this shitstorm to end more than Austin.

Victorious mood gone, he shrugged. "I don't know."

"Well, maybe you shouldn't hang around with people that could pull you down."

His eyes narrowed. That quickly, his positive outlook deflated, reminding him of all the depressing repercussions he still had to mend. Some of them included his behavior with Cord, but he was too busy resenting his friend's endless self-righteousness to sort things out at the moment.

Fuck it. He was done explaining. "You're probably right. I'm going to bed."

Alcohol might be the root of the problem, but those seeds were planted long ago and Austin had some major cleanup ahead of him. Analyzing his every move under Cord's shadow was draining as fuck. He couldn't do anymore tonight.

Cord looked like he had more to say, but Austin turned away before he had the chance. Making a quick detour, he grabbed *The Big Book* off the kitchen table and headed to bed.

Seven

Austin

"HEY, baby, it's me. I thought I might catch you if I called early in the morning." Austin stared at the empty side of their bed. "I'm in our bed. It's lonely without you. I...I guess you know what that's like."

His head tipped back. He'd left her countless messages and wasn't sure if they made any difference at all. At least she was safe and getting some sort of peace away from him.

"I know I've said it over and over, but I'm sorry. I'm doing everything in my power to fix this, baby. I'll do it. I swear, even if I die trying, I'll never stop trying to fix this, to fix us. You're my everything."

The longer he stared at the undisturbed bedding, the more he understood how wrong it was for only one person to sleep there.

"The house isn't the same without you. Cord's here. Things are fucked up, but he refuses to leave. I guess that's a good thing, because I don't want him with you, right now, anymore. I don't know. As much as I need to know you're okay, I'm afraid you'll move on without me and I don't want that. Maybe I'm being selfish. Probably. If you're not busy, call me. Please. I miss your voice. I love you."

Cord said his parents were managing the store all week and Ember still hadn't talked to him either. Cold comfort, but he'd take it. In fact, he grudgingly appreciated that his friend was staying clear of his wife, though how much longer that would continue was anybody's guess. It had only been a few days, but the guy had to check on her —and his house—at some point.

A rap drew his attention to the bedroom door, and he flinched. His nerves were worn to shit. A drink would settle them. But fuck that.

"I miss you. I'll call you later. Love you." He ended the call and stashed the phone under the covers. "What?"

"You want breakfast? I got some eggs cooking."

"I guess." He heard Cord move away and managed not to fall back into his miserable longing for December.

How long was the guy going to stick around? He wondered if Ember was still helping out at the hardware store in Cord's absence. Even in his drunken stupor he'd been able to tell she really liked working there. Sobriety had a way of showing him the logic behind her taking the job. Maybe one day he'd have the balls to tell her he was sorry for fighting with her about doing the responsible thing.

But she shouldn't have to work. Especially not for Cord. The plan was for Austin to be the provider. As much as she might need some independence right now, he truly believed she preferred taking care of their home. He needed to make that a possibility again, get his shit back in order.

Scrubbing his palms over his face, he focused on the next baby step and got his mind off his confusing feelings toward the man currently making him breakfast. He'd been reading that book and something that resonated was the mention of how easily alcoholics could shift blame on others. Cord was catching a lot of that, and Austin had to sort out how much was deserved.

Best Ember wasn't around, because no matter how Austin tried to show his appreciation, it usually spewed out coated in resentment. He could call her and leave messages with the good stuff. Keep some distance until he got a better handle on his moods.

Shoving the blanket back, he clambered out of bed and made his way to the bathroom. He risked a glance in the mirror as he washed up and decided to shave. The face that reflected back didn't look as haggard—or unfamiliar as it did a week ago, and that lifted his spirits a tad. He exhaled, stoking the cautious flame of hope.

A cramp instantly seized his belly and he doubled over the cold porcelain. Goddamn it. He should know better than to get ahead of himself. One tiny freaking step at a time. Like an inch.

He brushed his teeth and figured he'd shave later. Pulling a clean shirt over his head, he left his sleep pants on—good enough for breakfast. The smell of bacon and eggs drew him downstairs where Cord presided over the stove.

His observant blue eyes glanced over his shoulder the moment Austin entered. "Can you butter the toast? If I take my attention off this bacon it'll burn sure as shit."

Austin scraped some butter over the cardboard-like toast and tossed the slices onto a plate. He set it on the table and grabbed the coffee carafe to fill the mugs while Cord maneuvered the bacon onto some wadded up napkins.

He frowned as Cord blotted at the meat. "What're you doing?"

"Soaking up the grease." Cord poked at the strips one last time then poured the remaining fat from the pan into a glass bowl and set it aside. "And draining the fat."

Austin reached for the pan of scrambled eggs and piled half on his plate. "Draining the fat?"

"December showed me." Cord forked up a few strips of bacon, divvying them between their plates, and dropped into a chair.

Austin's appetite withered up and died. He forced a wad of eggs into his mouth and chewed mechanically. He'd read he had to take care of himself physically in order to stay healthy and resist the urges.

As much as he focused on eating a healthy breakfast and tried to keep his mind on the future, his brain wouldn't get out of the past. "She show you other stuff?"

His friend froze, fork in mid-air, and lips parted. His strong jaw and piercing blue eyes wore a mask of uncertainty, tinted with...pain, as he blinked in Austin's direction. Then his gaze narrowed and his features twisted with anger.

"Fuck you, Garret. I took care of your wife while you trashed your life—and hers. And you can own part of what happened. After. Later. Whatever. Fish somewhere else."

He wished he hadn't opened the subject, despite it simmering like a living thing between them. Hell, he couldn't see past the next five minutes without reliving every monumental fuck-up he'd orchestrated in the past. They kept piling on his shoulders, bearing down on him.

Own your faults. Take responsibility. There was some mention about forgiveness too, but he be damned if he was ready for that yet. "Whatever."

Cord dropped his fork and sat back in his chair. "Look, if you want to talk about it—"

"I can't." He wasn't quick enough to mask the agony and despair, and Cord heard it.

His friend visibly flinched and his gaze dropped to the table. They both contemplated their food and silence reigned. The strange little clock Ember bought for the kitchen ticked loudly, a countdown to an explosion Austin figured would blow them both away.

"Then leave it for now. Until you can. Until *I* can." Cord grabbed his plate and carried it to the garbage, dumping the remaining scraps into the trash.

Somehow he'd defused the situation. Austin fought against a softer emotion where his friend was concerned, and tried hard to see past his resentment and give *something* back.

"I appreciate that you're here." It was true, but saying it was like chewing off his own arm. His mouth soured then watered as a familiar thirst and urge took hold.

"No worries."

How did he minimize his living here like that?

Maybe Ember didn't want to see Cord either. He couldn't resist dropping another lure. "You could have stayed with her. Checked in on me, once I got home."

Cord set the plate down and turned to face him. His face looked suddenly pale as if he were going to be sick. "*Stayed* with her? How could I do that when I don't know where the fuck she is?"

"*What?*" Austin found himself standing nose to nose with Cord but with no memory of leaving the table. "She's at your *house*! Working in *your* store!"

Cord's forearm blocked against his chest. "The fuck she is! She came here after... after she left me and went to see you. She wrote you that letter, remember? It's in your dresser."

He remembered. He remembered the finality of every word, wanting to die before he even reached the end. But it wasn't in his drawer anymore. The letter was tucked in *The Big Book*, a constant reminder of the destruction left in his wake and the long road of reparation ahead.

But where the fuck was Ember? "*Where is she?*"

"I. Don't. Know."

He wanted to bash Cord's face in. Make him bleed. Terror and powerlessness crippled him and he staggered back. She was supposed to be at his house. He'd been leaving her voicemails. Fuck. What if she wasn't getting his messages? Absolute worry and terror stole his breath, choked out any oxygen left in his lungs.

Panting, he fumbled across the room, searching for some sign that she was near. His unsteady hand closed around the cow shaped saltshaker, wishing it was a beer, wanting to hurl it at Cord. "You have no idea where she is?" His mind couldn't accept that.

"I thought you knew. Jesus, Austin. She left us both. We wrecked everything."

"No!" He shoved Cord's chest, the porcelain cow shattering on the wood floor. "I told you to look after her!"

"Stop!" Cord snapped, gripping his arms.

He couldn't get it together, couldn't think. His entire world, everything he'd balanced his resolve upon was suddenly tipped on end and spilling shit everywhere. "You led me to believe she was safe."

Cord tightened his grip as he tried to shove him again. "I didn't want you to worry."

"Worry? *My fucking wife is missing!*"

Another cramp came, nearly crippling him to the ground. He grunted and doubled over in pain. Fuck. *Fuck!* Words tumbled out. "I can't do this. Where is she? Did she give up? Is it over—*really* over? Goddamn it!"

Strong arms banded around him. His wife—his pride and joy—gone. All. Gone. He leaned into Cord and fought for breath, hoping his heart wouldn't give out. He needed to find her.

Cord's support gradually eased and finally he was strong enough to stand upright again. Breath unsteady, his vision swam as he stared at his biggest enemy and only ally. "We have to find her."

"Austin. I've wracked my brain. I called the hospitals. Called anyone I thought she might crash with. My best guess is she's gone to her parents."

Fuck. He'd driven his wife home to those Luddites, and with the way Misha and Rona roamed, she could be anywhere. Maybe she wasn't even getting his calls. No, he couldn't think that. "The cops would have called if anything bad happened."

"True." Cord returned to his chair and sat, his hands draped between his thighs as he stared at the floor.

Austin raked a hand through his hair. "She found her parents, then. Okay. All right. I have to accept that." He didn't. It had been a comfort to think of her at Cord's house, despite his rank jealousy.

"We'll find her. When you're better. Keep calling and checking in with her. She'll hear it in your voice each day you leave her messages. Eventually, she'll call one of us back."

She'd call him, her husband. Cord was out of the equation at the moment. And also a factor he couldn't quite figure in without wanting to kill him, and right now he needed him.

She had to call sooner rather than later. She was out there. A giant fist seized his belly and he desperately wanted a drink. "Right. Exactly. I'll keep showing her I can do this and eventually she'll pick up."

"You gonna eat?"

Was he out of his fucking mind? He wanted to vomit. "I had enough."

His heart lurched when his gaze dropped to the floor. She loved those ridiculous salt and pepper shakers. He carefully gathered the broken pieces into his palm and placed them on the counter. Another thing to fix. Lord knew where she got them. Another irreplaceable thing broken.

He grabbed the broom and swept up the salt, while Cord silently watched. The guy had a fucking staring problem. Picking up the broken shaker, he slipped the pieces into his pocket. "I'm going to go get dressed. You should head to the store."

"I'm not—"

"You can't babysit me, Cord. You've done enough. You can stay around for a while if you feel like it, but hovering isn't going to keep me honest or sober. That's my job. So go to work. I'll see you later."

He couldn't recall a time his friend ever looked so conflicted, at least not since they'd both gained their manhood status. Confident, alpha males. A bit arrogant. So certain they had life figured out. Now, look at them.

An X-rated vision of Cord with Ember blinked behind his retinas and his gut tightened, sending bile up his throat. He ruthlessly shoved it away. "I...really need a day to myself."

It was time to put certain things into action. Austin Garret had work to do. And he couldn't get what he needed done with Cord looming over him every second.

Cord finally nodded. "Okay, I'll head out. You call if...if you need something."

If I plan to get drunk you mean. Someone should *really* write him a hero riff. Despite his friend's good intentions, Austin wanted to knock him down a peg, but he kept his anger to himself.

"I will. See ya later." Because there was no doubt Cord would be back. *Because he's your friend.*

After a long shower and several bouts of sitting around despite his earlier motivation, Austin contemplated the rest of the morning. He'd missed so many mornings, forgotten how peaceful they could be. However, without his wife there to keep him company, the peacefulness seemed more like loneliness.

It was the first time he truly considered how hard the silence must have been on her, the times he'd been home, but absent, sleeping it off. He was a shitty, fucking asshole.

She'd begged him to sit with her in the beginning, when he'd first lost his job, but he'd always made an excuse, not wanting to put on a happy front when his head was in the shitter. He'd give anything to sit with her now.

He glanced at her chair, the one she used when she sewed the buttons back on his shirts or worked on something for the house. He could almost picture her there, smiling up at him when she caught him watching her. His lips twitched in a half smile and then he frowned, seeing nothing but upholstery and the vacant surroundings.

The urge to take action beckoned again and the fear that the urge might morph into a craving for something else set him into motion. Clearing a spot on the floor, he dropped to the carpet and began counting off sit-ups. God, he was out of shape.

His muscles were sore and his back weak. At one time, he could do hundreds. Now he was lucky if he knocked out fifty. Dropping flat with a huff, he stared at the crack in the ceiling. Add that to the list of things that needed fixing around here.

Rolling to his stomach, he pumped out a few push-ups, which were more pathetic than his attempted sit-ups. How had he let himself go like this? It was probably a relief to December that he'd stopped pestering her for sex. He was disgusting.

If he was going to heal his insides, he might as well tackle the whole package. He decided he'd start a morning regimen to get himself back in shape.

Pushed to his limit, he wandered the hall and chuckled. Oddly enough, he sort of missed Cord. Was he out there, looking for her? The terror of his earlier revelation returned, stirring him up and reminding him of his priorities. He kept moving, searching for a distraction.

A half a pot of coffee remained, still warm, on the burner. A clean mug waited for him.

He'd never been much of a coffee drinker. He enjoyed a few sips to start the day, but after that he left the stuff alone. This morning, however, he brewed a second pot and consumed at least four cups.

When the silence grated his nerves to almost nothing, the temptation to find a drink multiplied. His breathing became labored, worse than when he'd been working out, though all he was doing was sitting, sipping coffee. Stillness suffocated him. The walls began to close in and he needed to get out. Fast.

Grabbing his keys and coat, he rushed out the front door and into his truck. The engine protested, but he got the old girl started. The interior didn't warm up until he was halfway across town. With a quarter tank of gas and nowhere to be, his escape could only last so long.

Passing the church, his mind recalled last night's experience. Would he go back there tonight? He still wasn't sure. He'd have to leave the house to get Cord off his back, but whether he made it to a meeting was anyone's guess.

He parked in a lot at the end of town. The liquor store was to his left, the hardware store to his right. If he wanted something all he had to do was go in and buy it. The disapproval of others wasn't enough to deter him, but it helped. No, this was about his own approval.

"You're not going to drink today," he said to himself, feeling like an idiot for speaking aloud, but also finding some comfort in the sound of his voice.

His gaze sought Cord's truck in the lot. He thought about all the times he'd been offered a job by his friend. Where would he be now if he'd taken Cord up on his offer all those months ago? December would probably still be with him.

December.

She worked in that store, alongside Cord. His hand rubbed across his brow, and he grimaced, rubbing the damp trace of sweat between his fingers. His attention skittered back to the liquor store and he swallowed.

He glared at the *Bay's Hardware* sign. Jealousy choked him, tightening his gut. He wasn't sure what brought on the tremors. Could be the temptation of drowning his turbulent thoughts in a bottle or the temptation to unleash on his friend.

The back of his hand rubbed across his lips as he debated. Why had he even come here?

He'd always liked that his wife and best friend got along, but lately, his gut couldn't take the image of the two being chummy. He'd somehow managed to compartmentalize the truth of recent events, tucking them away for a day when he was stronger, but sooner or later he'd have to face what happened.

He still believed, on some level, that he'd done the right thing in enlisting Cord as...what? A standby husband for Ember? She'd needed Cord, someone she could trust...and love. Someone to count on, like she did Austin—before he royally fucked everything up and left her adrift.

Jealousy was a stupid, soul sucking emotion. He'd picked the right guy, no doubt. What he hadn't considered in his narrow, alcohol soaked state, was that she would view it as rejection. And a shredding of the very fabric of their reality.

He had to get past blaming Cord. Had he really expected the man to be able to withstand the onslaught of Austin's demand and the temptation that was December?

He and Cord would have to *talk* about it. His stomach roiled at the very thought, and he forced his thoughts elsewhere. December might be MIA, but she was always in his head.

With a mental shake, he set the uncomfortable topic aside and considered his wife's recent employment. What had she done at the store? Did she work the register? Clean the shelves? Do something in the back with orders and inventory? He didn't like imagining her working there, but now he was curious and wished he'd taken the time to ask what her days were like.

Glancing at his watch, he sighed. It was late morning and he was sitting in his truck accomplishing nothing. Might as well be sleeping. "Fuck."

Plucking the keys from the ignition, he climbed out and made his way through the cold and toward the stores. Unsure which way he was going, he surprised himself when his feet suddenly pulled right and took him into Bay's.

No one was at the register, but he sensed people nearby. Passing a few customers, he weaved his way up and down aisles. If he had money he could buy the supplies to fix that crack in the bedroom ceiling.

In the tile section he found a stack of boxes just sitting there, needing to be stocked. The packaging was cut open, but not unloaded. It was an enormous shipment that blocked a good part of the aisle. What if the woman shopping over in home goods wanted to get through here with her cart? Someone could trip.

Austin eyed the shelves, noting that the tile was individually packaged in sets. Peeking in the boxes, he saw each set tied in pairs with plastic bands. Someone had left a box cutter on top of the cases, so he picked it up and sliced the band. Next thing he knew he was stocking the shelves.

As his body warmed, he removed his coat and tossed it aside. Each box he emptied, he collapsed and piled away to unblock the aisle. The obstruction was gone in a matter of minutes, so he proceeded to straighten the shelves and pull items to the edge where customers could reach.

"Austin?"

He didn't turn at the sound of Cord's voice. "Hey."

"What are you doing here?"

He climbed the metal shelves and pulled a flat of grout forward, stacking each little bucket near the edge. "Those tiles needed putting away and these shelves need organizing."

Cord was silent, but Austin could feel the weight of his thoughts, his ever-present stare.

Jumping to the floor, he grabbed the folded up boxes and his coat. "You got a dumpster?"

"Uh, yeah. In the back."

Nodding, he carried the trash to the rear. He didn't see Cord over the next hour, but sometimes he heard him speaking to customers. Austin wasn't into customer service, but there was plenty to do around the store that he could handle.

There wasn't time to consider if he was intruding—if Cord even wanted him there. Between the aisles that needed stocking and organizing, he kept himself busy. When he ran out of shit to put away, he found a push broom and shoved that around for a while.

"Yo, Austin," Cord called from the end of the lighting aisle.

"Yeah?"

"There's a shipment of lumber coming in. You wanna give me a hand unloading it?"

"Sure. I'll be done here in a sec."

It was easy, working alongside Cord when he didn't think about anything. Somehow, they'd found a reprieve within performing menial chores, working in the hardware store and that suited him just fine.

At six o'clock, when the store was closing down, he remembered how quickly a productive day could move. He hadn't even stopped to eat and was too busy to think about hunger—or thirst. But as the lights dimmed and the customers slowly disappeared, demons began to stir.

"You ready to go?" Cord spoke behind him, his presence a sudden bulwark against the resurfacing storm of need.

Shaking off the start of a cold sweat, he nodded. "Yeah. Let me just grab my coat in the back."

He walked his way through the store, trying to distract himself with a mental list of things he could do tomorrow. What would happen when they got home? Would they talk about him being the new self-proclaimed employee?

He didn't want to have that conversation. He didn't want to address the fact that he'd done what everyone said he should do months ago. Finally gotten off his ass and gone to work—for Cord. How fucking juvenile was he?

Cord waited at the front of the store with the keys in hand. Austin dug out his own keys and set his eyes on his truck—escape. Dreading the thought of Cord dictating his next move, the words left his mouth before he'd given them much thought. "I'm heading to the church."

Cord stilled, a thousand assumptions in his eyes. Austin couldn't bring himself to offer explanations he didn't have. He only knew he didn't want one-on-one time with his friend, so he marched directly to his truck and climbed in.

When he reached the church lot, there were only six cars. He didn't see the black Escalade and that made him uneasy for reasons he didn't understand. His stomach growled, emphasizing his hunger, but he didn't have any money to eat.

How had December afforded groceries? The simple thought brought his phone to his ear.

"Hey, baby, it's me. I'm getting ready to go to my second meeting. I miss you. I know I don't say it enough, but you're amazing. You've done so much to make our life happy. I just want you to know I appreciate all of it, even the stuff you probably think I didn't notice. I noticed."

His gaze remained on the doors to the meeting

as his thumb picked at the worn part of the steering wheel. "I worked today. At the hardware store. It felt good to get out and do something productive. Necessary on a mental level. Physical, too." He gave a rusty chuckle. "I let myself go. I know nothing's really changed, but I'm making progress. I can feel it, even if it's only a state of mind."

A small, bundled figure, likely a woman, entered the church. He sniffed, his nose cold from sitting so long in his truck. "Ember, I hope you're okay, wherever you are. I...I thought you were safe at Cord's. I'm worried about you. But I get it. We all need time to catch our breath once in a while."

Another figure entered the church and something inside of him twitched, as if hurrying him along like he was about to miss a train. "I better go. Feel free to call me if you want to talk." He laughed. "I'd even take you yelling at me if it meant I could hear your voice for a minute. I love you."

He leaned back in his seat and let out a long breath. If anything, the meeting was a place to grab a donut and a warm cup of coffee. Getting to the door was easier the second time around and the next thing he knew he was sipping a cup of shitty java and biting into a day old pastry.

He was grateful for the sustenance, even if it didn't fill him. Didn't ease the craving gnawing in his belly. He took a seat in the back and this evening he didn't waste time thinking about those sharing the room. His thoughts focused on himself.

The meeting had yet to start, but he'd begun on his own, centering his mind and reiterating all the reasons he was there. He thought about the passages he'd breezed over in *The Big Book* and decided he'd give it another look tonight when he got home.

When the meeting officially started, he cleared his mind of judgment, opened his ears, and listened. Some stories were harder to listen to than others. He wouldn't be sharing his shame with a room full of strangers. Not because of them, but because of him. It simply wasn't in him to exploit his lowest of lows.

It was odd how a stranger's story could tug threads to memories he'd all but forgotten. His father drank. He'd grown up in a house that always had beer in the fridge. When his mother passed away after his twelfth birthday, his memories were a collective slideshow of his father cracking open cans and not looking beyond the television set, unless to point out something Austin was doing wrong. It hadn't always been that way.

At one time his childhood home had been a happy place. His mother was always there to help with homework and patch his jeans. She cooked, not great, but frequently. They had a modest little rancher on the other side of town until his dad sold off their land to developers.

He hadn't talked to his dad in months. God, maybe over a year. Beyond the condition of his truck or the effect of the cold climate on his arthritis, there wasn't much his father liked to discuss. But show him a flaw and he'd beat it to fucking death.

He'd come to their wedding and met December a few times, but other than that, he never showed much interest in family, which was probably best.

In a way, Austin appreciated his father's absence, but maybe a small part of him resented it. December used to push him to invite his dad for a visit. He'd extended an invitation once or twice, but the man always had an excuse at the ready. And the few times he did show up, he always made a point to tell Austin what he could do better. It didn't matter that his father no longer owned a home, he had plenty to criticize about Austin's.

And after a while, his wife quit pushing. She didn't much care for his father's attention to detail and critical comments. Another failure on his part, not running interference and telling his father off when he harassed her.

They really didn't have much in the way of family. December's parents were hippies, joined by some ritual involving a hookah and togas. She'd always wanted a simple, traditional life. It was so easy to give her that. It killed him that she was likely back with Rona and Misha revisiting the unstructured lifestyle she'd spent years trying to escape.

The hour passed and the meeting concluded. What seemed abhorrent just yesterday had become tolerable. As he left the church, avoiding eye contact with others, he spotted the black Escalade pulling out of the lot. Harley had been there and somehow Austin missed him.

Out of curiosity, he drove past the diner and pulled in when he spotted the now familiar black vehicle. Harley was sitting at the same booth he'd occupied the night before. His dark hand flipped over the neighboring coffee cup before Austin made it to the booth.

"I hoped you'd be back."

The idea of being predictable grated on him, but he didn't know why. "I wasn't sure."

"Coffee?"

"Yeah."

Harley waved over the waitress and she filled his cup.

"You can leave the pot."

She left the coffee beside a small dish of cream and returned to the front of the diner.

"How's it going?" Harley asked, doctoring up his own mug.

"Good." Austin dumped a few sugar packets

into his mug and swirled in some cream. When the hot beverage hit his stomach he sighed. "Coffee's good here."

Harley chuckled. "No, it's not, but it's better than booze. How many have you had today?"

"Beers?" Austin asked, shocked he'd assumed he was drinking. "None."

Harley again laughed. "No, I mean coffee. Recovering alcoholics tend to live off the stuff. That and cigarettes. You a smoker?"

Was that true? It sounded a little stereotypical, but Austin did seem to be developing an obsession with it. "I've never smoked, but I've been drinking a lot more coffee than I usually do."

The man eased his weight in the booth, resting his arm casually on the back of the bench. "What are your thoughts on God, Austin?"

Here we go.

He didn't want to offend, but he also didn't want to get into some born again campaign to find his savior. He believed in God, had a special understanding about attending church on religious holidays, and didn't get too wrapped up in all the little rules.

"I believe there's right and wrong and a good man knows the difference."

Harley nodded. "I look at religion like a dick."

Austin choked and swallowed down his mouthful of coffee before it spit past his lips. "Excuse me?"

"It's fine to have one, but it's impolite to go waving it in people's faces or jamming it down their throats."

A bubble of laughter slipped out. The guy was definitely nuts, but Austin was growing fond of him. "Agreed."

"Good. However, I'm curious if you believe in a higher power."

"You mean like heaven and hell?"

"I mean like anything bigger and more powerful than you."

"Sure. I couldn't take on a tornado and I'd likely drown in a tsunami. Mother nature's stronger than me."

"Interesting that you went to the feminine explanation before the typically male theory."

Austin shrugged. "Women are impressive. Like any female, Mother Nature should be respected."

"Good man. But my point is that you believe some things are out of your control."

"Well, yeah. I never did great in science, but I've watched enough Discovery Channel to know the universe is way bigger than us. Who knows what happens in the next life? This one's hard enough to figure out."

"That's an important outlook to keep. Humble, to know we're merely men, not to be confused with the so-called gods."

"Trust me, I'm no god."

"Good thing too. Imagine how many times we'd abuse the privilege of turning water to wine," Harley laughed but Austin couldn't see the humor. He wasn't to the joking point yet. "What did you do today?"

"I worked. It's been a while."

"Economy's tough right now. Anything else?"

"I exercised a little. Called my wife."

"She away right now?"

Austin's lips pressed tight. "Yeah."

Harley nodded, allowing his confession a moment of silence. "I bet it felt good to have control of your day."

"It did. I barely stopped and didn't mind. I could have kept going, but...I ended up here."

"I'm glad. I was looking forward to talking with you some more. A week ago, what were you doing?"

"Nothing."

"Had to be doing something."

"I was lying on my couch drinking."

"By choice?"

"Yes."

"Really?"

Austin flipped over an empty packet of sugar. His knuckles were still banged up from the last wall he'd punched. Why had he done that? Had any of it been a choice?

Back then he'd promised December he wouldn't drink, but somehow it was the only thing he'd accomplished that day and the day before that and the ones that followed. Then he decided he couldn't take any more, wrote her a letter that basically massacred the last bit of normal his life was impersonating—albeit with the best intentions—and then he kicked off the week with attempting suicide.

He shook his head. "I don't know."

"Some people drink because they enjoy the taste of a good merlot. Some do it for fun and some do it because there's nothing better to do. I used to be in one of those categories, then I just did it to hide. I kept failing, you know? Even simple shit I'd always done I couldn't get right anymore. I couldn't take it. I was disappointing everyone—all the time. If I was sober for a second, they'd hit me with everything I was doing wrong. Fucking depressing. So I drank some more."

Austin knew what that was like. *Exactly* what it was like.

"It was like living in a coma. Things happened I couldn't recall, most of them I'm lucky I missed. But my wife...she was there and she suffered every minute I was too wasted to feel. Then she died."

Harley's admission hit him like a punch. His mind shifted to Ember and his worry tightened enough to turn his stomach inside out. He swallowed, physically fighting the sense that he was about to be sick. "I'm sorry."

Harley nodded. "Me too. I have a hard time

with God. Mohammad, Makah, Yahweh, they're all foreign. I don't like to think about karma. Did I mention a drunk driver killed my wife?"

Austin's skin prickled uncomfortably. No explanation was needed. He understood—loud and clear—the point Harley was making. His hand pressed to his pocket, feeling for his phone as he wanted to call Ember to see if she was okay, but she probably wouldn't answer.

"I eventually found another love, but nothing will bring back my wife and that's something I'll have to live with until it's my time to see her again."

"Is that when you stopped drinking, when you lost her?"

"What do you think? Put yourself in my shoes. I'm a raging alcoholic and the last person that loved me suddenly dies, killed in a car accident just because some asshole decided to run a red light."

Jesus, the mere thought made him want to find oblivion.

Harley shook his head. "Hell, no. That's when I drank the most. Days—weeks—were lost. I truly hit rock bottom, not that other shit you assume is rock bottom. I'm talking about the hell beneath all of that. But that was also when I realized I was powerless against my addiction. I should have stopped, but I couldn't. Drinking was literally killing me."

Austin hadn't died, but his visit to the psych ward was close enough. When they'd sent someone in to talk to him, he couldn't bear a single word.

But in the end, he was in hell. His wife had left him. He had no job, no money. His house was falling apart. His body was failing in ways too humiliating to even think about. Yeah, he'd found the other side of hell.

"I'm guessing, by the fact that your woman ain't around right now, you're beginning to see it's bigger than you, just like I realized it was bigger than me."

Reaching for his empty mug, Austin poured himself more coffee. "Her name's December."

Somehow talking about her didn't hurt like talking about other things did. She was the good in his life, his light to his darkness.

"We met when I was twenty. She was still a teenager, but legal. I fell in love with her the moment I set eyes on her. You know how you describe rock bottom? Our love was the complete opposite of that. There was love—the kind people assumed was as real as it got—and then there was what we had."

"She sounds like an incredible woman."

"She is."

"A woman like that deserves a pretty impressive man."

Austin nodded, shame and other unpleasant

feelings pressing down on him. "That used to be me."

"It's still you," Harley said, his dark eyes conveying his sincerity. "You're there. You just gotta clear away all the bullshit that's interfering with your potential."

"That's what I'm trying to do."

Harley reached into his pocket and pulled out a folded piece of paper. Sliding it across the table, he said, "You need to take inventory of yourself. Read the book, Austin. It's the best tool you got right now aside from your free will."

Removing a pen from his pocket he jotted down a number on the paper. "Once you've made your personal inventory, call me and we'll talk some more." He stood and dropped some money on the table. "Coffee's on me."

He'd just opened up his soul and the guy was leaving? A sudden dread of more isolation startled him out of his seat. "Harley."

The man turned as he shouldered on his coat. "Yeah?"

Austin took a breath. Another chance to talk would come tomorrow. It was something to look forward to. Then it clicked.

This was helping him.

A tentative grin pulled his lips. "Thanks." He took the paper from the table and placed it in his pocket.

Harley nodded. "Anytime."

Driving home, a sense of familiar yet strange contentment settled over him. While he was still torn apart and missing his wife to a point beyond pain, there had been something ordinary about his day, something basic and straightforward he hadn't experienced in some time. Something... soothing.

Perhaps it was getting out of the house and going to work, although Bay's wasn't his job. Or maybe it was finding Harley waiting for him, a sort of end cap to the past sixteen hours and vindication he hadn't made things worse.

As he drove, his brow tightened. Little puzzle pieces fell into place to make a picture of his day, one he'd lived through yet barely recognized. Today felt...better. Did that mean he was recovering?

He slammed on the brakes, nearly running a red light on the vacant road leading to his house as his mind whirled. If he was recovering, that meant he had a legitimate problem.

Alcoholic.

Fuck, it was the first time he'd actually considered the word and understood how much it described the last chunk of his life. No wife, no job, no control, nothing but that unyielding urge to take a drink and smother his discontent.

But today he felt a speck of contentment. He felt alive, like he had a purpose again.

He blinked through the startling revelation,

looking up in time to catch the green light cycling back to yellow, then red. He dropped his head back against the seat rest, feeling like a load of bricks had landed on his shoulders, but this time he had a clear frame of mind and could actually see what he was up against.

I'm an alcoholic.

His mind tried to shun the words, but the blaring, silent truth lodged in his throat like a painful pill he wasn't sure he could swallow. Then another realization broke through the haze. Harley was an alcoholic, but he was recovered. At one time he'd been *recovering*.

Passing through the traffic light as it turned green again, his mind moved a million miles a minute, all thoughts leading back to December. He wasn't going to merely be an alcoholic. He was going to recover from this, recover all he'd lost—his control, his pride, his purpose, and, goddamn it, his wife.

That was his goal. And it was so damn clear, so glaringly obvious, it focused all his energy toward the little pinhole of light suddenly recognizable at the other end of the tunnel.

He would get there. Step by step, day by day, he was going to make it through.

Eight

Cord

CORD WASN'T PREPARED for the coming weeks. He should have been, but Austin had changed so much he didn't think it was possible for him to revert back to old—positive— habits so quickly. Of course, that could change at any second, but over the passing of a relatively short period of time he'd been blown away by the transformation in his friend. Like a switch had been thrown.

Every morning Austin woke up before Cord, returned to the house sweaty and energized from his morning run before Cord even had a chance to brew the coffee. It was disarming in several ways, and although Cord appreciated the positive turn, it worried him about other issues—his own personal ones.

Austin would grab a quick cup while he was still scrubbing the grit from his bleary eyes, then would disappear to his room for a while. At first, Cord didn't know what he was doing in there. But as Austin became less closed off, he realized he'd been using the time to work out—like running was just an appetizer. The guy went from built to zombie to ripped faster than he believed physically possible.

And it wasn't only his body that was changing. His complexion took on a healthy glow and his attitude underwent a total transformation. The slovenly couch potato with ruddy cheeks, bloodshot eyes, and shit attitude was gone. Strangely, this worried Cord because he couldn't help feeling like he'd soon be displaced. If Ember knew all the progress her husband was making she'd likely come home and Cord's presence would be pointless. He didn't care what kind of man that made him. There had to be room in her life for him, too.

Austin usually showed up at work shortly after Cord opened the store, jumping right into whatever needed doing. Work was the easiest time of day for Cord where his friend was concerned. They could talk about store related things without issue. But at home their conversations remained stilted. He took what he could get, glad Austin was speaking at all.

Every night Cord heated up something easy for dinner and left it on the stove so Austin could eat when he returned from his nightly meeting. He was curious about the meetings and what actually took place. Austin frequently mentioned his friend Harley, who Cord assumed was his sponsor, but he never gave away more than small details.

"Harley gets these work boots that have a lifetime guarantee. If they dry out the company replaces the soles."

"My friend Harley told me about the compound he used to seal his deck. You don't carry it at the store and maybe you should. He says it's the best. I'm thinking about building a deck when the weather breaks."

It was ridiculous to be jealous of Harley. The man was Austin's sponsor, an ex-drinker who should only be relevant where recovery was concerned. Cord was thankful Austin found someone who understood what he was going through, but also resented that *he* couldn't be that friend.

He wanted to be Austin's confidant like he'd always been, but their relationship was damaged and Harley, apparently, was better suited for the job. Cord reminded himself daily, since Austin wasn't confiding in him, they were lucky there was a Harley.

Austin was slowly returning to his old self, but

he was somehow more estranged than ever. They never discussed December and that was probably for the best.

Cord left her a message nearly every day, okay, sometimes twice a day, just a quick update about how things were going. How Austin was doing. How he, Cord, missed her and wished they could turn back time. He'd only actually said that once, because he meant it, yet he didn't. He missed her so badly.

He worried about her, and if he was worried, what was Austin feeling?

His friend would sometimes mention her while making repairs around the house.

"December will be glad to see that fixed." But Cord wasn't sure she'd ever know.

The longer time went on with no word from her, the more he feared she might never come back. He didn't have the courage or desire to discuss his suspicions with Austin. The assumption of her return might be the only thing keeping him sober.

The phone never rang, but sometimes Austin's voice carried from his room, his tone pitched with tender affection the way it often had been when he spoke to Ember. Confusion and jealousy ate at Cord when he overheard muffled conversations coming from behind Austin's closed door. Was he talking to her and not merely getting her voicemail? He thought Austin would tell him if he actually made contact, but maybe not.

Something happened to him since sharing his bed with his friend's wife. The feelings he'd concealed all those years magnified and refused to go away, and were now stirring other things best left ignored.

For nearly a decade he'd done the honorable thing, but hearing her voice, her need that night, and knowing she needed him pushed him to his limit. He'd been weak and would likely grapple with the circumstances wrought by his actions for the rest of his life.

Story. Of. His. Life.

It had been weeks since Austin had taken a drink. Cord feared his presence was no longer necessary. His friend had given no hint about wanting to harm himself again. On the contrary, everything he did spoke of a need to improve his quality of life and build a better situation for when December returned.

By Austin's attitude, it seemed an inevitable outcome. He was just so damn sure of himself, of her. Meanwhile, Cord was turning into a fucking basket case.

He knew he should leave, but Austin never suggested it, and he couldn't make himself go. December was gone. Austin was all he had left in this mess, even if their relationship wasn't anything like it was before. Living with Austin felt one step closer to happiness, closer to December. Yet the truth was, he was more miserable than he'd ever been before. How did living with Austin make him feel lonelier than when he'd lived alone?

Yet he stayed, awaiting the day she'd come home and he'd no longer be necessary in their lives, no longer wanted. Every day that Austin got better, Cord's future looked bleaker. His friend's victory would be his loss, and it was never supposed to be that way.

With the arrival of April, came the wet weather. Remnants of snowdrifts dotted the town in tarnished eyesores. The ground squished like a wet sponge begging to be rung dry and the first sight of spring flowers really drove home how much time had passed. Days grew longer, and the winter that changed all of them, eventually melted away.

Spring was always a busy time of year at the store. After months of cabin fever, people were antsy to get a jump on summer. Outdoor fireplaces were purchased, lawn furniture went on display, and all those home improvements the cold weather prevented could finally get started.

Their seasonal hours extended, as customers tended to dawdle with the longer days. Austin never complained about staying later at the store. Somehow, he always made it to the other end of town in time to end his day with his friend Harley.

Then one evening, mid-April, just as he was

getting back to the house after a long day of unloading summer inventory, Cord came home to a surprise. Rather than being at the church, Austin waited for him at the kitchen table.

Hanging up his keys, Cord scanned the kitchen. Something was up. Was he finally throwing him out?

"Hey," he greeted nervously, searching for any telltale sign that Ember was there or might be.

"Hey."

The imbalanced energy of the room had him cautiously avoiding a seat. "What's going on? I thought you'd be with Harley."

"Not tonight."

Cord paused, sensing he was walking into a trap. "Everything okay?"

"Yeah. I wanted to talk."

Oh, crap. Hiding his many reservations, he feigned nonchalance and slid into a chair, the gravity of his friend's mood pressing into him with every pulsing second.

Austin drew in a deep breath and audibly exhaled. "I don't know where to start. I knew, but now..." His attention skittered to the counter. "How about some coffee?"

Not really wanting the caffeine, but sensing they could both use a few minutes to collect themselves, Cord agreed to the distraction.

Austin busied himself setting the pot to brew and waited, keeping his back to the table. "I want to thank you," he said, his voice low and muffled by the chugging of the percolating machine.

Not seeing his face made his words difficult to interpret. "For?" He wasn't being a smart ass. Cord honestly didn't know what he'd done that required gratitude.

Austin turned, leaning his hip against the cabinets. "Everything. You're a good friend. You stood by me when I was unbearable. You pulled us out of a financial hole I couldn't face or overcome on my own. You gave me a job when I desperately needed one and offered me work countless times, before, when I was too stubborn to accept. You looked after Ember when she needed someone." His lips pressed tight and his gaze dropped to the floor. "You were there for her when I couldn't be, when I asked you...well, you were there. I don't know how to repay you for that."

"You don't need to thank me, Austin—"

"Yes, I do. I...I guess what I'm trying to say is that I... Well, you're the closest thing I have to family. You're my best friend. One of the most important people in my life. You being here these last few months...sometimes I think it's the only thing that's kept me breathing."

His gratitude weighed uncomfortably, too heavy for Cord to bear. "It wasn't merely for your benefit."

"I know that too."

A hollow pain filled his gut as he debated the

profits of honesty. Austin was putting a lot on the line, addressing the issues he'd been too afraid to face. Cord owed him the truth. It would come out eventually. "I love her."

"I know. You felt something for her ten years ago—"

"Not like this," he clarified. "Not the way your best friend should love your wife, Austin. It's wrong. I think of her and I miss her. I call her, leave her messages, sometimes to let her know you're doing good, but also to tell her how much I miss her. I want her to come back..." He was a terrible person. "But not to you. Part of me wants that, but a bigger part wants her to come back to *me*."

Cord stood, unable to bear his own presence anymore. "I stayed here for you but also because this is where she'd most likely return. I'm Judas. Save your gratitude for someone that deserves it."

"Wait." Austin moved toward him, but hesitated. His eyes were troubled and lines of strain bracketed his mouth. Taking a deep breath that expanded his broad chest, he said, "The coffee's done." He turned and grabbed the mugs.

"Fuck the coffee, Austin. Did you hear anything I just said? I'm in love with your *wife*."

His friend's shoulders lifted as he stared down at the counter. "I heard you. I can't blame you, I guess. We...have to talk about it—without fighting. We *need* to talk about this."

"Why?" There was nothing to talk about. Pressing the subject would only end badly.

"Because I can't make amends with you until we do."

Fuck. He should have realized this was part of Austin's recovery. It didn't make sense to drag out all this garbage and ruin a perfectly good evening when they'd successfully ignored the elephant in the room for nearly three months. "Can't we just say it is what it is and move on?"

"No."

There it was. The final verdict, an unbreakable bone they'd likely fight over for the rest of their lives. This would be the end of a lifelong friendship. But it was part of Austin's recovery, and Cord wouldn't be the one to hold him back. His bitter self-pity abraded his soul.

He slid into the chair he'd vacated, a sense of loss already overwhelming him. "I'm listening."

Austin took his time carrying the mugs to the table. "I've come to understand that I resented you when we were kids. I was jealous that you had such a great family and I had a ghost for a mother and a father who ignored me—gave more attention to his next beer. When he did actually *see* me, he was sure to let me know he wasn't impressed.

"When we met December, you saw her first. Your whole face transformed. I followed your gaze until I saw what had you so captivated. Then she had me under her spell too. I never gave you the chance to talk to her, because I wanted her, and fuck my best friend or anyone else who got in my way—you already had so much. I lost all perspective once she spoke, I knew there was something special about her I couldn't figure out—didn't need to. I only needed her to be *mine.* I swooped in and did everything I could to steal her attention."

It was probably the one day all three of them would never forget. Cord's focus had been elsewhere, his attention on a different objective, stupidly hoping. But then he saw her, this little slip of a girl and he knew—just knew—Austin would see her too.

He knew his friend, knew his likes, and knew what attracted him. It was an inevitable moment and one he'd never forget. It had been the first and only time in his life he'd ever considered coming clean with Austin, and even then he'd waited too long. Everything changed the day they met December.

"I know she noticed you first," Cord added, wanting to make the retelling of their past as painless as possible.

"Maybe. But I had to work for it, really make her believe I was good enough to be her man." He laughed with a touch of disgust. "Sometimes I even acted like you, thinking how you would respond to things and what you would say. In the back of my mind, I knew I wasn't good enough for her and you were the better man, but I wanted her and I was determined to have her."

Well, wasn't that just fan-fucking-tastic? There was something believable in Austin's words, but Cord's mind couldn't go there. He couldn't accept that she'd fallen for someone imitating *him*. No one was that good of an actor and at the end of the day, Ember loved Austin—warts and all.

"Your memory's distorted, buddy. Yes, I noticed her. And yes, I wanted her. But she only had eyes for you. But that was *then*. Once you two became a thing I *never* intended to interfere. That's the truth, Austin."

What happened with Ember was a fluke. No matter the outcome Cord wanted, the truth never escaped him. December was Austin's wife. He never should have touched her.

Austin shook his head, his eyes narrowing. "We can't do this if we aren't being honest, Cord."

Fuck honesty. Austin wouldn't be able to handle the absolute truth and Cord was growing damn tired of the lies. But he had to keep his focus on what was right and not let another wrong impact their fragile relationship. Shit was broken enough.

"You might have shown her your best side, but it was all you, Austin. Even if you *were* trying to be like someone else,"—*me*—"it was you she fell in love with." And it pissed him off more than he could bear to think she might have been in some way duped.

Austin continued to shake his head. "We aren't that different, you and I. We share the same values, like the same music, watch the same shows. But you have depth I can't compete with. You're smart, Cord. Smarter than me. Remember when I teased you about being a shopkeeper? I convinced myself it was more respectable for a man to *make* his way in the world, rather than accepting what other generations built.

"I never gave you the credit you deserved. I'm fucked up. My own insecurities got the better of me. I was so afraid the act I was putting on would eventually fall apart and December would realize she'd settled way below what she deserved. Not being able to find work for so long...triggered something."

Cord kept quiet, like he always did to that sort of insult. A lot of people assumed inheriting an established company took less work than creating a new one, but that was bullshit. His dad retired when the bigger stores forced him to. It was Cord who kept the store alive, brought it back to life when it was under threat like all the other mom and pop's. He knew how hard he worked and didn't need to justify shit to anyone.

Austin glanced at the fridge, his thumb gliding slowly over the handle of his coffee mug. Despite

Cord's instinct to let the comment roll off his back, it scraped all the way down.

He liked having Austin working at his side, didn't really see him as an employee, rather, something more. It felt the same as when Ember had been there. Unable to keep his mouth closed, he admitted, "It's still a lot of work. You've helped me. Did you ever think my offer for you to work at Bay's wasn't only for your benefit?"

Austin glanced at him and nodded. "I know it's a lot of work. I know how hard *you* work, which is why I regret not realizing it sooner."

A bit of the sting eased. Maybe one day the three of them could work there. All together. That would be amazing. He was getting ahead of himself—*way* ahead. "Sorry, go back to what you were saying."

"When I lost my job, I slowly began to lose everything. December always adored you. I'd watch the two of you laugh and found myself thinking, that's the kind of guy she should have married. You've got something...more than me, and it makes her respond. I know I hid my insecurity, but as your success grew, so did my self-doubt. And I hated myself, because I had the best woman in the world, *and* the best friend, but I felt it all slipping away."

"No one was leaving you, Austin."

He held up a hand, his eyes briefly closing as if he were bracing for the sharp point of all this disclosure. Cord didn't know how much more he could hear.

"It was only a matter of time before I lost her. I couldn't manage my life, couldn't be the guy she deserved. And *you* became the biggest threat. *I* was losing."

"It was never a competition—"

Austin laughed coldly. "No shit. It killed me to see you handle everything with an ease I couldn't muster. Competing with you exhausted the hell out of me—"

"Damn it, Austin, it wasn't a fucking competition. I was trying to—"

"Help. I know. And you did. Meanwhile, I became such a pussy I lost control of everything. Even when I tried, I fucked up. So I just gave up and eventually—while you effortlessly took up the role of her hero—I admitted I'd never be you and she didn't deserve the real me."

Jesus. He hadn't realized Austin begrudged him so much. Had his friend's shitty childhood created this part of his adult self that Cord was only now discovering?

He frowned, not accepting he was better than anyone else. And irritated Austin couldn't recognize how great of a guy he was. He had no need to copy others.

"There's nothing wrong with the person you are. Do you think I'd have hung out with you if there was? I mean, we've been there for one another since before we could walk. I never saw you as somebody beneath me."

"I just never felt I measured up."

"Whose defective thinking is that? Don't tell me I laid that on you. I'm sorry your family wasn't there for you like mine was, but we don't get to pick our parents. I've never rubbed my home life in your face. We've always invited you to holidays and family dinners—you're like family. My parents adore you and Ember. Fuck, you have more of a friendship with my dad than I do!

"Christ, you want to talk about jealousy, whoever you tried to be, at the end of the day December saw the real you. Having loving parents and job security is one thing, but it will never compare to having a wife like her."

Austin brooded over his coffee, his mouth a taut line. "I took advantage of her trusting nature, sold her a jalopy hiding behind a luxury label. This past year, everything started to break all at once. I was losing it and so much of the darkness I hid inside spilled out. I didn't change. She finally got a glimpse of the real me. She trusted me. I was supposed to be the head of our household and half the time I'd been guessing how to be a man."

"Austin, faking or not, up until last year you were doing it. You were the man you appeared to be. You took care of her. You were a responsible guy, an honorable husband. The man she left...

that guy isn't the real you. That was the alcohol—"

"No. That was *me*. The alcohol gave me courage, a little breathing room to hide, but then it started to make everything worse. I couldn't take the pressure, couldn't be as perfect as you, so I just stopped trying, knowing she'd eventually give up on me."

"Knock it off," Cord snapped. "I've known you my entire life and the asshole I met this past year was brand fucking new. You want someone to baby you, and buy all this bullshit, you picked the wrong guy. I know you too well. I don't care how fucked up you think you are, she loves *all* of you. Be a man and appreciate the gift that is. You can't do that, you don't deserve her."

"She loves an impersonation of *you*."

What the fuck?

"*Enough!* You may resemble me in some ways. I resemble you too. We've been friends since day-care. But you're still you and that's who she loves. We're not interchangeable, no matter how you'd like to assume we are." This was the twisted thinking that unraveled everything before.

"I know we're not interchangeable. My greatest regret in life is being too fucked up to re-alize that sooner. What I'm trying to say—Jesus, I'm still fucking this all up—is that she deserved *you*, instead of me. I have to make that up to her. I need to *be* a better man, not just pretend to be one."

Cord pressed his palm on the table, trying to calm himself. It was impossible to keep his emotions out of the conversation when he felt so much regarding December.

"Well, you're getting there. I don't know what else to say." Cord had his chance. It didn't change shit, made things worse. "She'll always love you more, because she loved you first, and what the fuck difference does it make anyway when she's gone?" Besides, she was only a third of the equation anyway.

"You see? That's the good guy, the one who will back off because he believes it's the best thing for her. So it *does* make a difference, Cord."

This conversation was crossing a line he wasn't ready to cross. Nothing changed. *If* she ever returned, it wouldn't be to him. It would be the two of them, her and Austin, him on the outside always looking in, seeing *everything* he'd never have.

Tired of the unchanging truth he'd faced for far too long, he mumbled, "It doesn't make a difference."

"You're wrong."

His nostrils flared. They were going in circles. "How am I wrong, Austin? None of this shit matters."

"It does matter, because she loves you too."

Cord's laughter was cold and dry, and his chest

ached dully. "And look what that gets me. I accept your apology, Austin, or whatever this is you're doing. Making amends. I never realized how much you resented me for things out of my control. It is what it is. But I don't know if I'll ever accept the way things are.

"For years I kept quiet, buried my feelings. But then you lost it and didn't have the balls to ask for help." He couldn't be that sensitive guy right now, tiptoeing around his friend's fragile ego, worried he'd set him off drinking again. "I still haven't forgiven you for dragging her down with you, for hurting her and using me to get it done. You're the one that insisted she go to me no matter how much I begged you not to do that."

"I know. Fuck, Cord, I know I got us here."

It was startling how fast old rage could come to a boil. Before he realized what he was saying, hurtful truths started to overflow and he couldn't pull them back inside.

"And you know what? I still can't find the guilt any honorable friend would feel. I wanted her, I took her, and no matter how wrong I know it was, I don't regret it, because deep down I know a part of that was real for her too. So while you might see me as someone worth emulating, I assure you, I'm not. There's no promise I won't do it again."

Austin's hand balled into a fist on the surface of the table, the pink of his knuckles bleaching to white. "You're right," he said slowly. "December doesn't do anything half ass. I'm sure what you two shared was...real to her. As a matter of fact, I think it was too real. So much so, I think it's keeping her away."

Cord's jaw locked as his gaze rolled to the ceiling. Great, more blame. He was seriously ready to fucking snap. Patting his own shoulder, he sneered, "Right here. You want to put it all on me, go right ahead."

"That's *not* what I want. What I'm saying is maybe she doesn't regret it either and that's killing her."

"Great, blame me for all of it." And fuck Austin for throwing this shit out there. Blindsiding him. He'd made his own amends, saving his friend's life and sticking by him over the passing months, being taken for granted despite his efforts.

Had Ember felt that way too? Fuck, he wasn't thinking straight. Sounding like Austin, whining and...

"I blame myself," Austin said. "I pushed the issue. I knew what I was risking, and I was too fucked up to care. I gave up and got everything I deserved."

He should never have sat down at this table. Some shit was better off suppressed.

They turned quiet. The entire discussion dredging up issues too big to bury again. This would mark the end of their friendship, and despite the harsh words, his heart pained at the idea.

He couldn't endure much more. Should Ember come back, losing her all over again would rip him to shreds. It was probably time to say goodbye to both of them and lick his wounds in private.

"So what's the point of all this? You want me to leave?" It was the inevitable hurt he'd been avoiding for months, the only end there could ever be for his friend to truly get his life back on track.

Rather than answer, Austin leveled him with a determined stare and announced, "I'm gonna get her back."

Well, no shit. Cord mentally retrieved his items scattered throughout the house. His bag was somewhere upstairs and he had some laundry in the dryer. His drill was—

"And you're gonna help me."

His attention jerked to Austin's face. The line he'd been toeing since the New Year was suddenly behind him, crossed. He had a limit and he'd reached it.

Laughing, because what the fuck else could he do? He shook his head. "Look, Austin, I stayed here to try and make sure you got better. Let's face it, you're well on your way. Beyond that...my days of playing pinch hitter are over. Do yourself a favor and take me out of the equation and try to save your marriage by yourself—if it isn't too late."

He stood and dumped the untouched coffee down the drain.

"You don't get it."

Hearing all he could take, Cord let the mug crash into the sink. He turned and snapped, "No, *you* don't get it! Use your fucking head. If she comes to me I won't hesitate. I fucking love her! This isn't a game to me. And it shouldn't be to you! She's your goddamn wife! This is your marriage you're gambling with—*again!* Take what's left and leave me be. I can try to keep it civil for old time's sake. I'll always love you. Like...like a brother. But at the end of the day, where Ember's concerned, I'm not your ally."

"If there's nothing left," Austin muttered, "she won't come back."

"What the fuck are you talking about? You're here." A bitter huff of laughter crossed his lips. "I can't erase what happened or change how I feel. I'm sorry. You're gonna have to figure this out on your own."

"She'll only come back if everything's okay between us. I know my wife."

Cord really laughed then. "You're off your fucking rocker. This will never be okay. What I did...what you did...what we put her through, shit like that can't be fixed."

"Why?"

He pitied the man. He really didn't get it. "She cheated on you, Austin. You might have permitted the affair, fuck, you insisted on it to ease your own conscience, and I fucking well took you up on it. But that means nothing to a girl like Ember. Your marriage was her *life* and she broke her vows. You displaced the problem and made her responsible for a disaster that was never her making. You should know her well enough to get that she'll never forgive herself for such a transgression."

"You can't make it black and white. It's not that simple."

"Look," Cord said, rubbing the tension knotting his neck. "Paint it whatever fucked up color you want. If you two somehow manage to reconcile, I'll take that as a win because I know she'll be happy again. But count me out. You may see me as some sort of hero, but I'm only a man, and I have limits. I can't sit through the next few decades of your happily ever after. I just...want to know she's okay."

"What about me? Do you want to know if *I'm* okay?" The plaintive thread weaving through the words nearly got to him.

Demons reared and, for a split second, his bleeding heart interpreted his friend's words like the answer to his prayers. Cord shook with the sense of being exposed, instinct telling him to hide. Austin wasn't on the same page and never would be. Cord would make certain of that.

Common sense diffused his hope in the blink of an eye. A compass that always drove the needle back to Austin directed his entire life. He needed to get off this godforsaken path once and for all. He needed to start facing reality and find a life away from this man if he ever wanted some passable form of his own happiness.

God he was tired. Long before he ever loved Ember, he'd loved Austin. He'd accepted those feelings would never be reciprocated to the level he suffered, and recognized December as an extension of his friend, only to develop an independent fondness for her as well. He couldn't take anymore. It was enough.

Letting his exhaustion show, he shook his head at Austin. "You really are something unbelievable. *Yes,* I want to know you're okay too, but Christ, Austin, how much am I supposed to endure? You'll have her, so I'm pretty sure you'll be great. But who's gonna worry about *me?* Remember me? The guy who interrupts his life to help out his friends, opens up his house, his bank account, his company, and yes, his heart just to make sure everyone else is good?"

His heart felt like it was being sliced in two.

Austin set his elbows on the table and rubbed his face, the heels of his hands pressed his temples as he muttered something intelligible.

The kitchen seethed with unspoken secrets that would never be shared. Cord's hurt, which he would bear silently and alone, turned to fury.

"You wanna throw out apologies? I'm sorry I

ever let you talk me into this. I'm sorry I fell for her, but I did and what we shared... That's ours. *Ours*. You can't touch it and I'll never be sorry for that. You had years with her and will likely have a lifetime more. Me? I get a few fucking hours of memories and an eternity of knowing every other woman will come up short. I gotta get out of here."

Snatching up his keys, he left, not giving Austin the chance to utter one more fucked up word. Once he'd driven far off the property he pulled over and dug out his phone. His thumb found the contact by pure muscle memory and he waited for the call to dump to voicemail.

"Ember, it's Cord." What the hell should he say? "I know there's a long road ahead, but I gotta bow out now. I..."

Jesus, it killed him to say it.

"I think it's time you came home. I don't know if you're getting my messages or what, but... I can't do this anymore. I can't. He's doing great. He doesn't need me there anymore. I gotta get on with my life and you two gotta get back to yours."

Letting out a breath of frustration, he pinched the bridge of his nose. "I don't know what's gonna happen with the house. He needs someone to share the load, but it can't be me anymore. This... this is where you belong. You know it. I know it. Just...come back so we can all move on and leave the past behind."

His voice turned hoarse as he struggled to speak past his pain. "I don't want to hurt anymore, kiddo. I...I think about you all the time and I know in the end I'll lose. I'd rather quit on my own terms with the little bit of dignity I have left. Austin can keep his job at the store until he finds something better, but..." He was dragging this out and losing his will to say goodbye. "I promise, I'll stay out of your way."

His vision blurred as he stared at the taillights passing by. "I love you, December."

The phone slid from his hand as he ended the call, the lifeless device bouncing off the seat and falling to the floorboards. His body tightened, forcing back the tears attempting to escape. He stuffed every hurt, every bit of longing, and every forbidden desire down deep until his insides felt pulverized.

"Fuck!" His fist slammed into the steering wheel. *"Fuck!"*

He was tired of worrying about everyone else, tired of making choices no man should have to make. The one thing he knew was that he couldn't go back, couldn't go backward anymore. He was going to his own house and getting good and drunk once he got there. Sally fucking forth.

Nine

December

DECEMBER CAREFULLY PLACED her phone on the vanity, Cord's words scraping over her raw heart. She stared at her reflection. Hollowed cheeks, lacking any color, fine lines engraving a gaunt trail to her pale lips. The sensitive skin beneath her eyes wore the mark of too many tears.

Austin was recovering. It was evident in the multiple messages he left daily. Cord on the other hand...she wasn't sure if he'd ever heal. Perhaps none of them would.

For months she'd been hiding away on a ranch with Rona and Misha, but time had done nothing to mend her broken heart. Some days she couldn't get out of bed, weighed down by too much guilt. Others, she worked herself to the bone, barely able to make it inside before collapsing. How she passed the time changed nothing.

Rona couldn't understand the significance of what happened. December's parents had always shared an "open" marriage and so long as things remained consensual, her mother saw no harm in infidelity.

Shame ate away at December. Worry for the two men who meant the world to her left her paralyzed. The memories of failing her husband when he was at his weakest and threatening his friendship with Cord left her emotionally bereft.

Perhaps her leaving was for the best. Austin was getting his life together and that was her last request of him before she left. It shouldn't matter that he was finding success in her absence and couldn't achieve it when she was there. But it hurt admitting she hadn't been enough to make him well.

Staring at the mirror, she wondered what he ever saw in her. Her identity originated in him. Without him, she was nothing. Once he'd stopped sharing her table, her bed, participating in their life at home, she'd lost her purpose—lost herself.

She wasn't worth their friendship, yet that was exactly what she'd cost them. They built her up to be something she wasn't and she'd torn their relationship apart.

There was no reprieve from the ugliness brimming inside of her. What people saw on the outside…it was a façade, distilled, a fading beauty she no longer took pride in.

Gripping the polished edge of the vanity, she scorned the reflection in front of her. She wanted to shatter the mirror, break the woman she saw until there was nothing left.

This wasn't her house. This wasn't her home. The woman looking back at her wasn't who she was anymore. Her actions had misplaced her entire life.

Slowly, her hand curled around the knob on the drawer of the antique vanity and she tugged it open in tiny increments. Her fingers blindly closed over a pair of sharp sewing shears. The cool, heavy metal comforted her tired hand, then heated within her grasp.

Glaring at her reflection, suffering nothing but disgust for the woman she saw, she lifted a clump of hair from her shoulders and watched, impassively, as the blades cut through her thick mane. It was just another veil she used to disguise the ugliness that she hid inside. Time everyone saw who she really was.

She'd lost her husband's interest and then he'd betrayed her trust. Except hadn't she betrayed *him*, falling in love with another man? The one he'd given her to? And then lied, even to herself, denying anything so heinous—and wonderful—could be true. She'd made her bed the day she lay in Cord's. Her life was over. Ruined. Irretrievable. She'd tainted her past. And she couldn't bear to look at the woman responsible for the mess anymore.

Waves of chestnut wilted to the floor. She lifted another hank of hair and clamped the scissors shut, slicing away her worthless pride. The crunching close of the shears, over and over again, was a much-needed lash of penance. Breath choked in her throat as she gasped with each carving tear.

The heavy weight she'd worn all her life slithered slowly to the ground. Cool air touched the back of her neck and the tops of her ears. She silently wept as she watched the woman in the mirror transform in to someone she didn't recognize. Vanity would only shroud the hideousness of the secrets she kept, and the world should see how ugly she was. She couldn't bear the weight one more second.

Her mother's gasp startled her out of her trance. "December! Baby, what have you done to yourself?"

The shears clattered to the floor, landing with a brash clank. Stuttered breaths hacked out of her in broken sobs as her face collapsed into her palms.

Humiliated, exposed by her own hand, the

way she wanted. Let the world see her for who she is. She couldn't keep the pain in any longer.

Her pain wrenched from her gut. "I'm so ugly."

"Oh, honey, no." Rona rushed into the room and dropped to her knees, pulling December into her arms and kissing her damp face.

Tears fell unchecked as her entire body convulsed with the surging force of her erupting agony. She had to get it out. Expel every drop of poison inside of her.

There was no end to the agony consuming her. She'd ruined everything. Her heart broke for the two men she'd driven apart. She wanted to go home, but everything had changed and she no longer belonged, *couldn't* belong when her heart was split in two.

Rona hummed quietly as she rocked her in her arms. *"December Skye, please don't cry. All this pain will soon pass by."* Her mother's lips pressed into her bare neck.

"Nothing's ever hurt this much," December whimpered, too beaten down to lift her head. "It's all my fault and I can't forgive myself. I'm just so ugly."

"No, baby. Never that. Your soul's too pretty for that."

Rona's fingers combed through the soft, short spikes of hair covering December's head. The world would see now, see she had changed, see she had nowhere to hide.

Rona lifted her face and sighed, a sad but understanding twist pinning her lips.

"Did you think doing this would change who you are on the inside, December? It doesn't work that way, baby. I wish it were that simple, but it's not. You need to accept who you are and stop fighting the nature of the beast.

"All the little experiences, good and bad, they don't define us, they guide us and offer us options. You have to face what's happened and stop fearing it. What's done is done and only you can decide how it will change your life. You're too strong to let it break you like this. I know you're hurting, but it won't get better until you face your fears."

She'd tried to face it. She'd confronted Austin at every turn, hoping to find common ground, but even then he'd turned her away. The past year played like a broken record, grinding a wound into her happy memories so deep it couldn't possibly heal.

"It just hurts so much. I want to fix it, but I can't. I can't take it back."

Austin was getting better and she was falling apart more and more every day. What if she went back and he started drinking again? What if her return drove Cord away, forced him out of the town where he'd made his life? She couldn't bear to take so many risks, her selfish needs could drive them farther apart, because every time she tried to make things better, normal skittered further out of reach.

"Shh... don't think, baby. Just be still and the pain will eventually pass."

It wasn't clear how long her mother held her. Eventually her cries faded to shaky breaths and sniffles.

Once she settled, Rona softly kissed her nose and smiled. "I think short hair might be a nice change. Why don't you let me clean it up for you? Then we'll go show Misha and let him gush over how beautiful you are."

Sometimes she wished she was more like her mother. Rona could minimize every injustice down to nothing more than destiny, assigning all the blame to some force of nature. It was an insignificant way to exist, but at the moment December wanted to believe her pain served a purpose and was outside of her control, her circumstances the result of serendipity she had no business trying to solve.

She slowly nodded and her mother helped her to the stool. *Oh, God.* She looked like a boy.

"I think a pixie cut is adorable. Maybe I'll get one too." Her mother's fingers played with the short strands, brushing them this way and that. December shut her eyes, unable to bear her reflection.

The scissors snipped and her mother

hummed. The reminiscent sense of surrender soothed her frayed nerves and allowed her to relinquish control to someone much stronger. Strangely, it was the closest she'd felt to her old self in a long time. Austin had an incredible gift for helping her let go. So did Cord, even in the short time they'd...

Shivers chased over her shoulders as Rona blew the clippings away. "Hmmm, you might like it nice and neat, but I sort of like it messy. Just think, no more knots or sleeping on wet hair. This really is a cute cut, honey."

Maybe that was why she'd done something so rash, to feel in control of what she could no longer manage.

The scissors snipped one last time. "Done."

December reluctantly opened her eyes. Miraculously, Rona had turned the damage into something vaguely attractive. Her fingers slowly trembled over the feathery strands. It was different, but not the massacre it could have been.

Rona's hands rested on December's shoulders as she smiled, meeting her daughter's gaze in the mirror. She pressed her fingers to her mother's and squeezed. "Thank you."

Her mother nodded, pleased. "I like it. Will you do mine?"

She laughed, startled by her request. "Really?" Rona had hair down to her behind. She couldn't recall it ever being above her shoulders.

Rona shrugged. "Why not? Summer's coming and it'll be hot this far south. I could use a change."

Suspecting her mother was doing this to form an alliance with her more than anything else, December found it hard not to acknowledge the attempted solidarity. It was something she needed very badly in that moment, something she'd lacked for the past while. Maybe the tenuous relationship they'd built over the last several weeks was real.

"I love you, Mom."

Rona bent and kissed her cheek. "I love you too, December. It doesn't matter if you're short, fat, skinny, bald or buck toothed. There's only one *you* and no matter what mistakes you think you've made, you could never be ugly. You're beautiful inside and out. Now move, so I can get my haircut."

It took her a while to get through Rona's hair, which had started to dread in parts. Her mother was definitely the better stylist, and for that, December was sorry.

In the end, they looked like twin fairies. When they showed Misha, he said they were the prettiest Fae to grace his vision in a long time, which was probably some reference to an enlightening acid trip he'd once had. But then her father pinched Rona and asked if she planned on leaving him for a cute little lesbian. Her mom teased her dad, declaring anything was possible.

Her parents, perpetual children lacking all the grown-up burdens of ordinary adults, dashed off to bed. December could hear their laughter through the walls. It made her happy, to see her parents still so in love. But it also made her miss home. Miss *them*.

When she went to bed that night, she wondered how long she'd stay at the ranch. No one seemed to mind her presence and Rona and Misha were always happy to have her visit, but the house didn't belong to them and eventually she'd become an imposition. Her parents would drift to a new dwelling and, as much as she loved them, she didn't know if she could endure much more of the nomadic lifestyle she'd grown up in.

Her mother was right. She had a decision to make. It was either time to move on or...time to return home. Was she really considering not going back? No. In her heart she knew where she belonged, but she didn't have a clue how to get there.

Austin wanted her back. He said so, every day. But he also continued to say, "when he was better" and "when he was certain he wouldn't let her down again". When would that be?

Her worry remained. What if returning too soon sent Austin in the wrong direction and he relapsed?

Cord said he was moving out. What did that mean? Had they fought? Were they on bad terms again? Still? She was so cut off from her old life she had no way of guessing where things stood. They both kept her updated, but she sensed there was plenty they weren't telling her, trying to protect her even at a distance.

What would her return do to Cord? He told her to come home, said she belonged with Austin, but was that what he really wanted? Why should he bear the cross alone?

Her phone suddenly rang, jerking her out of her daze. She glanced at the screen and a longing took hold of her, fiercer than what she normally experienced when he called. Reaching to tuck her hair behind her ear, she shook her head, forgetting it wasn't there.

Drawing in a bracing breath, she decided it was time to at least take a small step. Her finger pressed the screen, cutting off the ringing, but she lacked the courage to breathe a single word.

"D—December? Are you there? Is that you?"

Her eyes drifted closed at the sound of his voice, her body pulsing with desire as it always did when he said her name. "I'm here. Hello, Austin."

"Oh, my God. I didn't expect you to pick up. I...Jesus. I can't even talk. Where are you? *How* are you? I miss you. I fucking miss you like crazy, baby. I can't believe I'm actually talking to you."

She smiled. He hadn't given her a chance to say more than hello, but his happiness was contagious and at the same time heartbreaking. "I'm... okay."

"God. December... I...keep talking. I just need to hear your voice for a minute. Please."

She giggled, shocking herself. "What do you want me to say?"

"Anything. I don't care if you say the alphabet, just keep talking. I can't believe you're on the phone." He sounded so much like his old self.

"Where are you?" she asked. "You're going to wake up the whole town."

"I don't care! Let them wake up!" He hooted like he was at a sports event. *"I'm talking to my wife!"*

With a laughing shush, as though his excitement might wake Rona and Misha, she covered the speaker end of the phone.

He sighed. "God, Ember, today's a good day, baby."

"Is it?" The muscles in her face tightened, recalling what it felt like to smile.

"Yes. It's been torture not hearing your voice, not knowing if you're okay. This is the best day I've had in a long time. Tell me where you are." His tone was so animated he sounded out of breath.

"I'm with friends."

"Rona and Misha's friends?"

Of course he'd figured out she'd gone to her parents. There really wasn't anyone else. "Yes."

"Where? Are you far?"

She debated telling him her exact location. "I'm about nine hours from you."

"Shit. Is the Jeep still alive?"

She snorted. "Barely."

"I can..." His words cut off. "If you need anything, I'm here. I could pick you up."

She hesitated, sensing he'd be there by morning if she told him that was what she wanted. But she still wasn't sure what she wanted. "I'm not sure what's happening yet, Austin."

"But you have to come home. I haven't had a drink in fifty-seven days."

Though she'd gathered as much from his many messages, the relief that swept through her was dizzying. "That's wonderful."

"I know it doesn't sound like much—"

"It's huge." She couldn't let him minimize such a monumental accomplishment. "You have no idea how happy that makes me."

"Then it makes me happy too. If you're happy, I'm happy."

"It should make you happy no matter what. You should be proud. I'm proud of you." She didn't want him to base his happiness on hers. Wasn't it clear she hadn't been enough inspiration before, that he'd succeeded only in her absence?

His voice got low and the shock of actually speaking to each other amplified. "I'm happy," he whispered. "I want to make you happy, too, Ember. I'm better now. I'm working every day. I'm eating right, exercising. I...*miss* you."

His emphasized words carried implications that set her skin on fire with longing she struggled to conceal. Her husband's virility, his possessiveness, had always been a potent part of their relationship. When his libido disappeared, she'd feared he was falling out of love with her. To know he still wanted her... It was an intoxicating temptation, one she'd never had much luck resisting.

Releasing a shaky breath, she whispered, "I miss you too."

"Come home, baby."

"I...I'm not sure, Austin. I'm scared."

His voice deepened with a soothing timbre he'd always used when they whispered in the dark after making love. "Tell me what you're afraid of."

Snuggling into her pillow, she let his confidence wash over her. That's how it had always been, she'd have concerns and he'd overcome any obstacle, his confidence the first step toward succeeding. His unshakable presence in her life was what made the result of his drinking so unbelievable.

To her way of thinking, nothing was more formidable than Austin Garret. Realizing he had an Achilles heel like everyone else was terrifying, a staggering reminder he was human, and therefore prey to his own shortcomings as much as the rest of the world. It should have been a comfort, to know he was as fallible as her, but she'd come to depend on his strength, taking comfort in the shelter of his shadow.

She'd battle anything *for* him, fight every demon, but she couldn't combat *him*. And when he'd started looking at her as the enemy, his shadow grew very, very cold. Every foundation she stood on crumbled.

"What if we fight again? I don't know if I can handle any more, Austin."

He laughed, a sound she'd worried she'd never hear again. "We're bound to argue, baby. I plan on being your husband for a *long* time. Fighting, from time to time, is inevitable."

"I'm not talking about arguing. I'm talking about the screaming, the breaking of our home, the rage, the animosity directed at me." She had to put it out there. She couldn't take any more hostility. It had gotten so bad in the end, her house no longer felt like her refuge.

His voice was so quiet she barely made out his words. "I wish I hadn't put you through that. I'll apologize to you every day for the rest of my life for hurting you." He sighed. "It won't be like that anymore, December. I swear to you, and this time I mean it. I may not always keep my temper, but I'll never treat you like that again. You're my partner, not my enemy. You were never the person I was mad at."

He couldn't make promises like that, especially not with the odds stacked against him. Addiction was a permanent battle with a daunting relapse rate. She'd educated herself well. Fifty-seven days were wonderful, but he was still at the beginning of a journey that would take the rest of his life. One drink and they could be right back in the seventh circle of hell.

When they fought, Austin had argued some valid points, claiming she continuously pointed out his flaws. He hadn't given her much to praise at the time, but now he was doing great and she didn't want to take that away from him, didn't want to focus on the weaknesses in his plan and snuff out his optimism.

"I'm not asking for perfection, Austin. I'm just looking for a measure of peace. I can't come home if it's tense and scary. My nerves won't tolerate it. At the end, you had me so tied in knots I was getting physically ill."

"I'm so, so sorry, December. Hearing that, and not realizing what I was doing at the time, it...it fucking kills me. This is your home and I took the security of it away. I want to put it back, baby. I want to rebuild everything we had, but stronger. I know we aren't over. We can't be. But I can't build it without you. You're the cornerstone of everything we are. I need you."

She didn't think they were finished either. What they had was too unique, too special to give up. But there were other obstacles, things she hadn't decided how to handle. Maybe she should ask now. They couldn't pretend it hadn't happened.

"What about...everything else?"

"One thing at a time, Ember. We'll address that in time and it won't be as horrible as you fear. Trust me. I know it's difficult, but try. I'm not worried about what happened with Cord. I own it, not you."

To hear Austin say Cord's name triggered a burst of emotion—and the driving need to be honest. She couldn't return under any false pretense. "I kissed him, Austin. Before you wrote the letter."

Silence.

"I'm not sure if I was being honest with myself or you when I told you we were just friends." The longer he waited without responding the tighter the vise in her chest twisted. "Please say something."

His shaky breathing rattled the phone. "Okay."

"Okay? That's it?" Nothing was okay.

"I know I should be angry, but I'm not." His voice was shockingly calm. "Not anymore. I knew what was happening, drunk or not. I'm not an idiot. You were both lonely and spending a lot of time together. I was making your life miserable, which made Cord all the more appealing."

She wasn't going to let him make up excuses

for her behavior. Not when it ran deeper than that. "I wanted you, Austin, but—"

"I know," he interrupted and she sensed he didn't want to be reminded of the person he'd been back then. "But I also know lust alone wouldn't make you kiss another man. Cord's a friend and... some signals might have gotten crossed."

Stunned, she pondered his insight. No way would she have broken her vows to scratch an itch. She had to make the confession if they ever wanted to move past their mistakes.

"Part of me cares for him as more than a friend. I've tried to convince myself otherwise, but...I can't. That's why I'm not sure I should come home. Until I figure out what all these feelings mean, I don't think it's wise to return."

"Ember, he wants you here. *I* want you here. Maybe being here is the fastest way to decipher how you feel. How long do you intend to be backpacking with Rona and Misha? You hate that life and you have better options here, where you belong. I promise the stuff with Cord will level out in time, but that can't happen until you come home."

"I'm worried about him, Austin. I'm worried about all of us."

"Me too, but I have faith in us. We'll get through this. We're already on our way. It's just gonna take some time. Whatever happens...I'll handle it—without drinking. I'm stronger now, so please don't treat me like I'm fragile. This whole process has made me clear and I feel...confident we can get through this. I know we can do this. I promise not to shut you out, but first you have to let me back in."

Her hand pressed into her chest. Taking that step and placing herself back in a vulnerable position was terrifying. He might be calm with her right now, on the phone, but she was concerned about the moment the three of them came face to face.

"Are you and Cord okay? He said he was moving out of the house."

The line went silent, even his breathing stopped. "You talked to Cord?"

"He left me a message. You're the only person I've spoken to since I left. But I always listen to your messages."

"Does he call you a lot?"

This was exactly why she was afraid to come home. She couldn't deal with the tallies, the competitiveness, the two of them fighting because of her. "He calls about as much as you. Sometimes twice a day. Sometimes more."

"Right."

Neither seemed to have anything to say. December shifted uneasily in the silence, then forged ahead. "Austin, what happened today?"

"I'd rather discuss this stuff with you face to face, Ember."

"But I'm not there and I don't want to come home unless I know what I'm walking into."

He sighed. "I'm on my eighth step, working towards my ninth. I have a lot of people to make amends with, but today I worked on making amends with Cord. It didn't go as great as I'd hoped."

"Did you two fight?"

"He got angry, but I kept my calm—for the most part. I told him I didn't hold what happened against him and I...confessed some things I wasn't too proud of."

He paused then quickly said, "It's hard to explain, because I haven't gotten to you yet on my list. You're the first person I wrote down, Ember, but you're also the most important. I don't want to say too much before I'm ready to really talk to you about everything, and that, I'm afraid, I need to do face to face."

He was being so open, stretching himself to accommodate her and ease her uncertainty. He was definitely reverting to the man she loved, which made her believe that the conversation he was putting off would eventually come.

"I look forward to that talk, Austin. You don't have to tell me anything you aren't ready to share yet."

"And that's why I love you."

"I love you too."

The line got quiet for a long moment. "Do you have any idea how long I've waited to hear you say those words to me again? God, December... Please...just come back to me. Come home."

"I'm trying." It was the closest thing to a promise she could offer.

Eventually she'd see him again. But her love for Austin was so encompassing it made difficult decisions impossible. The moment she put herself back in his presence she'd never find the strength to leave again—no matter how bad things might get. Because no matter how bad he was when he drank, the man he was when sober would always rule over her heart.

"Will you pick up next time I call?"

"If I can. I'm not always by my phone."

"Be by your phone," he entreated. "Be by it tomorrow night, same time. It'll give me something to look forward to all day."

She smiled, already suffering the effects of his charm. "Okay."

"I love you, baby. Things are gonna get easier. You'll see."

"I love you too, Austin. Goodnight."

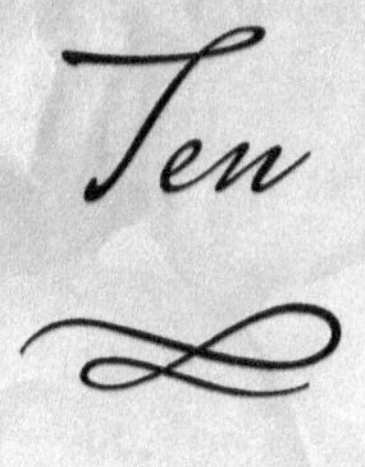

Ten

December

"NO, NO, NO, NO, NO!" December's palms smacked into the steering wheel of her Jeep. "We only have a little ways to go. Then I promise you can take a long nap." She turned the key again, but only a grinding click sounded. "Shit."

She hadn't wanted to tell anyone she was coming home in case she chickened out. After an emotional goodbye with Rona and Misha and thanking their friends for giving her shelter, she'd been driving all day. The sun was going down and she only had a little ways left to go, and barely enough money for tolls, let alone repairs.

Glancing at her surroundings, she considered

her options. She could stay at the rest stop for a while, give her car a chance to cool down, but chances were the old girl was at her limit. There was a funny smell coming from the vents and her gauges had stopped working about a hundred miles ago.

With no other option, she decided it was time to tell Austin where she was. Digging in her bag for her phone, she unbuckled her seatbelt and drew in a calming breath. *Send.*

"This is Austin. Leave a message."

Mentally cursing, she quickly prepared to leave one. "Austin, it's me. I'm, um... coming home. I wanted to surprise you, but...I'm sort of broken down at a rest stop and I don't know what to do." She glanced at the clock on the dash and realized why he wasn't picking up. "You're probably at your meeting. Please call me back as soon as you get this."

Tucking her phone on her lap, she fiddled with the radio, but that wasn't working either. As the sun disappeared, her surroundings didn't seem so safe. Truckers stopped to fuel up and the longer she waited the more uneasy she became. By eight o'clock she was starting to panic because he still hadn't called.

As a scraggly looking man passed by her window, she locked the doors. Maybe something was wrong with his phone. She dialed him again.

"This is Austin. Leave a message." It hadn't even rung.

"It's me again. It's dark now and I don't know what to do. I'm not really in the best place and I'm starting to get scared. Please call me."

Another twenty minutes passed and she considered calling a cab, but that would cost more than what she had in her purse. Even if Austin called in the next hour, it would probably take him another good while to get to her.

Her eyes were getting heavy after a long day on the road, but she didn't trust her surroundings enough to sleep. Her head jerked as she realized she'd drifted off. It had only been fifteen minutes since she last checked the time, but her eyes would not stay open the longer she sat in silence. Her lashes drifted closed again.

The shrill ring of her phone jerked her awake. Disoriented, she jolted and knocked the phone to the ground. "Crap. Don't hang up. Don't hang up."

As soon as her fingers scooped up the phone she accepted the call. "Austin?"

There was a lengthy pause, and a gruff, almost disbelieving, laugh. "Not Austin."

"Cord?"

He was quiet. He hadn't called her since the night he'd left the message telling her he was moving back to his own house and she should come home.

Figured, the first time she actually spoke to him she'd do something stupid like mistake him for her husband. Nothing was ever easy. "Are you there?"

"I...wasn't expecting you to answer. You sound out of it. What's going on?"

She appreciated him overlooking her mix-up, but didn't have time to think about her own problems. Why hadn't Austin answered and why was Cord suddenly calling her when he'd been adamant about taking himself out of the equation? She didn't want that, but she also didn't want to address her concerns over the phone.

She needed to get home, then she could deal with everything else. But first, she needed to lay her immediate worries to rest. Austin should have answered by now. "Is Austin okay? He's not answering. Did something happen?"

His breath echoed over the phone in a sound of disbelief. "Un-fucking-believable," he muttered.

"I'm sorry," she quickly apologized. "But I've been trying to reach him and—"

"Of course you have."

"No! It isn't like that! I'm stuck at a scary truck stop and I need someone to pick me up."

"What?" His voice instantly changed from irritated to concerned. "What truck stop? Where are you?"

Finally making headway, she sighed. "You

know that place where you get the river rock for Bay's Hardware? I'm just past that."

"What the hell are you doing there?"

"I'm trying to come home," she snapped.

He was quiet, then grated, "Austin knows you're coming home and he's not answering his fucking phone?"

By his irritated tone it was clear everything was *not* okay between them like Austin led her to believe. This wasn't the way she hoped her homecoming would go. "He didn't know. No one did."

"Austin's with his sponsor. I'll come get you. Lock the doors and don't move."

"Cord," she called before he could hang up.

"Yeah?"

"Thank you."

"No problem." The line went dead.

After a moment of stunned silence, December quickly hoisted her bag onto her lap and dropped the visor mirror. Using her phone, she tried to shine some light on her reflection. Fluffing her fingers through her hair, she fussed with the short, messy strands. Her other hand burrowed through her bag until she found some clear gloss for her lips. Anything to make her look less like a girl who'd sat in a car for the past eleven hours would be great.

She stilled. *What am I doing?*

Lowering the tube of gloss from her lips, she

blinked at her reflection. "He's not your husband." The whispered words broke the silence like a cannonball shattering a wall of glass.

Shamed, she bowed her head. She hadn't meant to react that way. She shouldn't care how she looked for Cord.

"This is so fucked up," she whispered.

Her joy at being rescued plummeted as she thought about what Cord picking her up might mean to Austin. Should she call him back and tell him not to come? It was dark, she was hungry, and eventually she wouldn't be able to hold her bladder like she'd been doing since the sun set.

She flinched as her phone suddenly rang.

Austin.

Slowly, she lifted it to her ear. "Hello?"

"Ember, where are you? I'm already driving. I'm so sorry. My phone was off because I was in a meeting. Tell me where you are and I'll get there as fast as I can."

"I'm at a truck stop," she explained stupidly.

"A truck stop where?" He sounded frantic. "What road are you on? Is there a mile marker?"

Nausea swirled in her belly. Maybe she should just call Cord and tell him to go back. She could wait for Austin to get there. Chances were they'd arrive within minutes of each other and her reunion with the two men would kick off on a very wrong foot.

"December, are you there?"

"I'm here." She pressed her forehead into her palm. "I'm on Route 6, somewhere near Meshoppen."

"Is there a mile marker you can see?"

She glanced around, looking for any sort of landmark. "There's a gas station called Mo's and a water tower in the distance, but it's too dark for me to read it."

"I think I know where you are. I can be there in about fifteen minutes. Stay on the phone with me."

She really needed to call Cord and tell him to turn around. "Why don't I let you go so you can concentrate on the road?"

"Fuck that. You're so close I can taste you. I can't believe you're here. Are you okay, other than the car problems?"

"Yes." She couldn't think. Her mind was distracted with what might happen when they both got there. Her anxiety spiked with each passing second. "Austin..."

"You should have told me you were coming home. I would have picked you up. That Jeep needs to go to the junkyard. We'll figure out a way to get you a new car once you get settled."

He continued to make plans for them as she stared at the dark highway. A truck pulled into the lot and her heart raced with recognition. Cord. He parked in the closest space, which was about twenty yards away from where her Jeep broke down.

"Do you want to get dinner when you get here? I haven't eaten and I'm sure you're hungry. We could grab something—"

"Austin."

Her stomach dropped as Cord's long legs unfolded from the truck and his heavy boots hit the ground.

"Yeah?"

"I..." She swallowed. "I don't think I need a ride."

"What? Did the Jeep start? I'll come meet you anyway. I can't wait another second to see you."

Her mouth was suddenly parched. "Austin, stop."

He finally silenced long enough for her to think, all the while Cord got closer. Shit. "I waited a while for you to call me back. Then Cord called—"

"Cord?"

She shut her eyes. "I didn't know where or how long your meetings lasted and—"

"Well, call him back and tell him I'm picking you up."

Cord neared her Jeep with long, steady strides. The sight of his tall body knocked the breath out of her. "It's too late," she rasped. "He's here."

Her insides tightened as shivers raced up her spine. The air turned thick. She couldn't move. Couldn't breathe. His intense gaze zeroed in on her, roaming over her like tiny fingers, touching everywhere.

"Ember."

She jolted at the snap in Austin's voice. "Yes."

"Goddamn it," he muttered. "I'll be there in less than five minutes. Just...tell Cord I'll handle it. I'll take you home, but ask him to wait with you until I get there so you're not alone."

"Okay."

"And Ember," he said in a serious voice. "I love you."

"I love you, too." Even if she did feel as though she was betraying him all over again.

She disconnected the call just as Cord's hand closed over the door handle. His mouth kicked up in a half grin as he signaled her to open the door. Gaze locked to his, she reached over and lifted the button. *Click.*

Slowly, he pulled it open. The sound of cars rushing by in the distance broke the silence and then he was all she could see, all she could breathe. Cord.

"Hey, beautiful." He leaned in before she could find her bearings.

His full lips brushed hers. Breath pulled deep in her lungs and her shoulders lifted as his mouth sealed over hers. Heat dipped low in her belly, tightening and thrumming through every nerve ending.

His strong hand slid around her bare neck and cupped the back of her skull, pulling her closer as his tongue teased hers. Her anxiety diminished as she melted into his dominant hold. *Safe.*

She hummed as he eased away, breaking the kiss, but keeping his face close. "I've missed you."

She couldn't breathe. She couldn't talk. Every part of her wanted to pull him back to her mouth and kiss him again.

"Let's get out of here," he said, wrapping his fingers around hers, and easing her out of the car. As her feet touched down on the pavement her knees wobbled. "You cut your hair."

Self-consciously, she tugged at the wisps covering her neck.

"I like it," he said, running a hand through the short strands and cupping the side of her face. "I can't believe you're here." He leaned in to kiss her again.

Belatedly, she stepped back and drew in a shaky breath.

He frowned. "Ember?"

"Cord..." She licked her lips nervously, tasting traces of him on her skin. She didn't want to hurt either of them, but there was no way out of this without someone getting hurt. "Austin called."

His expression sobered, his eyes narrowing

and mouth turning down. "Did you tell him I was already picking you up?"

"Yes, but he said he'd take me home. I'm sorry—"

"Well, I'm here and he's not. I'll get your bags." He moved to the back of her Jeep and wrenched open the tailgate.

The change in his mood filled her with nervous energy. And then lights flashed as Austin's truck barreled into the lot and jerked into the parking space next to Cord's truck. She wanted to look at Cord, but her unblinking stare was fixed on Austin's truck.

Anticipation burned through her and when his door popped open, her body trembled with an eagerness strong enough to knock the wind out of her. His feet hit the ground with nothing short of absolute resolve and his potency slammed into her like a drug.

There was her husband.

Strong and determined, he strode to her, stare fastened so intensely on her it was as though every frayed thread between them worked rapidly to knit his soul back to hers. Forever tethered, her soul reveled in recognition of its mate.

Her heart beat against her ribs, hard and full, as though his ability to finally *see* her was the sweeping motion to put all the shattered parts back together. Without a word spoken, she knew this was different. There was no diffidence, no hesitation in his stride. He saw her. He wanted her. And he wouldn't stop until he had her in his arms.

That was how it had always been. Potent. Unstoppable. Passionate, beyond any word or meager thought. Just—raw.

Entranced, she met his gaze. Intense purpose rolled from his pores. The heavy clip of his boots echoed in cadence with her breath. He didn't rush, didn't have to. He was that confident, a predator secure enough to bide his time. His whiskey brown eyes devoured her as he took that last step and she shivered.

"*Wife*," he growled, sliding his hands up the back of her neck and through her hair, pulling her into his kiss.

Breath rushed out of her, mingling with his. His tongue pierced her mouth, probed deep, and took without apology. Her knees gave out and he stooped, backing her into the door of the Jeep as his palms slid down her sides and roamed over her hips.

Putty in his hands, her neck loosened as he tipped her head back. Passion wasn't a bold enough word to describe the way he kissed her. Deep, consuming strokes of his tongue stripped away every defense she had, laid her bare, exposed, and willingly helpless against his magnetism.

Her center pulsed, thrumming heavily as blood pumped through her veins, heating her body to near combustion. He molded his body to hers. Every bit of his impressive hardness pressed into her softness. So lost, she was no longer sure she was standing.

His fingers teased her ear, pulling, erotically seducing. She wanted him right then and there. Her fingers pressed through the cotton of his shirt. He tasted like Austin. There were no traces of whiskey or beer or anything else. Just Austin.

A throat cleared. She vaguely recalled they were in a parking lot. Her eyes fluttered open, but as she tried to break the kiss his fingers tightened, guiding her jaw back.

"Not yet," he whispered over her lips, slowing the kiss to a sensual press of need and desire.

Her insides were searing. Heat churned through her body as her mind clouded under a haze of endless yearning. She'd feared he'd never kiss her like this again, but there was no feigning such chemistry. He mastered her. This was real and the most evident truth she had that her husband had returned.

His lips pulled slowly from hers and he chuckled, low, like they shared a secret no one else would ever know.

"Welcome home, baby," he whispered.

Lost, like a little girl staring into the eyes of her first crush, she embraced the sheer joy that they were together again. Pressing the back of her head into the cool glass of the car door, she sighed and opened her eyes.

Austin.

Her dazed head rolled as her gaze pulled to the left and the wind sucked out of her chest. The tranquil blanket comforting her ripped away as she saw Cord's expression.

Her bags dropped deliberately from Cord's opening fists with an ominous thud. His mouth was a flat line, his jaw a sharp blade against the moonlight.

"Cord," she whispered, her heart breaking.

Austin stepped back and narrowed his eyes at his friend. December quickly forced her knees to stiffen and took a staggering step toward Cord.

He held up his hand, his glare so cold it froze her on the spot. "Don't."

Austin's hand closed around her numb fingers. Her eyes pleaded with Cord, a million apologies running through her mind, but none of them fitting for how truly sorry she was.

Jerking his head to the side, he stared into the distance. His face tipped at an angle that should have appeared distinguished, but she read the agony in his expression. Though he might try to hide his heartache, she sensed it and it gutted her.

"Right." He turned on his heel and marched toward his truck.

"Cord, wait," she wheezed.

"Let him go," Austin said.

Shaking off his hold, she set her apologetic gaze on her husband. "I can't." She couldn't bear either of their disappointment. "I'm sorry." She turned and chased after their friend. "Cord, wait a minute."

He pivoted and she nearly tripped over her own feet as she staggered to a halt. *"What?"*

She cowered as he towered over her. Chin shaking, she whispered, "I'm sorry."

He shook his head. "No, you're not."

As he turned away, she grabbed his arm. *"Yes,* I am." Tears rushed to her eyes but she blinked them back. "I didn't know it would be like this."

"How the fuck did you expect it to be, Ember? You're married."

"I know!" she cried. "I don't know how to fix this."

Sucking in a long breath through his nose, he glanced at the sky then glared down at her. She saw the effort it took him to soften his glare, and it still wasn't enough to hide his hurt.

"You shouldn't have to fix anything. You didn't deserve any of what happened. So let me make it easy for you. There's your husband. Go to him."

At that, he walked stiffly to his truck and climbed in. The door slammed, the engine ground, and he sped away.

Austin's image shimmered in her peripheral as her shoulders shook with the effort to contain her tears. He slowly walked over, his bulk familiar and reassuring, but he didn't touch her. She lost sight of Cord's truck as the taillights faded into the night, and forced herself to look at her husband. His expression blank, his hands hung passively at his side.

It became too much. Lowering her head, she tried to hold it all inside and failed. With the unmanageable pressure of a single sob, she broke.

Eleven

Austin

AUSTIN SAW her going down and panicked. *"Ember!"* He barely caught her before she sagged to the ground. "Hey, hey, it's okay. He's gonna be okay."

"None of this is okay. I did this. *Me,*" she sobbed.

"You didn't," he insisted, pulling her stiff body into his arms. "C'mon. Let me help you up."

He carried her to his truck and belted her in. "I'm just going to lock up the Jeep. I'll be right back."

He hated leaving her, but needed a minute.

Fuck, this was not how he expected this reunion to go—not that he was complaining.

As he ran across the lot his brain quickly sorted out everything her sudden return meant. She was back. Home. Shit happened, and there'd be fall out later, but he couldn't stop smiling. His wife was back.

He locked the POS jeep and grabbed the bags Cord had abandoned, a sharp twinge of guilt rushing up his spine as he thought of the devastated look in his friend's eyes when he walked away. He quickly shoved the image back and directed his full focus toward Ember. He'd deal with Cord another time.

Once he stashed her bags in the bed of the truck he climbed behind the wheel, giddy with the sense of taking her home, but sidetracked by the distraught look in her eyes. Shit. Maybe this was too much, too soon.

She sat, staring blankly at the windshield. He let the keys dangle in the ignition and faced her. "Ember."

She shook her head.

"Baby, it's not your fault." It was his. He'd been the one to forfeit everything on account of his weakness. "You have to give it time. I promise, we'll get through this." He gritted his teeth and exhaled. "We'll fix things with Cord. I promise."

"I don't know what I was thinking. What kind of person am I? What kind of *wife*?"

"Hey," he infused a touch of authority into his tone and got her full attention. "You are a *good* wife. Do you hear me? You're not allowed to put this on yourself."

"I missed him, Austin. What does that make me?"

He swallowed. It hurt, the truth he saw in her eyes, but he'd put them in this fucked up predicament and he had no one to blame but himself. "A loving person, baby. It makes you a loving person. One with a big heart. Cord knows it too. He was just..."

Fuck, he still didn't know what to make of this clusterfuck. He couldn't regret the way she'd fit into his arms and returned his kiss after so much time apart, but the look on Cord's face... Even in the dimly lit lot, he'd seen the pain. And if he were honest, he'd *felt* it too.

"I love him, too," he whispered, mimicking her blank stare as he looked out the windshield. "I think we all just need a little time to adjust."

He had no idea how long it would take for the dust to settle. There was nothing in his past or hers that prepared them for this sort of fallout.

"How about...we get a cup of coffee before we go home." Baby steps. It seemed the only way he could approach mammoth problems anymore.

She nodded and wiped her eyes on a wad of napkins she'd unearthed in the side panel of the door. Had he known she was coming home, he would have cleaned up the truck.

He drove them to the diner he and Harley visited every night. His friend was long gone. The moment Austin heard all of Ember's messages he'd been a panicked mess. He'd given Harley the abbreviated version, confusion apparent on the other man's face, and then hit the road.

Guiding her to his usual table, the waitress greeted them with a smile, delivering a pot of coffee. Though he didn't usually eat there, he assumed Ember could use something in her stomach.

"Can we also get a slice of pie? Blueberry would be great."

The waitress nodded and left them alone. He reached across the table and caught Ember's fingers in his, pulling them closer. "You still like blueberry pie?"

Her smile was precious. "It's still my favorite."

It was good to know some things never changed. He smiled in return, the gesture so spontaneous, so easy. There hadn't been a great deal to smile about for some time.

The waitress left the pie and he poured them each a cup of coffee. It was hard not to wonder where the passion from twenty minutes ago had gone as she nibbled quietly, avoiding eye contact. The confusion of their weird triangle, or whatever the fuck this was called, crushed a great deal of her earlier excitement, and rightfully so. He had to get his head in the game and quit being so selfish.

He tried for easy conversation. "I have this new obsession with coffee. This is probably my tenth cup today."

She blotted her lips with a napkin. "That much caffeine isn't good for you."

He grinned stupidly, loving her for always looking out for his health. "I know. Eventually I'll cut back, but right now... it makes it easier."

Her gaze shifted to his, dark chocolate eyes under full lashes measuring his sincerity. God, she was beautiful. "Your hair's pretty."

A flush worked over her cheeks, which seemed thinner. She'd also felt lighter in his arms, now that he thought about it. While her favorite pie might still be the same, there had definitely been some changes.

"It'll grow back," she murmured, casting her eyes toward the table.

"Who says it has to?"

She shrugged.

He rubbed his thumb over hers. "What made you come home?" He still couldn't believe she was here. Maybe that was why he couldn't let go of her fingers, touching her made it real.

"I just... After talking to you..." She shrugged again. "I thought this was where I belonged."

"It is."

Those two words seemed to place so much

weight on her shoulders she shrunk a little, her small body curving toward the table. Damn. He wished he could make this easier for all of them.

"Look, Ember, I know this isn't how you want things to be. I wish I could have everything back to normal for you, but the truth is, *you're* the normal. You're the balance. Having you here...it's necessary for us to move forward. I can only do so much without you by my side. It's where you belong."

Her head lowered. "You're different yet so much like your old self."

"Isn't that what you wanted?"

She nodded. "Yes, but it's strange. I feel like it's been longer than a few months. I feel like I haven't seen you—this side of you—in much longer."

Because she hadn't. "Well, I'm back. That other side of me isn't going to return. I know I have a thick skull and it takes a while for things to sink in, but trust me, the lesson stuck. I don't want to lose you again and I intend to do every-thing in my power to prove that to you."

"It's just hard."

He swallowed, his throat tight. "I know it is. But if you give me the chance, you'll see. I'm more determined than ever. I know I have a lot of fixing to do, but I'm working at it every day. Give it time and it won't be so hard to believe in me again—to believe in us."

"I can't just go back to where we left off."

His breath held tight. What did that mean? "Because of Cord?"

"Because of us, Austin. I...need time."

She was still here though, so it was a win. "I can be patient."

"I don't know if I'm ready to..."

His hand tightened, his thumb dragging slowly over her knuckles. "To what?"

"I can't sleep in our bed."

His heart jerked as sadness nearly swallowed him whole. "I understand," he rasped, taking a sip of his coffee to ease the tightness in his throat.

Trying to lighten the mood, he forced a laugh. "For the record, sleeping there alone sucks. I now know what that feels like."

Fuck. He hadn't meant for that to come out sounding like a dig. It was supposed to be an apology of sorts. Her head lifted as her brown eyes narrowed.

"Do you? Do you think you'll ever know what it feels like to share a house with the person you love and fear you've lost their love forever?"

His fingers, suddenly numb, released hers. Beneath all that softness was a backbone made of steel and...venom. Venom he'd let seep into their life. "December..."

"I didn't think so."

Her words ripped open his heart. She'd changed. Or had she? Maybe he'd pushed the limits of her patience, taken it for granted. But he couldn't recall his wife ever making such harsh accusations before, unless they'd been blunted by the booze. Her anger and resentment cut and stabbed deep. He deserved all of it.

"You're right. I shouldn't have made light of what I did. I shouldn't make light of any of it."

"No. You shouldn't."

This was so much more than proving that he could stay sober. This was about immeasurable damage. Some of it could be repaired, but other parts...

What if they were always a little bit broken? She might forgive him, but she'd never forget. None of them would.

The road ahead was once again daunting. "I won't argue with you. Not about that. I did a lot of shitty things I'm ashamed of. I wish I could take them back, but I can't. We can talk about all of this, December. I plan to. But one thing I've learned from AA, one thing that stuck, is that there's no getting around the hurdles. Inevitably, we have to climb over them, or pull them apart—when we're ready. The best we can do is pace ourselves and take it a little bit at a time until we're sure we can land on both feet."

He didn't even know if he was making sense. But he couldn't act like this was hopeless. No matter what, he believed he could retrieve what they'd lost. Perhaps find something stronger in the end, because this time around he'd be honest—about everything.

The silence stretched and as he watched her he noted the signs of exhaustion, the dark crests under her eyes, the paleness of her skin. "How about I take you home now?"

She nodded, but looked hesitant. "Okay."

They drove in silence, his mind wandering to Cord and making sketchy predictions of the future. Would she sleep on the couch? In the guest room? It irked him that the sheets in the spare room probably smelled like his friend.

"You can have our bed. I can crash in the spare room." He didn't want to mention the couch because that seemed like a setback.

"I'm not ready to enter our room yet. The guest room will be fine."

Fuck. It was as if her having that hint of his friend somehow marked a point in the other man's column. He'd read that scent sparked memory more so than anything else.

It's not a competition.

But what if it was? It had been a long time since the three of them had been in the same place together—not counting tonight. He saw the way they looked at each other, felt the energy between them.

The one thing he hadn't been prepared to see was the determination and challenge in his friend's eyes, in total contrast to his words. It was as if the gauntlet had been thrown and Austin was at risk, him and his insecurities. May the better man win. Fuck, he shouldn't think like that.

But he wasn't used to Cord challenging him. Though he'd bowed out and told her to go to her husband, the truth was there for anyone to see. Cord wanted her and...part of Ember wanted him.

He glanced over at the passenger seat and saw she'd fallen asleep. His precious cargo.

He needed a plan. Somehow they had to work this out together. It wasn't fair for Cord to be upset with her on his account, not that he expected his friend to hold his anger very long. Ember wouldn't allow it. They needed to work out their shit—the three of them. She'd leave again before she'd allow her presence to drive a deeper wedge between a thirty-year friendship.

He swallowed, unsure if *he'd* survive a life without Cord. Currently, things were fucked up, and his best friend posed a threat, but, despite their recent estrangement, Austin needed him. Missed him. He needed his wife too. Jesus. There really wasn't an easy solution.

Twelve

⬿

Cord

THE DAY after the debacle at the truck stop, Cord hauled the broken display rack on his shoulder and roared as he hoisted it into the dumpster. *Piece of shit fucking frame.*

It landed with a crash and he kicked the dumpster for good measure. He was sick and tired of wasting time and energy on shit that couldn't be fixed.

Marching back to the store, he glared at the clock. Two minutes to open and he already wanted the day over. After a sleepless night, he had no patience for dumb fucking questions and retail bullshit. Not to mention facing Austin, if the jerk even made it in today.

He felt lightheaded at the implication. Wasn't sure which was worse, seeing the prick or knowing he was home with Ember. He shook away the carnal images assaulting his mind.

Unlocking the doors, he ground his teeth as he made his way to the lumber section. He'd have to build a new display today—which was just what he fucking felt like doing. The wood he needed was stacked on the top shelf, so he climbed onto the high reach and turned the key.

When the machine didn't start he turned the key again. "God fucking damn it!"

Climbing down he went to the front of the store to find a new battery. As the doors opened he paused. Dark rage took over him as Austin strode through the entrance, his eyes intent, his confrontational mood palpable.

Great. Another fucking delay he didn't need. It was clear the asshole wasn't there to work.

Cord stood at his full height and met the other man's irritated glare with his own. As Austin closed the space between them, the energy in the vacant store thickened. What, did he want to fight?

Bring it.

Cord's knuckles popped as his hands balled into fists. He took a quick step forward, widening his stance, and braced for the first swing.

Austin's arm snapped out the second he was within striking distance, and landed a right hook directly on Cord's jaw.

The jolting hit brought a delicious snap of pain that exploded from his face all the way to his shoulder. Cord gave a quick shake of his head, his brain rattling under the impact. He'd forgotten how mean of a punch his friend could pack.

"You upset December," Austin growled.

This was what he needed. No more talk about feelings. No more excuses. They were fucking men, and he was ready to end this once and for all.

Cord lifted his fist. "She should be used to being upset. You broke her in well." Maneuvering his way around Austin's bulk, he growled and plunged his fist into his ribs.

His friend grunted and snuck a shot square over Cord's kidney. "Fuck you. She doesn't need another reason to leave."

Cord spit on the cement floor, the copper taste of blood souring his tongue. He didn't have time for any more bullshit. Cocking back, he swung out and delivered a nasty right hook of his own. "Then don't give her one, asshole."

As his fist plunged into Austin's face, the other man's body twisted and staggered into a display of solar garden lamps. Plastic parts went crashing to the ground and crunched under Austin's weight as he shuffled to keep his footing.

This wasn't the drunken sot he'd beaten the

shit out of last winter. This was Austin in the best shape of his life. Cord never had the brute strength the other man possessed. Austin was a monster in a fight and it was only a matter of time before Cord was on the ground. He decided to go down swinging if that was the case.

Austin roared and charged, locking his arms around Cord's waist and barreling him into the end-cap of push brooms. Wooden handles clattered to the floor as Cord delivered a quick left uppercut followed by a right. His range of motion was limited with the way his back was wedged into the racks, but it didn't matter. He kept swinging.

Austin grunted, but held his ground. When Cord surprised him with a clean shot right to the nose, his head snapped back and he staggered back. He leveled Cord with a glare, blood tinting his teeth as he grinned.

Oh shit.

Austin pile-drove him into the display of garden hoses. They wrestled, too close to deliver any good hits. Grunts and curses echoed through the store and then white light exploded behind his eyes as Austin nearly KO'ed his ass.

Falling back to the cement floor with a thud, Cord blinked through spotty vision. Austin glared down at him and snapped, "You're invited to dinner tonight. At seven. She's making Italian. Don't be late." Pivoting, he marched out of the store.

Cord groaned as pain flared from his back and vibrated clear up to his face. His eyes blurred as he stared at the florescent lights above him and grinned.

He might be lying on the floor, hurting and tasting his own blood, but it seemed like it was the first time he and Austin had been honest with each other in a long, fucking time. He'd be there with bells on.

Thirteen

Austin

THE DOOR CLOSED with a soft click and Austin drew in a bracing breath of...calm. Ember's presence immediately leveled out his mindset, a comfort so familiar and right the world spun properly on its axis again.

"Austin? Is that you?"

She was upstairs, likely still unpacking the few belongings she'd used in her travels. Knowing Ember, she was knee deep in reorganizing everything just the way it should be. Over the past few months he'd been living from a laundry basket, making a quick selection and stopover at the washer and dryer before going on his way.

"Yeah," he called, preparing for her reaction to his inexcusable appearance.

"What did you do with the—" She halted midway down the stairs. "What happened to you?" Panic laced her voice as her hand lifted to her trembling lips. Was the damage that noticeable?

"Cord and I had a little scuffle, but everything's okay. He'll be here tonight."

"You...fought?"

Reaching down to unlace his boot—and hide a bit of the wreckage—he winced at the soreness in his side. "We had a meeting of the minds. Don't worry. I took the brunt of it."

Slowly, she descended the last of the stairs. "Let me see your face."

His lips twitched at the stern disapproval in her voice. She might be pissed off, but it was nice to know she cared. Tucking his boots under the bench, he rose and faced her.

Sucking in a breath she took a quick step forward. "Your eye's turning purple."

"Yeah. He got me good in the nose."

Shaking her head, her fingers tenderly examined the split on his lip. His lashes lowered as he luxuriated in the wonder of her caress.

The instant she stopped her gentle examination, he winced. Her touch was something he always depended on, like a limb or his hearing, and every time she took it away an unnamable emptiness pressed in, alarming and worrisome.

Glaring up at him, she said, "Go sit on the couch. I'll get a bag of frozen peas or whatever's in the freezer."

Fuck if he knew. Cord bought the groceries. Hiding a smirk, he sheepishly did as he was told.

She entered the den carrying a lumpy bag of vegetables and a damp cloth. He should be contrite that he'd upset her, but when she sat beside him, so close on the sofa, her breath mingling with his as she examined his wounds, he couldn't feel the slightest remorse.

Her brow furrowed and the deep hickory flecks in her irises darkened. He didn't wince when she blotted the cut on his lip even though it hurt like a motherfucker. No matter the pain, her nearness was the best medicine each and every time.

Her hair was so short, pixie-like and elfin, the delicate wisps softly spiking down from her ears. He never imagined her with short hair, but, surprisingly, he liked it. She didn't seem as hidden. Lots of things seemed new. Change was sometimes good. And maybe she'd cut her hair for a reason, though he couldn't figure it out—or maybe he was afraid to know the *why* of it.

"Why did you do this, Austin?"

He grunted as she pulled the tightening skin around his eye. She smelled amazing, like flowers and tea.

"Guys fight. It's how we work out our issues."

Her mouth twisted and she shook her head. "And what could you have possibly accomplished by beating the crap out of each other?"

"Some things needed to be said and we didn't have the words."

"I highly doubt that." The peas, cold and jarring, pressed against his eye. "Where else are you hurt?"

His side ached, but it wasn't anything that wouldn't heal on its own. Still, he wanted her to keep touching him, so he slowly lifted his shirt and pointed to the space above his hip.

As her gaze traveled to his exposed stomach her calm demeanor briefly crumbled, and he liked the idea of triggering a reaction inside of her with the sight of his improved body. Her sweet shape triggered plenty from him.

"You're bruising. I'll get more ice."

Her strides appeared agitated as she headed toward the kitchen. He stared after her, hungrily taking in the sight of her backside in those fitted jeans. She was likely exasperated with his juvenile behavior, but he smiled anyway, quickly blanking his expression when she returned.

"I don't like this Neanderthal behavior, Austin. I told you, no fighting. That includes with Cord."

He jerked as another cold bag shocked his warm skin. The hip was an extremely sensitive area of the human body. He'd give his left nut to spend some time reacquainting himself with *her* hip. Just a few minutes. That's all he needed. One little peek at her body and he'd be gone, lost in a wonderland of womanly slopes and softness.

The cold bag shifted, shocking his sensitive skin again. She'd done that on purpose. It was a strange sort of flirtation, poking at his injuries under the veil of caring for him. But passive aggressive foreplay was still foreplay.

He couldn't resist poking back. "Are you going to tend to Cord's wounds too?" His breath seized, his own words catching him by surprise. Of all the dumb shit to say...

She stilled, her gaze dropping to the floor.

He hadn't thought about the question before it left his mouth, but it was borne of honest curiosity. "Sorry—"

"Austin," she softly breathed his name, imploring and sad.

Damn. He was so out of practice, his cocky attitude was getting in his own way. Gently touching her chin, he directed her gaze to his.

"It's okay. I didn't mean anything by it." But he still wanted to know her intentions toward his friend.

Her dark lashes fluttered. He'd give anything to know what she was thinking in that moment. She tsked. "Your knuckles are bleeding."

"They're fine."

She tried to stand, but he caught her hip, curving one hand around it, silently begging her to stay. All evening she'd been mute, barely making eye contact, and then sleeping in the spare room where Cord had stayed.

When he'd left that morning she'd only mentioned unpacking and possibly having Cord over for dinner. The idea had socked him in the gut before he manned up. They needed to find balance again, so he figured diving in was best, hoping they'd eventually find something close to normal they could all abide.

Beating the shit out of his best friend wasn't part of the plan, but it just sort of happened and, oddly, it was a relief. They both seemed to have some pent up anger that needed to get out and hopefully, now that they'd tapped a tiny release valve, they could both manage a peaceful dinner in December's presence. Together.

"You should wash your hands. I'll find some peroxide." As she stood his hand fell away.

The distance between them was beyond the physical, an emotionally deep chasm he didn't know how to breach. It hurt and frightened him, but he had to remain confident they would eventually cross the void and unearth some impression of normalcy again. They were lost in this together. All of them.

Following her to the kitchen, he paused by the door as she struggled to reach the top shelf where they kept some first aid supplies.

"Why is everything moved to the back?"

Glad to be helpful, even if only fetching household items out of reach for her, he stretched and grabbed the peroxide and cotton balls. "Here you go."

Hesitating a moment, she took the bottle from him. "What happened to all our medicine?"

Cord threw it away so I wouldn't try to kill myself with generic cough syrup. "A lot of it was expired. If you need something we can go to the pharmacy." Which had been the truth all along. He needed only to drive to the corner pharmacy to find something lethal enough to end his life. Cord's little safety measure couldn't keep him from dying, but that was no longer what he wanted.

"It doesn't make sense to use this cabinet for a few cotton balls and Band-Aids anyway. This stuff should be upstairs with the rest of the medicine. It never made sense that we had it scattered upstairs and down. It should be in one place in case of an emergency. I'll take this upstairs when you're done. Maybe we can use that pantry for spices."

"I'll do it." He didn't want her seeing how empty the upstairs cabinet was, too. Eventually he'd have to tell her, but he didn't want to have that conversation on her first day home. "Do you need anything for dinner tonight?"

"I need everything. I have no idea how you've been surviving. There's nothing but soup and coffee in the cabinets."

He grinned. "It's been rough. You always took such good care of me."

Her jaw trembled as she stared at him for a moment and then quickly looked away. He dabbed the damp cotton on his knuckles and welcomed the burn of peroxide.

"I should probably make a list," she announced, snatching the notepad off the fridge.

"I'll go to the store with you." He frowned when he saw her shoulders tense, her back to him as she searched for a pencil in the drawer.

"That's okay."

Enough.

Approaching her slowly, he pressed his palms into her arms and whispered into her ear. "It won't always be this awkward, Ember. We'll figure it out. But you have to let me try to be your husband again if we're going to save our marriage."

Her shoulders trembled as he pressed his lips to her soft, exposed neck. A weak sound of distress left her throat. "Austin."

"December."

Her head bowed as she let out a shaky breath. "I...don't remember how to do this with you."

"Do what? We're just talking."

Her shoulder shifted. "No. We're touching. I haven't had your hands on me in a long time."

"Not true." He kept his hold loose, slowly moving his hands up and down her arms. "I kissed you last night."

"You surprised me."

It was like getting her into a cold pool. If he coaxed her in, inch-by-inch, she'd eventually get wet.

Last night the passion was there. Even if just for a passing moment, he glimpsed enough to know their chemistry remained. It might be the only bridge still intact after their time apart.

He played back their kiss from the night before. What had worked for her? He hadn't approached slowly, he couldn't. No. He saw what he wanted, what was his, and took it, without apology or reserve, the way he used to. Maybe she was thinking too much and he had to get her out of her head for a bit.

She seemed so sad he couldn't pretend he didn't feel the unease between them. But he refused to let go, of her or the hope that they could retrieve everything they'd lost together.

Sighing, he confessed. "I know, baby. I feel it too. It's like a weight we can't shoulder off with any real force. It has to be removed carefully and gradually, but this wall between us will come down."

She nodded silently. "I don't mean to make this more difficult than it already is. I'm sorry I—"

"Hey," he cut her off, not liking the shamed tone of her voice. Turning her so he could see her face, he said, "Don't you dare apologize for any of this. This is my mess and I'll be the one to clean it up."

"But it isn't all your fault. I—"

"I know. But that's not what got us to this place. We were here long before any of that happened."

Her gaze turned away. "I don't know how you keep overlooking what I did."

"I'm not overlooking it, trust me. I'm just trying to come to terms with it. I can't blame you for doing what you did when I was the one to insist on it, and the one making you so miserable to begin with. Me, December. None of this would have happened if I had been able to manage my life."

Her brow softened as she stared up at him. "How are you doing this? How are you suddenly so confident and...sober? Doesn't it bother you? Not drinking?"

"Not as much as losing you bothered me. I'm not saying it's easy, but every hour gets a little more tolerable. I try not to think about it too much and each day I survive without giving in, I'm stronger, and my demons...they seem to shrink a little. They'll probably always be there, but I think, once I face each one, they won't be as scary as they used to be."

He paused, thinking he owed her more honesty than that. It was fucking hard, but things could be much worse. He could see that now.

"It's failing *you* that scares me. That's real, Ember, because if *I* fail, I fail *you*. You're here. That gives me hope and a reason to believe I can do this, because it also tells me you haven't lost all faith in me."

Her mouth tightened with a sad smile. "I believe in you. I'm just worried..."

"About?"

Her shoulders lifted as she drew in a big breath. "I'm so afraid to say or do something and push you over the edge."

Moments like this, he wished he'd had Harley's experience and wisdom. Alcoholism wasn't a cut and dried condition. It had taken him months to finally comprehend what had happened to him and hour upon hour of trying to place the blame, even when the sole reason stared back from the mirror.

He'd been paralyzed. But the first step came when he'd admitted this was his cross to bear and he'd carry it always. *Always*. Once he came to terms with the commitment required, he'd been able to move forward—slowly. Ember couldn't shoulder his burden any more than she could be blamed for his failure.

He rubbed his head, forgetting for a moment about his bruise. "It was never anything you did or said that made me drink, December. It was me. It's a part of me, all the parts I don't like and could no longer hide. I was looking for a way to veil all those traits when I should've been facing what I could and working on what I didn't like. I needed to change. Not just stop drinking, but change all the things that made me want to drink. You were never one of my reasons and I don't want you thinking you were. I needed a complete psychological change."

"I don't understand what would make you suddenly dislike your life."

"Not my life. Me."

She frowned, a disbelieving huff of laughter slipping past her lips. "I'd never met someone more confident or self-assured than you, Austin Garret. How does that translate into disliking yourself?"

"Believe me, it does. So much of my...behavior came from a disquiet living in me. It didn't matter what those I loved did around me. I was deeply depressed, maybe from the time I lost my mom, maybe even before then. I don't know. It doesn't matter. All that matters is I've taken responsibility, become accountable, and I know I can't pass blame to anyone else. Not you, not Cord, no one. If I want to fix whatever is inside of me I have no choice but to address it head on. That's what I'm trying to do."

Her brow slowly knit as she processed his words. It was a lot of honesty, maybe too much too soon, but he owed her the truth.

"I feel blind. How could I not have known—"

"Because I chose to hide it from you. It was easy, because I was hiding it from everyone, including myself. It was when I could no longer avoid it that everything started falling apart. You *did* see it, Ember. That's why you worried, that's why you tried to reason it out of me. But I wasn't ready to face it myself."

"But why couldn't that happen when I was here?" She cut right to the chase.

"I wish I knew." Maybe it was the shock of actually seeing her go, the blow of knowing he'd pushed her far enough to take action. "All we can do is deal with what's real. This..." He motioned his hand between them. "We're real, Ember. We can do this, but you have to be truthful with me. I can still get hurt, but I've learned how to manage the pain rather than run from it. We need that honesty in order to heal. I can't fix anything if I don't know the reality of what I'm dealing with, even outside of myself. I'm done hiding."

She swallowed. "Cord kissed me last night. Before you arrived."

His breath froze in his lungs, turning heavy and sluggish. His first instinct was to turn and escape, but where would he go? No matter how fast he ran, he couldn't escape himself. Running solved nothing. "Okay."

"See? How do you hear your wife confess she kissed another man and simply say, 'okay'? It's not *okay*, Austin."

"Well..." he glanced at the table, his mind weary with thoughts of the road ahead. "Let's sit down."

Once they were both seated, he asked, "Did you feel anything when he kissed you?" She didn't have to answer. "I can tell by your expression you did. Was it...lust? Or more?"

"I felt...scared."

He didn't like that answer. "Of?" If Cord was pressuring her in any way...

"I was so worried you'd show up and see us, but at the same time I was terrified it wouldn't last long enough for me to remember."

Oh, that kind of scared. Fuck, it stung, but he'd asked for honesty. He nodded. A big man could come up with something to say—maybe—but he wasn't that big.

"The second his lips touched mine I was lost. Spinning. I didn't know up from down or where I was supposed to turn."

His jaw locked as he forced back the urge to lash out at the world. Her response to Cord was partly his doing—maybe more his part than theirs. She and Cord had lived their lives and continued their friendship while he had his head up his ass. He nudged their connection along, given them his blessing, because he was too weak to be the man she needed.

Cord was a good man. Austin wouldn't have trusted his wife to just anyone. Even at his lowest moments, he knew Cord would deliver. This was Austin's doing and there was no undoing it. *Climb the hurdle.* "So you kissed him back?"

She nodded, her gaze turning to the table.

Maybe brutal honesty was too much. The only way he could discuss this with her was if he dissociated, listened as though she were only a friend and not his wife. It wasn't an easy thing to do and he wavered between the bite of real consequence and being objective.

"Do you love him?"

"I..." Tears shimmered in her eyes. "I don't know. But it isn't lust. Not only lust. It's deeper than that."

Suddenly angry, but keeping his voice calm, he asked, "Why do you want to have him here for dinner?"

"Because he's hurting and we did that to him."

Not her. He did it. "So is it pity?" Cord wouldn't tolerate anyone's pity, not even hers.

"No." Her answer was quick and certain.

"Are you sure?"

"Yes. Men like Cord, men like you, they aren't

the sort of men you pity. I offered the invitation out of respect."

"Respect?"

She nodded. "I don't know how to explain my feelings, because I don't fully understand them, but pity isn't a part of what I feel for him. I wish it was that easy. Cord's strong and compassionate. All he ever wanted to do was help. I made him—" Her voice cut off as a sob hiccupped out of her, startling them both.

The storm brewing inside of him seethed and quelled in light of her sudden upset. This was all part of understanding. "You made him what, baby?"

Rubbing angrily at her tears, she confessed. "He didn't want to be with me that night. He begged me to go back to my room and it killed me. I couldn't handle being rejected one more time, but he said no and I...I died inside."

Guilt seared through him, churning his gut into rolling acid, slamming him in the middle of the chest. He should have known Cord wouldn't easily betray him. Austin had pushed her so damn hard it was painful to admit he'd put her under another man, but he had. In that moment, he truly accepted the reality of what he'd done, couldn't hide from the images assaulting his mind.

His stomach pitched and he felt sick. He'd honestly thought he was doing the right thing. "Jesus."

She wept quietly. More tears that were his fault.

"I'm sorry, December. I wasn't thinking clearly."

"None of us were." She wiped her eyes. "Austin, I love how commanding you can be, but at the end of the day, you can't order me to do something against my will. You aren't that powerful. I chose to walk into his room. I chose to give myself to him. Your actions, your letter, might have been the catalyst, but it was my decision. I won't let you take all the blame. I won't."

"Okay. Okay." She was getting too worked up and they had to bring it down a notch.

Maybe he was wrong to heap everything on himself. The stuff leading up to that, yeah, that was all him. But what happened after he surrendered his role... He didn't like blaming her. Cord was an easier target. "Cord doesn't do anything he doesn't want to do."

Pressing the palm of her hand into her eye socket, she smudged away more tears, leaving her lashes spiked. "I know. But I was the pitiful one. He had too much dignity and honor to betray you like that. He tried to protect me from making a mistake, but I was so upset, so broken. Eventually, it didn't matter what he wanted. He gave me what I needed, regardless of his own reservations."

Numb. That was the only way to describe what he was feeling. He should be enraged or sprinting off on a rampage, but all he felt was... numb.

Where was the fury? The indignation? The need for retribution? It was all missing. Nothing but cold reality settling over him. Cord had given Ember what she needed—exactly what Austin asked him to do. But at what cost to his friend?

There was a fine thread of disappointment that, if tugged, led right back to the source. Him. He turned her into that person. He ignored her to a point of delirium. Everything was a result of *his* actions.

No woman should have to suffer the horrifying way he'd behaved. He neglected her for months on end, yet she toughed it out, every day trying to get through to him only to have her love thrown back in her face, until he finally broken her.

It was a dangerous thread. Delicate. Too much tampering and a trap door would open inside of him and all the self-loathing and unforgivable qualities would surge like an avalanche, suffocating all of them.

Better to appease one demon at a time and deal with each issue individually. That was how he'd begun to regain control of his life, by slowly chipping away at each little issue, one fucking dent at a time.

He was clueless how to fix this, though. Drinking had wedged a knife in their marriage, twisting and disfiguring their union until it had become unrecognizable. The situation with Cord was something different. There was the matter of fidelity, but more than that there was the issue of December's guilt. *Wait. That's it.*

"Do you feel guilty—"

"*Yes!*"

"Let me finish. Do you feel guilty about what happened or guilty because you *lack* guilt about breaking one of our vows?"

"I..." She frowned. "I feel...guilty about what happened."

"You don't sound too sure."

Her face pressed into her palms. "I don't know! All I ever wanted was a normal life, a wholesome marriage. I never thought I'd be capable of adultery. I feel disgusting when I think about what I've done."

"Is that how you categorize it, adultery?"

"That's what it is, Austin."

Maybe. Maybe not. "Would you be able to... kiss another man? Other than Cord."

She drew back, a look of horror on her face. "No!"

"Good, because the idea of you kissing someone else makes me see red. Seriously fucking ballistic."

He breathed through that reaction and thought hard. A complete change. Leaving past destructive habits and behaviors behind. Everything that dragged him down and made him lash out. That was the requirement to get sober and stay sober. It was everything AA seemed based on. He and Harley discussed the approach often and Austin placed immeasurable faith in such a theory, saw it as a plausible way to repair something that appeared unfixable. Maybe that approach could also be applied to this conundrum, but he wasn't quite sure what he was dealing with. The first step was making an honest appraisal.

Since their fight this morning, his urge to unleash on Cord seemed to have vanished. Weird. But not a guarantee. His wife and his best friend had done more than kiss. They'd slept together. Fuck, it still hurt to admit that, even to himself, but the initial sting had faded a few degrees. Maybe saying it out loud...

"You slept with Cord."

A sharp sound of distress emanated from her throat, stealing his attention.

"December." He waited for her to look at him. "Let's call it what it is. No more sugar coating." He drew in a deep breath. Let it out slowly. "You... slept with my best friend. He slept with you, my wife."

"Austin, please." Her face dropped to her palms again and he caught her wrist, gently pulling her hands away.

"Hey. I'm not saying it to accuse anyone of anything. I'm just processing."

"It's too much."

"Is it? Say it out loud."

She shook her head in protest, but he waited. After a long, struggling moment, she murmured, "I slept with him."

She wasn't looking at him, but he was studying her for any signs of distress—any new signs. "What do you feel?"

"Horrible."

"Really? Shut your eyes, Ember. Be honest with yourself. I know what it is to face tough thoughts. Think about that night. Think about how you were feeling, how he made it better for you—"

"I don't want to do this, Austin."

"Because you're afraid you'll hurt me or because you're afraid you might admit something you don't want to face?"

"Because... I don't want to hurt anyone, not you, Cord, or me."

He took both her hands in his and leveled her with a stare. "I can handle the truth, Ember. Trust me enough to give me honesty."

Her mouth firmed into a thin line and her eyes slowly closed. Her breathing, though silent, turned labored.

"Are you thinking about that night?"

"Yes."

"Now..." He kept hold of her hands and swallowed, bracing himself for the truth. "How do you feel when you think about that night?" Her hands pulled back, but he tightened his grip. "We can handle this, Ember. Together."

Her lips trembled, her voice pitched so low he had to lean in to make out her words. "I feel—*felt*...relief."

He wasn't sure whose hands were shaking worse, his or hers. "Go on."

"I couldn't understand or make sense of anything happening in my life. I just wanted to feel nothing—or someone, something worth breathing for. And he...got me through."

Austin drew in a silent breath. A new appreciation filled him, along with a blazing shard of pain. Knowing how it felt to be utterly lost, he never wanted her to feel that way. He should have been her strength, but he'd been so weak. Gratitude, for what his friend had done, what he might have prevented... It was definitely gratitude.

"I know you see this as something weak, but you are strong, December. It took strength to do what you needed to get through."

"It didn't feel that way."

"Were you scared?" he asked, recalling how alone he'd felt and how terrified he'd been that he might never be able to touch normal again.

"I was, until..." Her head slowly shook, her eyes still closed. "It wasn't desperation or a purely sexual experience. It was something else, something more."

Maybe that was why he couldn't find the anger. "It was emotional. For both of you." He realized what he needed to know, what he already knew. "You made love."

Her hands pulled away again, so quick this time he didn't have the chance to retain the connection. But, still no anger. He hadn't seen it as merely sexual involvement when he'd written that letter. It *should* have been more. He'd expected it to be. But while his wife needed someone strong to love her the way she deserved, he realized now how deeply overwhelming this was for her and for that he was sorry.

"Austin?" Her eyes shimmered with unshed tears. "How did it come to this?"

He knew how. What he needed to know now was how to move on. "If there was one consistency in my life, December, it was my desire to see you happy. Even on my darkest days, even when I was the cause of your misery, I never stopped wanting that. Knowing I was hurting you, made hating myself so much easier. I don't want you to hurt anymore. More than anything else, I want to see you happy."

Her shoulders slouched as she folded her hands in the shelter of her lap. "It never used to be this complicated."

"Things are just tangled up right now, but we're sorting it out. It's a big deal that we're talking about this. Most couples wouldn't be able to handle that."

A tear slid down her cheek and he hung his head in shame. If he could just take her pain away, remove the guilt. He'd do anything just to see her happy again.

Then it hit him. It didn't knock him in the head or flash in his mind like a light bulb. It was subtle, a gentle touch, a feather's push in the direction he needed to go. There was nothing abhorrent about his thinking when it possibly meant seeing her happy again.

He set his elbows on the table and forced himself to say the words. "Tonight, when Cord comes over, if he tries to kiss you again, you have my permission to let him."

Her head jerked up. *"What?* No!"

"Why? Does the thought of kissing him suddenly repulse you?"

"No, but it's wrong."

"Says who?"

"Everyone. Marriage. Tradition. Every pillar we stand on."

"The only opinions that matter here are ours." Well, and Cord's.

"Austin, stop. This is exactly how we got into this mess."

"No, it isn't."

"Yes, it is. You can't tamper with these things. Marriage is supposed to be inviolable."

He frowned, unsure what that word meant. "*In*-what?"

"Inviolable. Never to be broken. Sacred."

But it *had* broken. He leaned back and folded his arms over his chest. He weighed the consequences, trying to see the ones that eluded him before.

He needed to physically see them together, her and Cord. Every other option felt too much like running away from more demons. He couldn't run anymore.

"Ember, hiding from the truth implies shame and that's where the guilt comes from. In my mind, you didn't violate our marriage. Cord did exactly what I asked of him, exactly what I thought you needed when I couldn't be there for you. I should have known it would backfire, because that's the loyal wife you are. But we can't ignore what's done. So, kiss him if that's the way things play out."

"That will only make it worse—"

"I don't think so," he said, his thoughts racing as he considered his feelings, but really tried to comprehend hers—the ones she was too afraid to acknowledge. His wife could not feel guilty for this. They had to see it through. And fuck, wasn't that something he never envisioned? Ever. But he was getting past feeling threatened by those who continuously proved to have his best interests at heart. "Strangely enough, I'm not opposed to it."

She stared at him, eyes wide and disbelieving. Was there also some hint of hope in her expression? "And if you find out you are *opposed*, will you two beat the crap out of one another again?"

"I swear I won't lay a hand on him." He paused, recognizing the confidence and sincerity backing his words. So unexpected, it sort of knocked him off his axis in a good way. "Maybe it will give us all a new perspective." *A complete change.* "I just want you to be happy, baby, and be truthful with yourself about your feelings."

"Breaking our vows again won't make me happy."

"That's not what this is. We're confronting an issue to unearth the truth. Think about it. This isn't just about me. It's about you, us, and Cord has some say too, you know." Jesus, he hoped he was speaking the truth. His gut told him he was.

"And what about *your* feelings, Austin? Don't you think I want you to be happy, too? This can't be the answer."

"Figuring all this out will make you happy. And *that* makes me happy."

She didn't look convinced and he suspected she was harboring fears that this could send them into a tailspin that ended in absolute devastation. "I swear to you I won't drink or fight with you or Cord about this. I'm giving you a pass, Ember." His tone involuntarily infused with certainty, telling her this was best, being insistent, the way he'd taken the lead before.

He truly believed this would help. He'd cut off his own dick before he'd voluntarily hurt her again.

He wanted to see them kiss, interact intimately, not just to see what they looked like, but to know how she'd react when it happened. He couldn't imagine it on his own. Forcing it out in the open seemed the fastest way to remove her sense of shame.

Quietly, he said, "None of us will know how we really feel and what to do about it until we confront the issue honestly."

"I can't do it, Austin." But her resolve visibly wavered before his determination.

"Why? Don't you want to kiss him?"

"No!" She stood and snatched up the dishcloth, wiping down the counter, which was spotless.

Curiosity rolled into something more and he paused, trying to understand what he was feeling. He didn't have time to analyze the strange urge to actually see her do it now that he'd put it on the table. He tried to ignore the odd sensation, but it grew stronger.

It was almost as if... he didn't just *want* to see them together, but part of him actually *needed* to see them. Like there was an empty space, a void to be filled. Fuck, the odd current pulsing through his veins freaked him out, so he put his focus back on his wife.

"December, look at me."

"I don't want to."

"Because you want to kiss Cord?"

"Jesus, Austin. No!"

So transparent, he almost laughed. "You're lying."

"No, I'm not! Now stop saying things like that. This conversation is *over*. I'm going to the store."

The feet of the chair squealed across the tiles as he quickly stood and caught her arm, bending her back in his arms before she could find her balance. His dick was inexplicably hard and he had no fucking clue why after such an emotionally draining conversation. Maybe it was some territorial shit, but regardless, he needed to make one thing clear.

His mouth brushed over hers in fast warning then stole in for a deep kiss, his tongue piercing between her lips and drawing out a startled gasp. His palm cupped the back of her head, fingers sifting urgently through her wispy hair.

It was deep, slow, and demanded her full attention. He didn't pull away until he sensed her dizziness. When he exposed her like this, she had nowhere to hide. How had he forgotten the way she responded to being mastered? She blinked up at him, her gaze drowsy and confused.

"Remember something, Ember. No matter what, I'll never stop loving you. No matter what." Slowly, he untangled their bodies and steadied her.

Unblinking, her gaze crawled over him, begging. "Austin, don't do this."

"No one is forcing anyone to do anything. I'm just telling you, if you're saying 'no' for my benefit, don't. Do what's right for you, baby. Nothing will ever stop me from loving you. *Nothing*. You're the most important thing in my life, and I refuse to see you denied. There's no room for shame in our marriage."

Fourteen

Cord

CORD PARKED beside Austin's truck and debated backing out of the driveway and returning home. He wasted several minutes eyeing the gutters and the gable of their house. It was a nice home. Modest, but spacious, the kind of house that was rarely built anymore.

His gaze turned to the old shed with cross-beam barn doors. Someone should go get Ember's Jeep. He could skip dinner and go down to Al's, talk to him about getting the vehicle towed back to town. But was it worth fixing? Ember would need another car soon. Austin had probably taken care of picking up the piece of shit already.

The porch door opened and Austin stepped out. He didn't move past the top step, just sort of watched over him with a blank expression. The sight of the shiner his friend sported sent a jolt of satisfaction through him. Good to know he wasn't the only one wearing battle scars. His jaw had been killing him all day.

Sighing, he opened the door and climbed out. *Let's get this over with.*

He had no idea what being there would prove, but he didn't have the heart to turn down Ember's invitation. And a tiny part of him gloried in the hope it bugged the living shit out of Austin that she'd invited him to dinner. Funny that he could love the guy and want to yank his entrails out at the same time.

"Hey." He paused at the base of the porch, staring up at his friend, the air eddying out from the house lightly scented with basil and garlic. He loved Italian.

"Hey."

Avoiding Austin's stare, he climbed the steps and entered the house. It had been his home for several months, but never while Ember was in residence. Her presence changed the entire feel of the place.

Something by Louis Armstrong played quietly from the back of the house and the closer he came to the kitchen the more the delicious scent of homemade sauce intensified. Pausing at the threshold, he watched her.

She was mincing something at the counter, not yet aware of his presence. A vat of thick, red gravy slowly bubbled on the stove beside a steaming pot of boiling water. The air was warm, sultry for a spring night and one of the steamed windows was cracked, the parted curtains dancing under the slight breeze. It was amazing what a woman like Ember could do to a room.

The little paisley sundress exposed her shoulders, and he noticed that she'd lost weight. His heart pinched, knowing it was because of him. Him and asshole. The short hair looked good on her, feminine in a way most women couldn't pull off. Sensing Austin's approach, he cleared his throat.

Ember turned, her lips parting and falling short of a smile. "Hi," she whispered.

"Hey." Unsure how to proceed, he glanced at the stove. "What you making?"

"Angel hair with meat sauce."

Breathing in the scent of country ribs and sausage he nodded. "Smells great."

Blinking, she wrung her hands on a stained dishcloth.

Well, this was just great. A hiss came from the stove as the water boiled and splashed on the surface. "Looks about ready for the pasta to go in." *Let's get this show on the road.*

Turning, she quickly snapped open a bag of stiff spaghetti and dropped it in, giving it a quick stir. She faced him again, this time her gaze moving just past his left shoulder.

He felt the weight of Austin's stare on his back and his gut locked uneasily. He shouldn't be here. They should be working on their marriage and he was—once again—in the way.

He got a grip. December had been gone for months. Months he'd worried about her. Missed her. There was something between them and he wasn't going to dismiss it, regardless of that demented phone call he'd made when he'd tried to bow out. Told her to come home because he'd cried Uncle.

Ignoring the other man's presence, he pushed his way into the kitchen and leaned his hip against the counter. "So...How are you? Really."

"I'm...I'm okay. Really. Glad to be back. Home."

"Good. Good. You look good, kiddo." Fuck, where was his fabled silver tongue? "Glad you're okay. And back." He hesitated, and then said, "I missed you a lot."

"I missed you too," she whispered, her fingers working through the chopped basil on the old cutting board, her wedding ring catching the light.

He frowned when he saw her glance toward the dining room before returning her attention back to the herb. He looked over his shoulder and stilled.

Austin tipped his head in her direction and Cord scowled. He didn't need him hovering, making shit more awkward than it already was.

Cord looked back at Ember. "Can I do anything?" The sooner they ate the sooner he could leave.

"No, everything's pretty much done, thanks. Why don't you just relax? Dinner should be ready in a few minutes."

Relaxing was suddenly a foreign concept. Nodding he headed to the dining room. Austin went into the kitchen and lingered. Cord heard them speaking in low voices, but couldn't make out their words. Didn't care to hear them either.

The table had Ember written all over it from the fresh cut blooms filling the antique jug in the center to the delicately folded linen napkins resting on the plates. She'd even provided a pitcher of water, dripping with condensation from the evening heat. She'd thought of everything, meticulously putting effort into each fine detail. That was Ember.

Austin strode in to take a seat at the head of the table. Cord found his place, closer to the chair Ember usually occupied. Thank God for the music to fill the thick silence.

Austin broke first and hissed, "That was a cold welcome."

Frowning, Cord kept his tone low. "Well, we're not in fucking Kansas anymore. I can't pretend this is just another dinner at Austin and Ember's."

"Why not?"

Rolling his eyes, he snapped, "What do you mean, why not? Shit's changed. This whole thing is weird and uncomfortable."

Ember came into the dining room with a bowl full of greens and deposited it on the table. He and Austin watched her move as though she was putting on a performance just for them. She went toward the kitchen without a word, shooting him a sideways glance, nerves evident in her blinking eyes and the tiny lines of strain around them.

Tearing his gaze away as she vanished from sight, he caught Austin staring at him. "What?"

Austin nodded. "You're right. This is nothing like it used to be."

What the fuck did *that* mean? Reaching for the pitcher he poured himself some water. It was getting damn hot in here.

"So maybe you should stop pretending and just be natural."

Cord set his glass down with an irritated click. "Natural?" He laughed. "There's nothin' natural about this, Austin. Stop trying to force shit."

He shrugged. "I'm not forcing anything. I just want everyone to be at ease."

Ease? There was nothing easy about this.

Ember bustled back to the table, this time carrying a basket of warm garlic bread wrapped in a checkered cloth. She gave him a shy smile. Cord watched her, his lips curving into a grin, despite his confusion.

Austin's words slowly took on new meaning. Jerking his gaze back to the other man, he scowled.

The second Ember was gone, Cord growled, "What the hell are you doing? What is this?"

Austin shrugged and Cord recalled a time his mother had tried to fix him up with her canasta partner's daughter. He'd walked into a typical Sunday dinner and immediately felt cornered into some underhanded dating ritual. This reeked of similarities. He had to be misreading something.

Quickly looking over his shoulder to make sure Ember was out of earshot—God she was beautiful—he sent Austin a fierce glare. "I think your meddling has done enough damage for one lifetime. I'm not a monkey and I don't dance. Whatever you're trying to accomplish here, stop."

Austin shrugged, appearing unconcerned.

"And stop shrugging like that."

"I'm not trying to accomplish anything—"

"Yes, you are," Cord snapped. "I know you. You're up to something. If you're worried I'll make her cry or something, trust me, that's my last intention. Now, knock off whatever you're scheming and let's just get this over with."

Austin poured himself a glass of water and

took a long sip. "Fine. We can pretend, if that's what you need."

"What the hell's that supposed to mean?"

He shrugged again—*the fucker.* "I'm just saying, you don't have to pretend everything's okay. We talked. Talked a lot, about a lot. I know it's not okay. So does she. But we're done acting like it is. We, Ember and I, have decided pretending isn't healthy. We're only interested in the truth—whatever it ends up being."

"What do you mean, the truth?"

Austin shrugged again. "We're being honest."

His brow lowered as he narrowed his scowl. "You're being fucking weird. I don't like it."

"Well, I'd say all of this is a little weird. I'd rather know what we're dealing with, than run scared. I'm facing it, acknowledging the true situation. Maybe you can't."

Cord's spine stiffened at the implied challenge. "Are you fucking with me?" He jabbed a thumb over his shoulder in the direction of the kitchen. "Ember's in the kitchen, asshole. Why don't you try thinking about your wife for once?"

"Oh, but I am. She's mostly all I think about, my main focus."

Cord slowly drew back, digesting his implication. He stared at the door to the kitchen and jerked his glare back to Austin.

Austin folded his arms over his chest and arched a brow. "You want her."

His head moved like he was watching a tennis match. Back to the kitchen to make sure she was still preoccupied and then back to the man he was about to kill. "*Are you out of your fucking mind?*"

Another fucking shrug.

Cord ground his molars. "What the fuck is wrong with you?" he demanded, keeping his voice low.

A dry laugh passed the other man's lips. "Lots of things. Tonight I'm focusing on this problem in particular."

"Which is what?"

"My best friend's in love with my wife, and I'd like for it not to be a problem."

Cord's chest seized, his heart missing a beat.

Austin was entirely too calm. His stare moved past Cord's shoulder. "She's right there, in the kitchen. You could go say hello to her—this time without all the awkwardness and self-deprivation."

Slowly sinking into his chair, Cord gaped at him. "You're out of your goddamn mind." Shaking his head, he muttered, "Don't push me, Austin."

"Or what? We already brawled once today. Besides, I promised Ember there'd be no fighting tonight."

"It would only take one shot for me to knock you out. And believe me, asshole, I'm motivated."

He shrugged *again*. "If you want to hit me

where it hurts, my face shouldn't be your target. Besides, that would just make you look bad. I gave her my word. You hit me, I can't hit back."

Cord was tempted to ask if he was drunk. Unable to decipher the rules, let alone grasp whatever game Austin was playing, he lashed out. "By the way, my store isn't a boxing ring."

"I don't think there'll be any more violence."

"You're a fucking idiot. I'm leaving." He tossed his napkin on the plate and levered up from his seat then halted his movements.

Ember carried in a large bowl of steaming pasta that smelled incredible, her gaze fastened squarely on him. Cord tried to smile, but knew he wasn't convincing anyone. She sighed. "Dinner is served. Dig in, boys."

Austin reached for the salad and placed a mix of leaves and cut tomatoes in Ember's salad bowl. He then filled his own and passed the serving dish to Cord, who had no choice but to sit back down. Ember filled her plate with pasta then shoveled a heaping pile onto Austin's.

"Cord?" She nodded for him to lift his plate, holding the utensils above the bowl.

Mutely obeying, he watched as she filled his dish the same as she'd filled Austin's. Equal, down to the two links of Italian sausage, twin meatballs, and cut of country pork.

What the hell is going on?

Trying to do his part and act indifferent, he

lifted the breadbasket and placed a slice on Ember's plate. When he passed the basket to Austin his friend arched a brow and grinned.

One punch. That's all it would take.

"*Mangia!*" Ember announced with a shaky smile. Good, at least he wasn't the only one picking up on the awkward as fuck ambiance.

Wait. Did *she* know what Austin had suggested?

He'd said they talked, a lot...about everything. Cord glared at the other man's head as he shoveled in a bite of angel hair.

The damn meal was ruined. Ember's sauce—which Cord typically loved—tasted sour on his tongue. The meat was flavorless. Even the homemade bread was without the delectable punch of flavor he usually experienced. It had nothing to do with Ember's cooking, however. Nope. Judging by the sounds of pleasure coming from his idiotic friend he imagined the meal tasted as incredible as ever. It was Cord's confusion that dulled his senses.

All he could focus on was Ember, the sight of her glass pressing against her lips, the shift of her dress caressing the tablecloth. She wasn't doing anything but sitting and eating—and occasionally giving him that timid smile—yet she'd distracted him to the point of obsession.

Rays of sunlight intensified through the windows, tinting the blinds in soft pink, painting

Ember in a golden glow. She'd never worn makeup that he could tell, and tonight he spent a little more time valuing the dusting of freckles on her nose. If he breathed slowly enough, he could detect the soft fragrance of her perfume beneath the pungent aroma of Italian cuisine.

By the time Austin was on his second helping, Cord's body had begun to react to her presence despite his efforts to calm himself. His throat turned dry and he repetitively swallowed, trying to maintain some modicum of composure. Had she always held her fork like that, delicately balanced on her middle finger? Jesus God, there was something wrong with him. He was ignoring all his self-imposed rules of maintaining his distance.

Filling his glass, he guzzled down the cool water. Blinking toward the ceiling, he wondered if the room was getting hotter. Maybe it was the spice of the gravy.

"I made strawberry shortcake for dessert," she softly announced. Her gaze went to his plate and she frowned. "Cord? You barely touched your pasta. Is there something wrong with it?"

Breath labored, he worked to disguise the effect she was having on him. The look of concern in her brown eyes could be his undoing. He wondered what it would be like to take Austin out of the equation?

'Of course not, honey. It's delicious, as usual.'

She'd smile, hidden meaning simmering in her gaze. 'Good. I made it for you.'

'You always take such good care of me. I love you.'

'I love you too.'

"Cord?"

He jerked out of the daydream to find her frowning at him. "It's delicious, Ember."

Biting her lower lip, she stared at him a moment longer then nodded. "I'll clear some room and bring out the cake."

The second she was gone the asshole in the room spoke up. "You're wasting your time fighting it."

His fork clattered to his plate. "What the fuck is wrong with you? Stop shoving me at your wife!"

Austin stared past Cord, his face filling with concern.

Shit. Ember stood in the doorway, eyes wide, frozen in place, clutching a white frosted cake heaped with strawberries.

Goddamn Austin and his stupid ideas. "Ember—"

"I...I forgot the knife." She quickly placed the dishes on the table, her steps clumsy, and fled to the kitchen.

"Great," Cord snapped, bunching up his napkin and tossing it on the table. "Enjoy your fucking cake. I'm out of here."

Austin opened his big mouth, but Cord was

done talking to him. Reasoning with Austin was like trying to discuss physics with a chimp. "*Shut it*, Austin."

He detoured to the kitchen, unable to take his rage out on her. "Ember, I didn't mean—"

"It's okay." Her fingers twisted into a dishcloth and then she dashed away a tear.

Fuck. Tears? Not tears! His concern shifted into panic. "It's *not* okay. I don't know what Austin told you—"

"I know what he's up to. I told him not to do this."

She fucking knew her husband was messing with him? It didn't make any sense. "*Why* is he doing this?"

Now *she* shrugged. "He's Austin. Once he gets something in his head..."

Cord rubbed his palm over his face and squeezed. "What does he expect to gain from this? He's just making an uncomfortable situation worse."

"He's trying to fix it. He doesn't understand, because he wasn't there. He thinks if we put everything out in the open the guilt will go away. He thinks it's best to deal with it."

"Deal with it how?" He wasn't a fucking puppet Austin could jerk around.

"I don't know. I barely understand what I'm feeling right now. I can't pretend to understand what he's going through. Or you, for that matter."

All thoughts of her husband vanished as he focused on the 'f' word—*feelings.* Fuck if he knew how to describe any of the mess inside of him. "What are *you* feeling?"

Her face tightened and her hand pressed into her chest, her eyes betraying her show of bravado. "Here. It hurts. I don't know how to make it stop, Cord."

"Hurts how?" He took a slow step closer, keeping his voice low.

Eyes pleading, she looked up at him, her mouth tight with worry. "When I'm near you, my heart beats so fast I'm afraid it'll explode. But I know I can't... I can't express what's inside of me. Then this unbearable ache takes hold. It just... hurts."

"Wanting," he rasped. Fuck if he didn't know exactly the word to describe that ache.

She sniffled and shook her head. "W—what?"

"It's wanting. Longing. Like something's empty in there because I can't be with you."

"Yes," she breathed.

He shifted another step closer. His fingers gently brushed over the high arc of her cheekbone and catching a tear.

"He's playing with fire," he whispered. "If he thinks pushing us together again isn't going to have repercussions, I worry for his sanity." For the sanity of all of them.

"I'm so tired of getting burned." Bitterness

laced her quiet tone, but then she softened, lowering her lashes and leaning her face into his touch.

He dipped his head. "Maybe it just has to burn out on its own, this thing we've started." *Maybe in several lifetimes.*

Her mouth compressed and she remained silent.

"I want to kiss you, Ember. Not because Austin's scheming, but because I need to stop that ache for a second so I can breathe again."

His head dipped closer as if in some sort of trance. Slowly, his lips brushed over hers. She murmured his name softly against his mouth and his body shivered, quaking with pent up desire to fully taste her again, acknowledge this connection they were fighting.

His hand ghosted to the back of her neck, barely caressing her silky skin, but feeling all those tiny hairs rise under his touch. His lips opened over hers, his tongue gently coaxing its way into her warm mouth.

Taking his time, he nudged her until her back arched slightly over the counter. His other hand closed over her hip, the warmth of her making his palm twitch and his fingers tighten. Like the soft blossom of a flower, she opened under him.

Her palms rested on his chest, heating his skin through the cotton of his shirt. His heart thundered wildly and his temples pounded. She pressed upward, deepening the kiss, her fingers creeping to lace around his neck and pull him closer.

His body hardened, shifting and fitting over her small form until they were molded together. Heat. The burn to have her intensified, scorching his insides, and firing off every natural instinct to claim her.

Soft sounds keened from her throat as the kiss went on. Her fingers tightened, pulling, pleading. Blood pumped to his cock as his need shifted into something dark and possessive, and passion became an inferno raging inside of him, impossible to bank.

Breaking the kiss, she panted and stared into his eyes, breathless, wearing an expression of fear and wanting.

"I should go," he whispered, somehow regaining control.

Leaning in, he brushed his mouth over hers one last time. It was a farewell of sorts, but one he wasn't certain they could uphold. Whatever Austin had hoped to accomplish here, Cord was certain it wasn't this.

He wanted his best friend's wife with a frightening intensity, and was determined to have her again. Fuck the right and the wrong of it. Fuck Austin for encouraging the temptation.

A flicker of regret lanced through him before he ruthlessly stamped it out. Ember was caught in the middle even more than before, and he hated that, but he'd figure it out. He was gonna do what was right for her and he knew, in his heart, he was part of that.

"Thanks for dinner," he whispered, helping her find her balance. "I'll see you soon."

Cord turned and flinched inwardly as his friend's blank stare met his from the doorway. Austin's brown eyes studied him and he couldn't get a read. His first instinct was to protect Ember.

Locking his jaw, he marched toward the front door, knocking Austin with his shoulder as he passed. "Outside. *Now.*"

When he hit the porch, he sucked in a bracing lungful of air. Austin's footsteps echoed and the second he stepped onto the porch, Cord turned on him. "I'm done with the fucking games, Austin."

All cockiness was gone. Austin held up his hands, expression still unreadable, and made a show of shoving them into his pockets. "This isn't a game, Cord."

"No shit." He paced. "Jesus. It's never enough for you. You just keep pushing and pushing—"

"Do you regret it?"

He pivoted and scowled at him. "What?"

"Kissing her. Making love to her. If you could take it all back, would you?"

He shook his head. "You have problems."

"So do you."

He angled forward, shoving his face into

Austin's. "No. I'm done regretting shit. You want to play games? Go sit at the kiddie table and leave her out of it."

"You think I'd let you have her? You can't threaten me, Cord, not where she's concerned. You know it. I know it. And Ember knows it. This isn't about you and her or me and her or even you and I. It's about *all* of us. When you get that, you'll see that what I did tonight was for her. Not me. Definitely not for me." He glanced over his shoulder and back to Cord. "Now, if you'll excuse me. I have to go check on my wife."

Cord stood on the porch a few seconds after Austin left, seriously debating if this was some sort of waking nightmare. He needed to get some distance. Taking the steps two at a time, he hustled to his truck and fled. Whatever this was, he couldn't be a part of it anymore.

Fifteen

December

THE FLUFFY TOWEL wrapped around December's damp body as she stepped out of the shower. Steam kissed her skin, locking in the slow burn from Cord's touch that had yet to fade. Exiting the bathroom in a cloud of mist, she froze in place.

Austin, pulling on a pair of lounge pants, met her gaze and slowly rose to his full height. "Hey."

She swallowed. After cleaning up from dinner she'd busied herself making preparations for tomorrow's breakfast and anything else she could do to avoid meeting her husband's eyes. Showering was her last resort. "Hey."

He glanced at the bed. "Are you sleeping in here tonight?"

She hadn't made up her mind yet. "Do you want me to?"

"It's your bed—*our* bed."

"You didn't answer my question."

Leveling her with a stern, yet somehow vulnerable glare, he said, "Yes, December, I want you to sleep in our bed."

"I'm sorry." She glanced away, still unable to meet his gaze. "I don't know how to act."

And I don't know how to feel, only that I do. I feel so much...for both of them.

"Then don't act. Just be yourself."

"I'm not sure I know who that is anymore."

His steps drifted to the nightstand. His watch lightly clicked against the finish as he removed it. She'd forgotten about how he always took it off before bed. So many little rituals she'd never took notice of suddenly seemed monumental.

She went to her dresser and found a nightgown. Pulling the white cotton over her head, she slid her arms through the sleeves. She always slept in the same gowns, fine cotton covering only to her upper thighs. Tonight, it didn't seem enough. Perhaps she should slip on panties. Would he notice?

Hanging the towel over the quilt rack, she fussed with it until all the wrinkles were smooth.

His heated form pressed into her back, startling her.

"Sorry," he whispered, pressing his lips to the back of her neck. "I didn't mean to startle you."

With twitchy movements, she delicately shouldered him off and slid onto the seat at her vanity. Her hair didn't take the time it once had. Missing the ritual of braiding it, she brushed the short strands twice for good measure.

Her gaze remained focused on the mirror, but followed Austin's reflection. He folded down the blankets of the bed and glanced around as if considering he might be forgetting something. When he looked at her their eyes met in the mirror and she quickly dropped her gaze.

From the beginning of their marriage, they'd shared a room, a bed, and their bodies except for the time after he lost his job. It was the conclusion to their day, the time they always reconnected. Austin believed one of the secrets to a healthy marriage was kissing, every day, for several minutes. She'd come to expect those kisses and long caresses. She expected them now, sensed their approach, but her body was nervous and tense, her mind undecided.

Her gaze caught on an object that didn't belong, the little porcelain cow that used to be in the kitchen. Squinting, she noted the webbed cracks and dried glue. Slightly worse for wear, it now sat on her dressing table. Picking it up with a delicate touch, she turned it in her palm.

"My cow..."

A beat of silence passed and Austin's voice came like a slow whisper entrenched in regret. "I, uh, dropped it."

Her gaze lifted to the mirror, finding his reflection as he licked his lips. There was a story there, a part of the missing puzzle that took shape during her absence.

"I glued it as best I could, but it probably won't hold salt anymore. I'm sorry."

Her chest pinched. She loved those silly kitchen knickknacks, but not nearly as much as she loved her husband's ability to fix something she loved, his sincere regret for damaging something even a small as a saltshaker. "It's okay."

She traced the surface with a fingertip, feeling smooth china between the tiny chips. Broken but repaired. It seemed significant. With all its chips and damage, she still loved it all the same—perhaps more, because now she saw his effort to put something broken, back together again.

She carefully placed it back on her vanity, thinking that a good place for it to stay, a reminder of his effort in small things and big, to rebuild what was. She continued to comb out her hair, her gaze returning to the mirror and dropping back to the tiny figurine. A warm press of hope expanded in her chest. If he could fix little things he could possibly heal them—heal her.

Placing the brush on the glass tray, she stood. Austin reached for his lamp and half of the room dimmed. The decision seemed to be made for her, a relief than having to choose for herself. She climbed under the sheets and turned off the other light. Darkness descended. There was something special about the dark. It let her hide.

Lowering her head to the pillows, she curled to her side, but her eyes remained open. Austin shifted and his body spooned into hers. His hand crept over her hip as he whispered, "This is nice."

Panic rose as her heart beat rapidly. Her mouth went dry. He wasn't doing more than resting his palm on her hip, under the covers, over her nightgown. Yet somehow it seemed epic.

Minutes passed, dragging into unmeasured spans of time. Was he asleep? Was he thinking about where his hand rested? Did he expect her to make love with him? When the questions became too numerous, she bolted off the pillows and sat up.

"Ember? What's wrong?"

She couldn't breathe. "All of this."

His lamp clicked on. "What do you mean?"

Unable to look at him, she waved her hand numbly in the air. "This. This bed. Dinner. It's all wrong."

Scooting closer, he brushed a comforting hand

down her back and she flinched. She was having some sort of anxiety attack. Tightness twisted in her chest and her throat burned as she tried to swallow, each breath scraping in and out of her esophagus.

"Ember. Ember, look at me." He shifted in front of her, gripping her fists. "Shhh, baby, look in my eyes. It's okay." Unclamping her fingers, he drew her palms to his chest. "Breathe with me."

Her fingers spanned his tanned skin as she watched and felt his chest expand and contract. She tried to match her breathing to his. Slowly, the burning in her lungs faded and the tingling of her skin quelled.

"Good girl."

She'd never hyperventilated before, if that's what that even was. It was scary and gone before she could even make sense of it.

"Here. Take a sip of water."

Her fingertips were numb and her balance was off, but she did as he said, hoping the water would ease the lightheadedness.

"Is it me?" he asked, eyes downcast with concern.

She shook her head. "I don't know what it is."

Pursing his lips, he sat beside her on the mattress. "Do you want this, Ember? Us?"

Of course she wanted them. "Yes."

"If you don't, you need to tell me."

Gathering up her courage, she turned to him. "Austin, I *love* you."

"I know you do, but maybe I'm not who you want anymore. *What* you want. This whole thing with Cord—"

"Stop. Tonight was a mistake. It can't be both of you, Austin. A decision has to be made. You're my *husband*. A marriage is between two people. I'll sit down with Cord and explain things to him."

"Explain what?"

She didn't know. "The situation."

"Which is?"

I don't know. "That you're my husband."

He sighed. "Ember, there are physical affairs and then there are emotional ones. Even if you weren't sleeping with him you'd still be in love with another man."

Her arms ached as the blood chilled in her veins. *Can't I be in love with two?* She tamped down her wistful inner thought. "But you're my husband. You're the man I'm meant to be with. It's just the way it is. Over time...these feelings will fade."

"And what do we do in the meantime? I'm done hiding from obstacles in my life, December. The minute I start hiding again everything starts reverting to a place neither of us want to go."

"Maybe I need counseling."

"If you want to talk to someone, that would

be fine, but they'll only be able to walk you through the truth. At the end of the day, you're the one who has to take the steps."

She needed a break. There were so many issues bombarding her at once, she jumped to a different one. "I don't know if I can sleep with you again."

"Ever or right now?"

"Right now. It's...too soon."

"Okay."

"It's not because of Cord." She wanted him to understand that. "*This* has nothing to do with him."

"Okay."

"It's because of us. You hurt me, Austin. I put myself on the line so many times and battled some crushing demons of my own in this bed while you were on the couch. My confidence, my appeal, it all got ransacked. I can't just hit a switch and go back to the wife I was." *I'm broken but I want to heal.*

His eyes flashed with disappointment, his face tightening with regret. "I understand."

"But at the same time, I feel like we should just push through the intimacy. I can't take all this worrying and wondering if we'll ever be right again."

"We *will* be right again, December. So long as you want me in your life and accept the mistakes I've made. Try to forgive me as best you can—because I *am* so damn sorry for everything I did—I'll work every day at righting the wrongs. It may not be the marriage we left behind, but it will be ours and it *will* be right again."

Her fingers pressed into her temples. "I'm so confused."

"I wish I knew the ending, baby. I'd tell you what comes next. But neither of us will know until we try. I can wait, if that's what you want. It's not about physical needs. It's about the emotional connection with the woman I love. Until you're there, present and ready, it won't be real. I want it to be real, Ember. Nothing has to happen right now."

He sounded so much like the man she met years ago, strong, determined, and patient. She couldn't find balance between this man and the one who cast her off. She thought she understood why he'd sent her to Cord, desperate to provide some semblance of care when he was incapable.

But deep down she feared the bad Austin would come back. She feared if bad Austin did return, that she'd be too wrung out to argue anymore. What if he came back, if the misery and lies came back, and she just... gave up. She was trying so hard to be strong.

It was a real fear, because she loved him so deeply, she wasn't sure she'd ever choose a life without him, even if the life with him wasn't happy anymore. And she didn't want to be *that* girl, the one who suffered over and over, too weak to love herself enough to demand more. She wanted to respect herself enough to have the courage to demand what she deserved in this life.

She resented the possibility of weakness, in her, in him, but there was no guarantee. The only truth she knew was that she *did* love him. Then. Before. Now. Forever. But what if that was her problem?

"Talk to me, baby."

"I do love you, Austin—to a fault. No matter what, that'll never change."

He nodded, leaning toward her, his love written large in his gaze. "Me too."

She studied their hands wrapped as one. Somehow love managed to overshadow dignity, it was that big and that all-encompassing. Some days she was unsure who she loved more, herself or him. If he went back down that dark road, she feared she'd go with him because someone had to watch out for her husband, and if that happened they'd be lost forever—together but apart.

She'd follow him. In sickness or health, weakness or strength. That might make her weak as well, but there was nothing easy about her decision to love him. It would be her burden as much as her salvation, and she'd never know which, until she tried.

Once she admitted that undying love to herself she could no longer deny the truth. She didn't examine that realization too intensely, but sort of recognized all the possible outcomes if they failed. Not that she expected him to relapse. He seemed so strong now. But anything was possible and she had to prepare for absolutely anything if she intended to stay.

She was here and she didn't want to leave again. It was time for her to commit to her surroundings, commit to him, and put herself back in the game. All in. Win or lose, she was here for the long haul.

Her fingers, curled around his, squeezed a bit tighter. "Maybe we should try."

"We don't have to. I'm in no rush. I want you to be ready."

She wanted to push through this wall and get back to normal. The distance and awkwardness was killing her.

The chemistry was there. There were times when her knees went weak even catching his scent. She needed him to take back the upper hand, be the anchor that always kept them grounded, and decide this was right for *them*. But now, when her emotions were high and her fears lay bare, she wasn't sure if intimacy was something to force.

Yet she wanted it to happen. She wanted to prove she could be with him again, to take the risk, and believe he wouldn't disappear back to the couch or stop talking to her for days. She needed to be with him to prove to herself that things were getting better between them, and that this wasn't an act. She needed to know this—that Austin was solid enough to depend on.

If this part of them was broken, everything else would become twice as daunting. They needed some shred of normalcy back in their marriage—she needed that shred.

"I need you to do this for me, Austin. I need you to get me through this."

His head turned, his brows forming a deep V above his nose. "Ember, I won't force you to do something you aren't ready to do."

Her anticipation might be worse than actuality. If they crossed this bridge, maybe she'd be able to reflect on her feelings rather than hypothesize about them, fearing the worst.

"I need you to, Austin," she pleaded, knowing she didn't have the strength to do this on her own. "You've always been the aggressor. I don't know how to overcome this on my own."

"That's fine, but it doesn't have to be—"

"Tonight. I want to do it tonight. Waiting will only build more pressure between us."

He looked to the floor and she had no way of guessing what he was thinking. "Ember, forcing this could give you another reason to hate me."

"I don't hate you. I won't hate you. You're my husband. The only thing I've ever felt good at is being your wife. I...I need you to be my strong husband right now. I need you to take control. You know what I need."

"That's not the only thing you've ever been good at."

"But it's the only thing I've ever been able to do with complete confidence." Until her confidence was shaken to the core. "I need to feel like your wife again. Maybe the first time won't be perfect, but it will be progress. For a year, I felt like I was standing still, aging, and bartering with every god to give me back my husband. I desperately wanted this connection with you. I think if we let nature take the wheel and stopped trying to decide for ourselves everything else will come a little easier."

"You're sure?"

Terrified, but sure. She nodded. "Please."

He gave a tentative smile, his reservations clear in his brown eyes. "Lie back."

With shaky motions, she eased into the pillows. Her pulse rapidly fluttered as he waited, obviously collecting himself. Everything around them put her on high sensory alert. It was as though her skin could count every fiber of the sheets beneath her. Her nose took in the faint scent of coffee sitting on the counter downstairs. Her nightgown felt heavy on her skin as she waited and very soon, if he didn't do something, she would scream.

He stood and rounded the bed. The light clicked off but then he went to the bathroom and turned on the dimmer, cracking the door just enough so she could see him through the shadows. The mattress dipped as he eased in beside her. One big hand drifted over her thigh and lifted her nightgown.

She trembled, wondering if this was what virgins felt like during regency times. Every natural instinct fled, leaving her clueless and inexplicably frozen.

The covers rustled as he rolled to his side and eased closer. Her breasts tightened as her chest rose with each nervous breath.

Leaning close, he nuzzled the side of her throat with his nose, sending jolts of titillating shivers down her arms. It was as if he'd never touched her before, as though she'd never been touched.

Washed away were all the memories of prior moments of intimacy. There was only this moment, these slow caresses and tender awakenings to something she'd all but lost yet never stopped wanting.

His mouth kissed slowly over her throat as his fingers whirled in delicate patterns over her trembling thigh. Tipping back her head, her eyes drifted shut as his lips made a teasing crawl to her jaw and then her ear.

"December," his husky voice rasped, breath tickling the shell of her ear and driving her toes into little points.

Her thighs pressed together, sluggishly scissoring through the pressure building low in her belly. Friction, slight and delicious, traced beneath his fingertips as his touch drifted higher toward her sex, getting lost in that soft crease between her thigh and hip. Her spine arched languidly.

His mouth traveled to her collarbone, his tongue soft and hot, tracing the delicate curve. Leaving her hip, his hand slowly unfastened the line of tiny buttons on her gown and parted the cotton. His touch shifted under her clothing, pressing softly to her belly as his nose nudged the cotton away from her shoulder.

Warm lips pressed into the smooth expanse of skin leading to her breasts. She trembled as his body rolled closer. Cool air tickled her thighs and belly.

Uncovered, her sex contracted but the heat of her arousal didn't cool. Her body thrummed with need, hollow, and wanting to be filled. He parted her gown, exposing her breasts, and her nipples puckered tightly, chilled and needy for the heat of his mouth.

It had been so long since he'd touched her like this. Always so attentive and in control, he unraveled her, stripped her of every façade until she was nothing but carnal energy and deep-seated desire. He *mastered* her.

His fingers trailed down her bare arms, closing gently around her wrists and lifting them. "Hands up here, baby," he said, pressing them slowly into the downy pillows. His will alone restrained her, and she complied.

Her back arched, her breasts rising into the shadows. He slid a knee between hers and worked his way up her body, calloused hands skimming sensually over her sensitized sides. His lips dragged from her bellybutton to the valley between her breasts and then his mouth, scorching and wet, closed over her rigid nipple.

She cried out, startled by the acute sense of pleasure. His hands bracketed her ribcage, cushioning her breasts and cupping her curves. Dragging her head along the pillows, her knees drew up, embracing the weight of his hips, the strength of his body.

Heat burned low in her belly as desire transformed into dark need. The fabric of his sleep pants formed an annoying, yet sensual barrier against her heated skin.

His lips teased and nipped at her sensitive nipples, as his body rocked in a slow glide over hers, each brush of friction provocation for more. The scruff of his jaw rasped over her delicate flesh as he kissed the plump sides of her breasts. His mouth pulled at her skin, marking her, knotting her insides tighter.

Dragging the hard edge of his jaw over her soft belly, each coarse hair like a tiny blade of illicit pleasure, he licked and kissed her skin. His breath teased the cooling trail left from his tongue as his hands drifted down to her knees. He scooted lower and her eyes closed under a wave of emotion so similar to shame, yet so very different. She sensed the heat of his gaze in the dim lighting the moment it settled on her sex.

She was so wet, so ready...physically. His touch brushed softly over the dusting of hair covering her sex. A thick finger gently parted her without intruding. Emotionally, her body began to panic.

They were so close. The intensity, the significance of this coupling overwhelmed her. Biting her lips, she fought the urge to demand he stop. Her hands inched upward. Unable to fight the complex feelings bombarding her, she opened her mouth—

His finger sank deep into her sex. Her body lengthened, accommodating the intrusion as he simply held his touch deep inside of her. The soft tickle of his hair trailed over her belly as he rested his head just below her navel. Her personal panic took a backseat to concern.

"Austin?"

He shook his head and she frowned. Lifting her arms, she gently brushed her fingers over the top of his head, unsure what he was feeling but recognizing the intensity of his emotions.

"I'm sorry," he rasped.

Oh, God, he couldn't leave her like this. Despite the war waging inside of her, she needed them to finish. She'd been so concerned about her own challenges she hadn't questioned his.

What if he couldn't have sex with her? Make love to her? What if it was gone and they were both too lost to ever find each other again? His breath, hot and ragged came out in a broken exhalation as his finger slowly withdrew. Something wet touched her belly.

His voice was broken, gravelly. "I hate myself."

Is he crying?

A new panic took hold. She scooted lower and caught his face in her hands. His face pinched in agony, turning away from her.

"Austin, talk to me. Tell me what happened."

Mouth pressed tight, eyes sealed shut, he barely seemed to breathe. "How could I have let us go? I didn't mean to do this to us."

"We're not over." She pressed closer and turned his face toward her with insistent fingers, no matter how he tried to hide his anguish. "Austin, we're not over. We're fixing it. I promise. Please don't stop."

"I think about how much I need you, and see how you'll sacrifice everything to be there for me, when for a year I did nothing but turn you away when *you* needed me."

"It's no sacrifice, Austin." She shook her head quickly. "Being with you like this will never be a sacrifice. Not because it feels good or because of a sense of obligation, but because I love you and when we're together I feel that intangible love we share taking shape into something evident and undeniable. Please don't beat yourself up like this."

"I don't deserve to touch you like this."

"Stop it. That's not true. I belong to you. Do you hear me? You're mine and I'm yours, and until I tell you otherwise, that's how it will always be. That's how we're supposed to be."

His head hung between his shoulders. "I didn't expect it to hit me so hard."

Her throat contracted, all the significance slamming into her harder than before. It was a lot to take in. A lot to process. "You're not alone. I'm feeling it too."

The tension in his face eased by a small degree, his gaze, wrought with questions and doubt drifting to hers. "I never wanted to hurt you, December."

"I know." And in that moment, that raw acknowledgement seemed to provide all the understanding they needed to share.

He'd never made a conscious decision to hurt her. He loved her. Though she didn't fully understand alcoholism and all its implications, she did know Austin.

It had probably killed him to wake up day after day to the damage his intoxicated choices had wrought, knowing he'd hurt and humiliated her when he'd never intended to do more than love and honor her. Take care of her.

It was then she realized she needed to forgive him in order for him to forgive himself. That stranger who had slept on their couch and taken advantage of her kindness, that wasn't her husband. That wasn't the man beside her now. *This* was the Austin she'd made vows with. The other one was the enemy, a shared enemy, one they'd both strive to avoid from here on out.

She smiled at him, tenderly pressing her lips to his. "Make love to me, Austin. Heal me. That man who hurt me, he's gone. Right now, all I need is you, my husband whom I've missed to the point of pain. Please. Make love to me...now that I've finally found you again."

~

Austin

Austin pushed aside the anguish choking him and managed to look into her eyes, overwhelmed by the sincerity there, and all he could think was *why*.

Why did she love him? Why had she come back? Why had she not given up on him and found someone better? Any flicker of awareness was banished in the face of what he felt between them now, no one else there to shield the truth—not even Cord.

Humbled by her gracious acceptance of every wrong he'd done and her incredible willingness to forgive, he was shaken to the bone. His wife did indeed love him to a fault. It was a gift he wasn't sure he'd ever be worthy of, but one he would spend his life trying to earn.

Without haste, she eased back, sliding her arms from her delicate white gown. In a trance, he stared, breath stolen by her immeasurable beauty. Such an offering, such an altar to worship upon, to honor and cherish.

She'd suffered—it was apparent in the jut of her hipbones, the delineation of every rib, and the shearing of her glorious hair. He'd violated her trust. Allowed a toxic presence into their home, malignant and insidious, and seeing her now, so welcoming and accepting...it brought him down too many pegs to count.

She would always be better than him in so many ways. He might never have her capacity for tolerance, her graceful way of forgiving others, but he envied those qualities and would do his best to find them within himself.

Love. That was the truest truth he could offer her, and the greatest tool to help find their way out of the dark. His love seemed so small and insignificant, cast in the shadows of all that was December, yet it was the biggest emotion he knew.

And for her, it was everything she wanted, and something he could provide, because she set the terms within his reach.

Slowly, he removed his pants. The chilling sense of exposure rattled his senses, stripping him of all pretense and leaving him vulnerable. He'd never been one to overthink the act of making love, but this was monumental and suddenly he was a frightened wolf more fragile than any lamb. She was his everything.

Facing her, breath stuttered into his lungs. Her arm lifted, her hand reaching for him. His fingers laced with hers, so delicate and small. He'd always filled the dominant role in their relationship, because Ember needed it, but like a mirror in a funhouse, the world suddenly turned upside down. It had never been more apparent or undeniable that *she* was the one with absolute supremacy, with all the power. Admitting the truth brought about a peaceful sense of surrender. Neither of them was strong enough to face this alone.

He could open jars and rotate her tires, do all the stereotypical, masculine chores and be the dominant lover when she needed to surrender. He could carry her up the stairs when she was tired, tote in the groceries, bring home the paycheck, and hold her umbrella in the rain, but at the end of the day, her strength would always outdo his.

"Make love to me, Austin."

Breathing in her sweet scent, he lowered himself to the bed. Her limbs, smooth and tapered, wrapped around him like a welcoming cocoon. His body hardened the moment their skin touched. Heat from her flesh burned him in the most pleasurable way as he fit his body over hers, careful not to crush her with his weight.

Her soft breasts cushioned his chest as he burrowed his face in the curve of her neck. He simply breathed her in, drawing comfort from the familiar fragrance that belonged only to her.

"I love you, Ember."

He couldn't stop shaking. The heat of her sex caressed his cock and he gasped at the sensation. Lifting up, he carefully aligned their bodies, but didn't penetrate. Rising so he could look into her eyes, he met her stare. A million thoughts passed between them, yet not a single word was spoken. He breathed in, never taking his gaze from hers, and sank into her heat.

Home.

Her lips parted as she sucked in a deep breath. He waited, not quite ready to move. Hot, sultry heat wrapped around his length, burning passion scalding his soul. They fit together perfectly. How had he ever gone without this amazing connection?

"Are you okay?" he whispered.

A tear slowly slipped from her lashes. She nodded tightly then reached for his face, gently cupping his jaw and pulling him into her kiss.

"This, Austin." Her mouth breathed life into his soul. "This is everything I've held my breath for, everything I've longed to feel again. Not sex, but you." Her lips, tasting of the salt of their tears, moved against his. "Your love. That's what this is and I can't live without it. I need you, Austin. I'll always need you."

He kissed her passionately, unconcerned with time or any other distractions outside of that moment. His body slowly began to move, sliding languidly over hers, their connection delving into the depths of their souls.

Lost together, they'd come undone. All he'd forfeited was suddenly found.

There were no words for what they shared. It was something sacred and only theirs, something outsiders couldn't feel or fully understand. It was a love that had survived distance, endured trauma, and, somehow, breathed again.

Sixteen

Cord

THE HOURS HAD BEEN UNBEARABLE, slowly stretching into days. Days folded into weeks and hope eventually seemed nothing more than a hoax Cord was meant to suffer for the rest of his life. He hadn't seen nor heard from Ember or Austin in weeks. And he refused to be the one to call.

He'd expected this to happen, warned himself it was inevitable. She and Austin were likely back to normal and he was nothing but an unpleasant memory they'd made a pact to avoid. Austin's little experiment at dinner seemed like one last fuck with Cord's mind.

Like any grieving victim—and oh, how he loathed seeing himself that way—he digested the truth in stages. Some days the rage inside of him was so great he wanted to kill his best friend—*ex*-best friend—for taking away what had never belonged to Cord in the first place.

Sometimes, there was nothing but quiet acceptance laced with a touch of contentment. His friends had reunited and the shitty world was as it was meant to be once more. But most days, there was only emptiness.

He wasn't sure what he expected to happen after that kiss. Foolishly, he'd let his heart believe there would be more. There had to be more. But... nothing. *He* was nothing. No matter what, he wouldn't be the man who broke up a marriage, and couldn't allow Ember feel responsible for the same. He simply loved her too much.

He'd lost both of them...the woman he loved, a sacrifice required for his friend to move on, as well as a friendship he'd depended on for decades. And though Austin didn't deserve his compassion, Cord couldn't deny it was there, insisting he do the right thing. Fuck his life.

It was for the best. Maybe someday they'd all be able to sit at the same table again, but without the awkward after effects of broken vows and secrets. Sure.

Cord could have called, but his pride demanded she take the first step. He couldn't afford the whiplash of being in the middle any more. Despite his challenge the last time he left them, he couldn't be the bad guy.

But there were no calls. No visits to the hardware store. No more invitations to dinner. Christ, he'd accept another boxing match just to know they remembered he existed. But there was nothing.

His mother, Norma Jean, came out from the storeroom. Her cheery yellow T-shirt completed the sunny picture she made in her white denim skirt and flip-flops.

"Cord, I found a new line of linens I think you should order. They have a great selection of shower curtains with matching hooks for each set. The price is pretty decent, too. I don't like the new selection our usual company's offering this year."

"Okay, Mom."

Though his parents ran the store for thirty-five years, when he'd come of age they'd done what his grandparents had done, and passed the majority of responsibility on to him. He was grateful for the opportunity, though it hadn't been his first career choice. But since boyhood, he'd been stocking shelves and running to fetch his father's coffee. And it had been an unspoken expectation, one he'd accepted. It was good and familiar and he believed he did the job well.

His parents managed the store on Saturdays and Sundays, but all the big decisions now went through him. They were happy to pass on the legacy and eager to slide into retirement after working all their lives, his father at the store, and his mother managing their home and overseeing the woman's touch at Bay's.

She placed the catalogue on the counter by the register. "Kathy Lynch just ordered this set. Isn't it darling? I love the palm tree hooks."

He glanced at the picture. It wasn't his style, but he could see women getting a kick out of such detailed accessories.

"I'll call them today. Why don't you put together a list of ten patterns you think will sell?" Sometimes it was nice to have a woman's perspective. Like Ember's. But hey... She'd forgotten he existed. His gut cramped, but he bore it.

"You got it." She paused, before taking the book back to the storeroom. "Did I tell you we saw Austin and Ember at the market?"

His belly clenched again, differently, as curiosity reared its head. "That's nice." Asking for more details would only cause him pain.

"They asked about you. Haven't you seen them lately?"

His parents knew he'd lived with Austin over the winter, but not the details. He'd simply told them Ember had family obligations elsewhere and he'd agreed to help Austin with the bills in exchange for Austin helping around the store. "I saw them about a month ago."

"I wonder if Ember will come back to the store. Customers constantly ask about her."

"Probably not, Mom."

"Oh." She hesitated and he could tell she had something on her mind.

"What?"

"Cord, honey... When Ember went to visit family, were her and Austin on good terms?"

Sighing, he considered lying, but never in his life had he been able to pull the wool over his mother's eyes. "Not really."

"But now she's back?"

"Looks that way." He busied himself scanning the store for a customer. Anyone would do. Shit. The place was vacant.

"You should invite them for Sunday dinner."

"Mom."

"What? You three are friends. Best friends. If you haven't seen each other in a while, maybe a good family meal is just what's needed."

"I'll ask them."

She scowled. "Don't you lie to me, Cordovan. Now, tell me what's going on."

"Nothing. I gotta go change the bulbs in the fan display."

She grabbed his wrist. "That can wait. Talk to me. What's going on with you three? First, December worked here, then Austin. Now neither of them ever visit the store. I haven't seen Austin— aside from bumping into them at the market—in over a year. He looks good, but Ember… What did she do to all that beautiful hair?"

"Her hair's still beautiful."

"Oh, Ember will always be a stunning girl. I'm just shocked she'd make such an extreme change. Usually women ease into short hair. It concerns me, that's all."

He frowned. "Why? It's just hair."

Her lips thinned as she glanced away. "Hair is a woman's glory, Cord. Back in my day, it represented a female's femininity. The nuns would shear the hair off any girl who flaunted her…sensuality."

"What the heck are you talking about, Mom? It's a haircut. There are no nuns involved and those days are over. She cut her hair because she wanted to. You're overanalyzing."

She lifted a shoulder. "It's a huge change, Cord. A drastic one. I can't help but think it's a symptom of something deeper."

Defensive, and now a bit concerned, he put the topic to rest. "That's ridiculous. She wanted short hair so she got it cut." He forced a smile, desperate to distract her. "Go make your list of shower curtains."

"Maybe. Maybe not. I think I'll ask her why she cut it all off when she comes for Sunday dinner."

His spine stiffened and he turned back to her. "You will not."

She laughed. "I most certainly will. That girl's facing something and I know she doesn't have a mother nearby to talk to. You *will* invite them to dinner this week or I'll call her myself."

"Mom..."

"Cord, they're your friends. I've known Austin since he was a baby. When Emily died, I promised to look after him the way a mother would. I'll expect to see them this weekend."

"They might have plans."

"Then the following Sunday. Either way, I expect you to invite them and let me know when they'll be at our table." She slid the catalogue off the counter and marched toward the back of the store.

He hated when his mother manipulated him. And what the hell was all that hair mumbo jumbo? It was *hair*. Aggravated, he decided if his parents wanted dinner guests they'd have to do the inviting themselves.

Over the following days, his mother made no mention about dinners or the happy couple. Cord wasn't foolish enough to believe she'd forgotten their conversation, but he appreciated that she wasn't harping on it. She'd likely bring up the subject again, though, and he'd just avoid it.

On Sunday afternoon he went to his folk's house. His dad had been on a Japanese movie kick and Cord walked in to corny Kung Fu fights playing on the screen with delayed audio.

"You're still watching this crap?" he asked, plopping onto the couch.

His dad laughed. "I can't get enough. Your mother just ordered a six disc set she saw on an infomercial."

His parents had become addicted to infomercials since retiring. Cord's Christmas presents no longer consisted of things he wanted, but things his parents emphatically declared he couldn't live without. He now had a closet full of upside down tomato planters, blankets with sleeves, rotisserie ovens, countertop grills, vitamins, and countless exercise contraptions he didn't know how—or care—to use.

He sipped his beer and tried to follow the badly translated fight scene on the television. How could anyone watch more than two minutes of this crap?

"We need an *'As Seen on TV'* display at Bay's. The people will love it."

"Maybe." Cord could do an end cap of cleaning products and supplies, but he drew the line there.

"Use a coaster. You know how your mother gets when we have company."

Cord reached for a tacky crocheted coaster and stilled, unease suddenly washing over him. "Who's coming over?"

"Austin and Ember. Your mother said she told you."

His blood ran cold. "What?"

Not taking his eyes off the screen, his father said, "I thought you knew. She called Ember last night. The two of them were on the phone for almost an hour. What's the big deal?"

The big deal was his mother never gave him the chance to ask. Well, that wasn't true. But she never checked with him a second time. What if he'd asked and they declined and she'd called, thereby putting them in an uncomfortable posi-tion and—"Damn it." He stood and went to the kitchen.

His mother poured some powder into a pitcher of water and smiled at him. "Stir this for me, Cord." She left the long wooden spoon bob-bing in the browning liquid.

He swirled it around. "Austin and Ember are coming?"

"Is that a problem?" his mother asked as she checked on the roast in the oven.

"Yes, it's a problem. I told you I'd ask them."

"And you didn't. And I told you if you didn't I would. Wash your hands."

Frustrated, he went to the sink and turned on the water. "You shouldn't have done that, Mom."

"And why not, Cordovan? Those two are des-perate for family and we're it. I don't understand why you're so reluctant to share a meal with people who have always been close to you. This is ridiculous. Get the good plates off the top shelf for me."

He reached for them. "You don't know the whole story."

"That's because you refused to tell me what's going on. Maybe if you'd told me I would have considered your side, but you didn't, and I did what I thought was best. Go get the blue tablecloth out of the hall closet. The checkered one, not the one with snowmen."

Grinding his teeth, he marched to the closet and yanked the tablecloth off the shelf. Why did his mother have to interfere with shit that wasn't her business? He held out the tablecloth and growled. Son of a bitch, he'd grabbed the fucking snowman cloth. Turning he went to get the right one.

"You fold that back up the way it was, Cord. Don't mess up my closet!" she yelled after him.

He managed the store, owned his own home, and hadn't depended on his parents for well over a decade, yet one Sunday dinner and his mother had the ability to make him feel like he was seventeen again. He returned to the kitchen with the right tablecloth.

"The leaf for the table is in the garage. Go get it and put it in."

"Yes, ma'am."

After battling with the clutter of crap in his parents' garage, he finally unearthed the table leaf, wrapped in a packing blanket. Sweating, he stepped out into the baking heat and stilled.

Ember.

She and Austin held hands as he knocked on the front door. Drawing back, Cord watched as his mother greeted them, pulling them into a loving hug and hustling them inside.

Right there, that wholesome welcome into his parents' home was one of the things Austin claimed to hold against him. Fuck him. He didn't deserve Cord's mother's cooking, or her hugs.

Hefting the table leaf, he carried it into the house. No matter how much he intended to ignore them, Ember's voice climbed inside of him from the other room and burrowed deep. Damn it. Once he had the table extended, he centered the tablecloth. There. He'd done his part.

Deciding to go watch Kung Fu with his dad, he turned and came to an abrupt stop. Ember stood in the doorway holding a stack of plates.

"Cord."

He swallowed. "Ember."

"How...how have you been?"

"Great." The lie flung from his lips without thought and somehow he managed a smile. *Not that you cared enough to fucking check.*

"Good," she said softly, a trembling curve to her lips. "Your mother asked me to set the table."

He stepped aside. "It's all yours."

She carefully stepped around him. "It was nice of your mother…"

He walked away. He couldn't do it.

He simply didn't have it in him to face her alone. Not when her delicate fragrance assaulted him, laced with traces of Austin's scent. Not when her voice tightened every muscle in his body. No. He wouldn't put himself through that anymore.

Cord chugged a beer, not acknowledging Austin's presence in his parents' house, and endured the Japanese film while responding to his father's small talk with the necessary grunts.

Ember's voice continued to wreak havoc on his senses as she chatted with his mother in the kitchen. Austin strolled into the living room and the tension knotting Cord's shoulders tightened to an excruciating kink.

"How's it going, Reed?" He threw Cord a glance. "Hey, Cord."

For Austin, his father picked up the remote and paused his movie. "Austin. How are ya?"

They shook hands and Austin settled onto the chair beside his father. "Doing great. Back to work and feeling good."

His dad nodded. "That's great, son. How's that little wife of yours? Still cute as a bug's ear?"

Austin grinned. "As always."

"Good. Good."

Cord was going to throw up. His 'friend' and his father bonding was enough to drive him out of the room. He rose and made his way to the fridge. His mother whisked the gravy as Ember mashed the potatoes by hand.

"I think that's wonderful, Ember. You let me know when the classes start. I'll be your first student. Did you hear that, Cord? December's going to be teaching a quilting class at the craft store."

"Awesome."

His mother glared at him, likely appalled by his manners. He didn't have the heart to glance at Ember. She was probably glaring too.

"Well, I think it's a splendid idea. Cord, go get a bottle of soda from the pantry."

Glad for the distraction he turned and his steps faltered. Ember was staring at him, those dark eyes wary, her expression wounded. He quickly left the kitchen.

What did she expect? While their life was moving along the right track, Austin working again and her signing up as a sewing instructor, Cord was stuck where he always was, passing Sundays with June and Ward Cleaver to the soundtrack of Japanese subtitles and senior citizen gossip. He simply had no interest in women anymore. Women other than December.

He set the soda on the table and a second later his mother announced it was time to eat. The men wandered in and his father took a seat at the head of the table. Austin sat across from Cord, an empty chair beside each of them. His mother carried the roast to the table, December on her tail with the sides.

There was a moment, after his mother took the seat at the foot, where Ember appraised the remaining chairs. Yup. There it was. Her making up her mind and settling to Austin's left. Cord had to be the stupidest motherfucker in the entire universe.

"Pass the potatoes," he grumbled.

The platters rotated around the table in a shuffle of courtesies and clanking serving spoons. Cord focused on his plate and barely glanced up to pass the salt.

"This is delicious, Norma Jean," December complimented.

"Thank you. I know the boys always enjoy a good roast. Cord, honey, did you want another beer? Austin, can I get you one?"

The three of them paused.

"Water's fine, Norma Jean. Thank you, though," Austin said.

"You sure? Cord?"

His hands couldn't seem to move as he stared at his plate. "I'm fine."

"I brought an apple pie for dessert," December changed the topic, a touch of nervousness lacing her tone. "I braided the crust just the way you like, Reed."

His dad made a happy grunt of approval. "Got yourself a good woman there, Austin."

"You know what, Mom," Cord interrupted. "I think I will take another beer."

"Sure, honey."

He met December's gaze across the table. He wasn't sure what he was expecting, maybe to see her brown eyes angered, or perhaps Austin glaring at him, but he found nothing of the sort. She simply watched him, curiously, her brow pinched in—wait, was that pity? Oh, fuck that.

His mother handed him a cold bottle and he twisted off the cap. "Did I tell you I met someone?" The lie came out of nowhere.

"You did?" His mother grinned with excitement. "What's her name?"

"Uh, Kate," he quickly decided. "She's incredible. Tall, blonde. You know how much I love blondes."

"I didn't know you had a thing for blondes," his mother said.

"Me neither," Austin commented, his eyes now following him closely.

Uncaring about the challenge in Austin's glare, Cord went on. "Always have. She's great. Really independent. Owns her own company." He had no idea where the fabrication spun from, but the more he went on the easier it became.

"You should have invited her to dinner," his mother said, a regretful pout twisting her smile.

"Yeah," Austin agreed. "I'd love to meet her."

Cord's expression hardened. "What the fuck does that mean?"

"Cord!" his mother quickly chastened him.

Austin shrugged. "I don't know any blonde entrepreneurs in the area."

"Got to watch out for those business types, son. Raised like you were, I can't see you tying on an apron and playing Mr. Mom."

Embarrassed, he glared at his father. "Excuse me?"

"I'm just saying, you have to think of these things when you get involved. If you ask me, you'd be better suited with a girl like December, someone who takes pride in the home and knows how to really look after a man. Like your mother. She worked in the hardware store, but when you were a baby she was home with you. That's something hard to find and worth its weight in gold if you ask me. Wouldn't you agree, Austin?"

"I would. And I'd challenge anyone who implied a homemaker wasn't as independent as any entrepreneur. It's a labor of love." He leaned to his left and kissed Ember's cheek. "And she does it masterfully. She's incredible."

Cord plugged up his mouth with his beer before he said something he wouldn't be able to take back.

"Excuse me," Ember whispered as she rose from the table.

He watched her walk down the hall to the

bathroom and suffered a pinch of regret. Was she upset? Taking another sip of his beer, he stood. "I'll be right back."

Austin's stare burned into his shoulders as he left the room.

The faucet ran and soon the bathroom door opened. Ember jerked to a stop when she saw him waiting there. Her gaze skittered to the floor. "Pardon me."

She stepped around him and he grabbed her arm. "Are you okay?"

"I'm fine, Cord. Excuse me." Shouldering off his hold, all of his bravado fell away.

No matter the turmoil inside of him, he couldn't bear to see Ember hurt.

Your fault, dickhead.

Schlepping his way back to the table, he sat. "Sorry about my language, Mom."

"Apology accepted. So when do we get to meet this Kate?"

Sighing, he proceeded to do damage control. "Probably never. I don't think she's right for me."

His mother tsked. "Don't listen to your father. There's nothing wrong with a woman who works outside of the home. Being a full time wife and mother is probably one of the most challenging jobs there is, but it's not for everybody. That doesn't make one type better than the other."

"Let's just say she's not who I want and leave it at that."

After dinner Ember served her pie and his mother brought out coffee. The longer he sat in their company, the weaker he became. His combativeness dulled to bitter acceptance he honestly hoped would one day turn into happiness for his friends. But that day wasn't today.

When they finally left Cord felt like he'd been dragged through hell and back. There was no denying Austin and Ember were back on their feet. It was time to wave the white flag and admit defeat. Part of him wished there was a Kate, although he did prefer brunettes.

He returned the table leaf to the shed and went to say goodnight to his parents. His dad was sound asleep on the recliner and his mother was washing dishes at the sink. He kissed her cheek. "Thanks for dinner, Mom."

She nodded, but didn't face him. Shutting off the spigot, she rested her hands on the lip of the counter and quietly asked, "Did you have an affair with her, Cordovan?"

Immobilized, ice suddenly encased his heart in an attempt to shield his shame. "What?"

"You heard me."

Bowing his head, knowing she'd see through any lie, he whispered. "Yes."

She sighed, a soft whisper of breath announcing her disappointment. "Austin's your friend, Cord. How could you do that?"

"You wouldn't understand. It's beyond complicated." Scuffing his shoe on the floor, he waited for her condemnation, but she remained silent. "It doesn't matter anyway. They're together again and happy."

She turned, a frown tightening her face. "It *doesn't matter*? That girl is hurting. At first, I didn't understand all this strained energy between the three of you, but then I saw the way she watched you—the way you watched *her*. I think it matters very much."

"What would you have me do, Mom? Break up their marriage? She's where she wants to be. I'm staying out of it."

She nodded. "Okay." She gave a sad smile and sighed. "I always worried about you two."

"Who? Me and Austin? We're fine. It is what it is." Who needed a best friend? Who needed... He let that thought trail off and perish along with the other futile hope he'd nurtured.

"No, honey. You and Ember. I've watched the three of you over the years. I know you felt more for her than platonic affection. I've never seen you look at other girls the way you look at her. I know she's special to you. I'm sorry, sweetie. Love isn't always fair."

Disliking the idea of being so transparent, he forced a grin. "I'm fine. I'll *be* fine."

"Does Austin know?"

Austin suggested it. "Yes. I don't really want to talk about this, Mom."

"Okay, but I'm always here if you need me." She patted his cheek affectionately. "Here. Take these leftovers."

"Thanks, Mom." He hesitated, disappointed that his mother would lose something from all of this too. But he had to establish boundaries. "No more invites, okay? Best I don't see them anymore. You can," he added hurriedly. "But I'm out of it."

Sadness washed over her face. "If you say so, honey."

Seventeen

December

DECEMBER SUCKED IN A QUICK BREATH, held it, and knocked on Cord's front door. *This is a bad idea.* Wondering why she'd come here, she quickly turned to leave. She couldn't do this.

She was almost off the porch when the door opened. Her shoulders tightened as she shut her eyes, wishing she could disappear.

"Ember? What are you doing here?"

Shaking her head, she refused to face him. "Nothing. Sorry to bother you."

"Wait." He stepped onto the porch. "Is something wrong?"

Glancing up at the sky, she shook her head. She couldn't do it. No matter what, there was still shame and guilt. "Everything's fine."

He stepped in front of her. "You look like you're on the verge of tears."

Refusing to cry, laughter was her only other option, the chirp of emotion totally inappropriate and insulting. This was crazy. *She* was crazy. And now she was laughing in a situation that was the farthest thing from funny.

Cord's brown furrowed with concern. Once she composed herself, she lowered her head in disgrace. "Sorry."

"Are you sure you're okay?"

"Nope. I'm not really sure of anything anymore." She shook her head, unable to acknowledge the embarrassment consuming her. "Sometimes I guess you have to laugh." *Or cry.*

"Right," he said slowly, his eyes intent as he studied her.

God, he was gorgeous. She tried to convince herself she'd embellished her memories, but he was handsomer than ever. Despite her wonderful reunion with Austin, part of her heart still felt empty. She sometimes thought Austin felt the same. He had to miss that decades-old friendship. *The one I'm responsible for wrecking.* She shut that recrimination down. "I should go."

He frowned. "Why did you come here?"

"Trust me, you don't want to know."

"But...I do." He stepped in front of her again. "Tell me. Is Austin okay?"

Biting on her lip, she glanced up at the sky once more. "He's fine. Austin actually was the one who suggested I pay you a visit."

His shoulders tensed and he drew back from her. "Why?"

Because he's nuts—like his wife. "I don't know. He thinks after last night's dinner we needed to talk in private."

Why had they accepted Norma Jean's invitation anyhow? Ember knew they would likely be springing themselves on Cord when he clearly wanted space. He hadn't even called... Though his mother could be darn persuasive.

He tipped his head, but she couldn't read him. "Do *you* think we need to talk? Seems weeks have gone past when we could have done some... talking."

"You don't want to know the things I think, Cord." She laughed again, looking every place but at him. "I think if I walk through that door it will only be a matter of minutes before we're all over each other. I think that I've been avoiding you because of that fact, and what that means about me..."

He took a quick step back, his expression suddenly cautious. "But you're with Austin."

"Yes, I'm definitely with Austin."

"I don't get it."

She chuckled, and to her ears the sound was a little more honest, revealing her confusion and frustration. "Me neither. I shouldn't be here. I just... I don't get how a man as territorial as Austin can constantly push me toward someone he should see as a threat."

"I'm not a threat. You're his wife. I'm doing my best to respect that."

"Cord... How respectful would you would be if..."

His jaw ticked and he growled, "If what?"

Her gaze lowered and she murmured, "If I told you we had his consent?"

"What?" His face contorted with panic, and she fought the instinct to physically soothe him.

This was such a stupid idea. Another bad decision. How many rounds would she take on this merry-go-round before she got off, admitting once and for all every turn scattered her commonsense and left her acting on emotion?

It was totally selfish of them to keep pulling him back into their confusion when he so obviously wanted out. "Forget it. And try not to look so revolted. No one said you had to act on it."

"It's not the idea of kissing you that's revolting. It's the idea of Austin giving *his permission* to allow another man to kiss you. What the fuck is wrong with him? He has to stop this shit!"

She threw discretion to the wind. "He knows how I feel about you, Cord. How it began as friendship and grew to be…more. Much more. Longing. You said it. I need you in my life too. I miss you. *He* misses you. And after last night, well, he sent me here."

"Jesus Christ. You have to go." He paced away, his tension evident in his jerky strides.

"Which is exactly why I was leaving." She turned and stepped down the stairs.

Suddenly, he snapped, "What about *your* consent?"

She'd been so close to the truck, so close to walking away and returning to her husband. Back to a good life, a wonderful life, yet with that piece missing… But she halted at his question.

So. Close.

She and Austin discussed Cord daily. Her feelings never wavered, but she'd been…managing them. Austin, however, was impatient with the progression. While she tried to ignore her marked affection for his friend, Austin liked to poke and prod at the tender spots, dissect it until he fully understood what was there.

His new determination to share *everything* meant he wouldn't give up until he fully understood her attachment to Cord. It was difficult enough to know she loved this man without her husband pressing her. Physical distance merely left it simmering, unrequited, and some days it was all-consuming.

With a concerted effort, she turned back to

Cord and looked up at him. He stood on the porch, his eyes tormented and her heart ached. "I don't think I'll ever have the strength to tell you no, Cord. That's the problem."

His chest rose with labored breath. "Why is he doing this? This can't be what he wants."

"He says he wants me to be happy."

He balked. "Aren't you? Things sure look back to normal from where I stand."

"Most days, yes, but then there are those quiet moments when my mind wanders to you and a sadness takes hold of me that I can't shake. There's such an empty space in my heart."

"Ember, I don't want to keep doing this. It isn't easy—*for anyone.*"

She let out a dry laugh. "I know. Not for me, not for him, but most of all, not for you. I hate myself for putting you through this again and again. I wish I could stop and let you get on with your life. I never wanted to hurt you, Cord."

His mouth pressed into a thin line, indicating he had plenty to say but intended to remain silent. He shut his eyes and said, "You guys seem good now. Let that be enough."

Her head lowered. She'd been fighting this for so long. Perhaps she was more her mother's daughter than she was comfortable admitting.

"What if it's never enough, Cord? What if years from now I still want you as much as I do now?"

"Don't say that." His hands balled into fists at his side.

"I'm sorry, but I have to wonder. It's a worry that keeps me up at night, lying beside my husband, part of me always wishing you were there. The way things are, I can't go an hour without thinking about you, worrying if you're okay, wishing I could touch you. We opened up Pandora's Box that night and...maybe I don't want to shut it."

His cheeks darkened as he glared at her. "Goddamn it, December. Stop it!"

"I can't!" she snapped. "I've tried! I try so hard not to see you that way, to remember how we used to be, but I can't."

"Please stop..."

"Tell me how. How do you fight it? I try not to feel it. I try not to want you. I've stayed away from you for a month! It killed me that you didn't reach out. I've tried. I hated that my parents never honored monogamy. The things I saw growing up... It was corrupt and wrong and I swore I'd never be like them in that way, but when I make love to my husband, I'm sad you're not there."

"*Stop!*"

She flinched at the lash of his voice. She hadn't expected to confess so much, hadn't intended to bare her deepest, most shameful secrets. Her vision wavered before a wall of tears as she faced him and the truth she'd been hiding from for too long.

"I want you, Cord. Denying it is useless. I know it. Austin knows it. You should know it too. If he's willing to accept it—"

"He's not!" he growled. "He doesn't know what the fuck he's doing! He's playing with something bigger than he can fathom and he's gambling everything that's keeping him alive! Go home, Ember. Go home to your husband."

Her eyes closed as sorrow bled from every nerve in her body. She'd bared all, confessed the truth to him, and he still somehow managed to find moral ground. Unlike her. She was going to break again, along those same fault lines.

Somehow she remained standing. "I'll go. But I want you to know this wasn't a conclusion he reached overnight. We talk about it, the two of us. He wouldn't suggest I come here on my own unless he fully trusted you and was certain he could handle the repercussions."

"And what happens when the repercussions fall on *you*? He's a goddamn idiot."

"No, he's *not*," she all but growled, hardly recognizing her own voice. "He loves me. He's quite aware of his shortcomings *and* mine. He even knows a few of yours, Cord. He may have a lot of flaws, but he's no idiot."

"Go home, Ember. This conversation's over."

His words hit hard, forcing her to take a step back. Her gaze fell as she admitted defeat. "My behavior, even sharing my deepest secrets, it must seem despicable to you."

His tone darkened with disapproval. "We *all* did this, December. We've all behaved despicably."

Shame tightened her heart and she nodded. Her eyes closed under the weight of so much unresolved pain, her tears fighting to slip past her lashes. "I'm sorry we involved you in this," she rasped.

Her wooden movements somehow got her in to Austin's truck. Maybe now, her husband would let go of his obsession with Cord, ignore their transgressions like she'd suggested from the beginning. Forget that she loved him too. The same as she would learn to do, for the rest of her life, because each time she and Austin made progress as husband and wife, the mention of Cord jerked them back to a place neither of them seemed capable of leaving behind.

Her shaky hands struggled to get the key in the ignition when the door ripped open and she gasped.

"Move over," Cord growled, crowding her and leaving her with little time to scoot from behind the wheel.

"Wh—what are you doing?" He snatched the keys from her as she slid over.

"I'm going to kill your husband. You can watch."

"Cord, I don't want you two fighting."

He grumbled something she didn't understand as he did a quick K-turn out of the driveway.

"Cord, please don't start a fight with him. Yell at me."

He shook his head and made a sound of disbelief. "I'm not gonna fucking fight with you, Ember. You people amaze me. What the fuck did he think would come of this? You'd come here with his *permission*, and I—like some hard-up half-wit —fall to my knees in gratitude? Man, does he live in a fantasy world."

"You're driving really fast."

"That's because I'm really fucking pissed off."

"I shouldn't have come," she muttered, wishing she could go back in time.

"Well, you did and now this is where we are. Maybe you two will finally get it through your heads why shit doesn't work this way."

Yanking the wheel, they barreled up the drive to her house. He slammed on the brakes, and her palms braced against the dashboard as the vehicle shuddered to a halt maybe a half-inch before it slammed into the barn.

Throwing the shifter into park, he gripped the wheel and seethed. Waves of energy emanated from his tense form as her heart pounded about a hundred miles a minute.

"Cord?"

He didn't answer. The screen door opened with a snap and Austin stepped onto the porch, a frown on his face. Taking the steps, he slowly approached the passenger door and opened it, his eyes making a quick assessment of Cord's palpable tension and her unsteadiness.

"You okay, baby?" His voice was soft, unthreatening.

She nodded tightly, then glanced at Cord. Austin followed her gaze, at the same time gently edging her out of the truck. "Go in the house, Ember. Make some coffee, okay?"

Her hand slid out of his as he helped her down from the truck, placing a kiss on her temple. She looked back, and he nodded.

Her steps toward the house were hesitant, fearing a fight might break out at any second. Cord had yet to release the steering wheel or acknowledge her husband.

Austin braced his arm on the passenger door and spoke in a low voice, his words not meant for her. Everything about her husband's body language spoke of calm control and she put her trust in him.

As she stepped inside she lost sight of them and hurried to assemble the coffee maker. She'd give them a minute to talk and herself a moment to catch her breath. Her ears remained focused on any sounds of possible hostility, but everything was strangely quiet. Too quiet.

She crept to the front window and stood beside the curtain, carefully peeking out. Her husband's voice carried over the hum of Cord's truck.

"...if you'd just listen for a half minute! This isn't how it ends, Cord. You know it can't. Our life doesn't work without you in it."

"Seems to have worked just fine over the last month."

Austin's head bowed as he rested his arm over the frame of the car door, his intensity thrumming through the air.

"You have to believe our distance wasn't to hurt you. Things were...fragile. I'm trying my best to do the right thing, and first and foremost, my focus is on Ember. She needed time to adapt, to remember our home as a peaceful place and see that the broken parts could be repaired. But we're far from fixed."

Her heart swelled and she bit down on her lip, leaning her weight against the wall.

Cord's response rang out, loud and clear. "So don't go breaking shit again, Austin—including your vows."

She couldn't imagine Austin letting that pass and braced herself, straining to hear the response.

He sighed loud enough for her to feel his tension, yet his remarkable calm didn't waver. Keeping his voice level, he said, "Come inside. Just talk with us. You drive away now, you'll crush her. Is that what you want?"

Silence. Time marched on...and on, as Ember held her breath. Then the truck's engine silenced.

Taking a quick glance, her heart pumped hard as she watched them approach the porch steps. Bolting back into the kitchen, she set out three mugs and tried to slow her breathing.

The screen door creaked open and snapped closed, and her shoulders tensed. She sucked in a deep breath as she turned and spotted the two of them in the foyer. Her stomach pinched as her heart raced into triple time. With shaky hands, she poured coffee, wincing as the droplets spattered and hissed on the element.

"We're going to talk," Austin announced, stepping into the kitchen. "Like civilized people."

Cord folded his arms over his chest and leaned against the jamb of the door, his scowl pinned on Austin.

Her husband pulled out a chair for her. "Take a seat, baby."

Her body lowered onto an old wooden chair and she folded her arms to still her trembling. She couldn't look at either of them.

"My wife is in love with you," Austin broadcasted and all the breath left her lungs. "At first I thought she was just attracted to you, but over the past month I've accepted it's more than that."

Cord remained silent.

"I know you love her too," Austin continued. "As do I, which is why I've decided to do this."

"What, exactly, do you think you're doing, Austin?" Cord growled.

"I'm letting it happen."

Cord's chuckle was cold. "Letting it. You're a real asshole. Like you're the boss of Ember's gratification. Or of mine, you cocksucker."

Austin's agreeableness disappeared as his glare turned hard and settled on Cord. "She's my wife."

"She's also her own fucking person."

"I know she is," he snapped.

Sensing his gaze, she lifted her face to look at him and his tone gentled. "I know you are, Ember. You can speak up at any time. I'm only trying to make this easier for you. I know the things we talked about in bed when there was no sense of judgment threatening our discussion. If I, in any way, misrepresent your feelings on the subject I want you to tell me. Deal?"

Her breath was shaky as she nodded. They had discussed so many dark emotions late at night under the security of shadows. In the light of day, however, confessions didn't come as easily.

She truly appreciated what he was trying to do for her, even if it was frightening. Her fear was for the damage this might do to Cord. Their friendship was already strained, likely beyond retrieval, so maybe there was nothing left to lose. As far as Austin speaking for her...it was a relief.

She nodded again. "Thank you."

Her husband turned his attention back to

Cord. "I know my wife." His eyes narrowed. "Because she's mine."

"Fuck you," Cord hissed.

Austin's hand slid to hers and squeezed, a silent show of solidarity, the acknowledgement that she'd always belong to him and he'd always belong to her. It was how it had always been, how they both deemed it should stay.

"Do you trust me?"

Her belly swooned. "Yes." She trusted him with every bit of her soul.

"Does the idea of sleeping with Cord excite you?"

Her gaze lowered to the table as awareness sent chills racing over her skin. Shame seemed the appropriate emotion, but her love for Cord overshadowed the guilt and pushed it away. Her thighs pressed together as her body reacted.

"Yes," she whispered.

"This is bullshit," Cord growled. "I'm out of here."

"Open your dress, Ember."

Cord stilled, one foot out the kitchen door, his back tensing before her eyes. Her breathing turned labored as she stared at the table and swallowed.

Cord turned and growled, "Knock it off, Austin." His long legs crossed the floor and he crouched in front of her. "Ember, you don't have to do this. He isn't the boss of you. You can leave.

With me or I can take you somewhere else, but you don't have to put up with this—"

She somehow found her voice, and reached to set her hand against Cord's cheek. "I know I don't have to do this. I'm not under duress or being held captive, not even emotionally. What he's doing... It's for me. For us. Because he loves us."

"But—"

Shifting her fingers to his lips to stop his protest, she looked into his eyes. "Austin knows me better than anyone. He knew what I needed before I had the courage to admit it to myself. I...I hate being in control. I need for him to relieve me of it, just like you relieved me of it that night. Do you understand?"

His handsome features tightened and he shook his head. In a near whisper, he said, "In a fucked up way, maybe, but not like this."

Despair flooded through her being. She was at a loss and cast a glance at Austin.

"Ember," her husband's voice gently cajoled. "Do you want Cord?"

Through numb lips, she forced the answer. The truth. "Yes."

"Do you consent to what we're doing right now?"

Relief competed with despair and gained the upper hand. "I consent."

"Do you want *me* to leave?"

Her husband needed to be a part of it as much

as she needed him there for support. "Please stay," she whispered.

Cord stepped back as Austin's knuckles slowly lifted her chin. "Hey. Remember everything we talked about. You have my full approval. I've thought about this for a long time." His thumb dragged over her lips. "If you want him, show him. You don't have to hide anymore. Give me honesty. Give *us* honesty. It's what we deserve."

Her fingers trembled to the first button of her dress and fumbled.

"Do you need me to help you?"

She nodded and her husband shifted closer, sending Cord back another step, but he still remained in the kitchen. Her chair pulled back from the table with a slow drag, the scrape of wood tightening the tension flooding the quiet room. Austin took her hand and helped her to stand.

His body blocked her view of Cord as he looked into her eyes and slowly unclasped the tiny buttons running down the front of the simple cotton dress. Halfway through, their breathing became audible. She could sense his arousal and it heightened her own.

When the last button was opened, he pulled the fabric apart and it slid down her arms to rest on the back of the chair. Austin preferred her without a bra, something she'd grown up rarely wearing, so she stood in only white lace panties and her sandals. Bracing her hand on her husband's shoulder, she toed her shoes under the table.

Her nipples tightened with the sense that they were both watching her and gradually she lifted her gaze, signaling to Austin that she was ready.

His lips brushed over hers. "I love you. No matter what, I love you." He stepped aside and she sucked in a breath as her gaze collided with Cord's.

He stood still as a statue, a myriad of emotions chasing over his face, but his stare never left her. "You're a jerk, Austin," he growled. "Ember, it doesn't have to be—"

"I want to. Me. This is my choice, and Austin gave me the courage to make it."

His chest lifted as he continued to stare, his conflict evident. His resolve was weakening. She could feel it. And see the physical evidence.

"I think you want me too," she whispered, hoping she was right. She'd never forgive herself for pushing him to do something he truly didn't want to do.

Cord's head tipped back, his gaze fastening to the ceiling, his Adam's apple protruding as the muscles of his neck tightened. He whispered something.

Austin stepped behind her, his hands resting on her waist, his knuckles then purposefully brushing the side of her breasts, creating chills that raced over her shoulders.

"Isn't she beautiful, Cord? It's an incredible

feeling to be wanted by such a woman, something I've never been able to walk away from. Can you?"

"Why are you doing this?" Cord's jaw noticeably locked, the words forced through his teeth. A turbulent show of emotion played in his stormy blue eyes.

"Because I'll do anything to make her happy so long as she's not putting herself in danger. I know you'd never hurt her. She's safe with you." His hands slid over her ribs and cupped her breasts. "She's offering you everything. All you have to do is find the courage to take it. No more games, Cord. No more hiding behind lies."

Her knees went weak as her husband's calloused hands caressed her needy flesh. Austin's mouth teased over the side of her throat as he whispered, "Are you turned on, baby?"

"Mmm," she nodded, sinking into him.

She couldn't describe her state of arousal. Such intense emotions and desires flooded her as she leaned into Austin's hold while staring into Cord's beautiful eyes. A greedy part of her psyche warned her not to overthink this. Her darkest fantasy, about to come to life—she hoped.

"Do you want me to hold you while Cord touches you?"

Her breathing accelerated. *God, yes.* Please. The distance Cord kept was killing her. Why wouldn't he take those last few steps separating them? Didn't he recognize her need, feel his own?

She could *taste* her husband's will, trying to coax him closer.

"Answer me, please." Austin's mouth closed over the lobe of her ear and her thighs reflexively pressed together.

She sucked in a breath as the press of his erection ground into her backside, his arousal spiking her own to dangerous heights. "Yes, please."

His tongue dragged down her throat to her shoulder. "Then ask him."

Her gaze focused. Cord wasn't looking away anymore. His dark jeans bulged under the clasp of his belt. His chest lifted with each labored breath and the veins in his arms swelled as his hands balled into fists.

His expression was blank, but his eyes spoke volumes. The desire swirling in his intense stare was tangible.

"Please touch me, Cord."

He breathed a curse and quickly crossed the kitchen, not stopping until his hands reached for hers, wrapping tightly around her wrists and yanking her forward. She was tugged out of Austin's hold and Cord's mouth was on her, devouring, demanding, distracting.

Her head fell back as he took. His large palm slid to the back of her neck and held her in place for his penetrating kiss as his body molded over hers. His full lips pulled at hers as his other hand dragged down her spine and settled on her ass, squeezing possessively. Her body was on fire.

"Fuck, Ember."

Fingers ghosted up the back of her thigh. *Austin.*

"Does he kiss you good, baby?"

She whimpered and inched back from Cord, ending the kiss. His breath beat against her throat as the weight of his jeans, his solid erection, dug into her.

"Tell me," Austin whispered, his fingers teasing softly at the curve of her ass.

Her gaze lifted to Cord's uncertain one and a shy smile twitched at her lips. "Yes."

"And Cord..." Austin left the question open.

Cord was silent, his mental debate evident. "She's your wife."

"She'll always be my wife, but she cares for more than just me. She needs you too."

Cord's face lowered to her shoulder, as he whispered, "Do you really want this, Ember? Want *me*? Be honest. I can handle the truth."

Her cheek brushed against his, her mouth turning to press into his warm skin as she breathed in his unique scent. "Yes, Cord, but only if you do. Only if we all do."

On a deep inhale he was kissing her again, this time even more possessively as he lifted her from Austin's touch, high into his arms. The world spun as her back was pressed into the cool kitchen wall and she gasped.

"Let's take this to the living room," Austin said, but Cord didn't move.

His insistent mouth devoured hers as his hands closed over her breasts. "Who's touching you, Ember?"

Memories from that night, of how he'd dominated her mind, body and soul, flashed behind her eyes. "You are, Cord."

"That's right." His cock pressed against his jeans, abrading her tender sex through damp lace as her body wept for him.

Austin cleared his throat. She broke the kiss and Cord growled. Her heavy lidded eyes found her husband watching them, his gaze dark with lust and traces of need.

"Let's go to the living room," she suggested, echoing her husband's suggestion, and Cord lowered her feet back to the ground, all the while glaring at Austin.

She reached for both their hands, reminding them this was about all of them, and led the way. It was almost comical how much they resembled each other, both in their worn black t-shirts and well-worn jeans. Both aroused behind the faded denim.

"Ember makes the rules," Cord announced and her excitement knocked down a notch. She thought he understood.

Panicked, she looked to Austin. Her husband recognized her distress immediately and amended. "You can make any rule you want, baby."

Licking her lips, she sent Cord an apologetic glance and said, "My first rule is that Austin makes the rules."

Cord rolled his eyes. "Unbelievable."

Resenting the sudden jolt of self-consciousness, she tightened her lips. "It's what I need, Cord. If he says stop at any time, it's because he sees something we're missing. I want him to have that authority. It's important to me."

She saw the wounded look in his eyes, disguised by another glare directed toward Austin. When he looked back at her his expression softened. "I'm trying to understand."

"Thank you."

Her gaze drifted to Austin's and he mouthed, "I love you."

She merely nodded, disoriented by her brief role as the decision maker. She always preferred the submissive role when it came to intimacy. Her husband, the only man to know her intimately before Cord, understood that. He helped her discover that quality in herself. Her desire always diminished the moment she was called upon to be the aggressor.

Austin, always so in tune with her, crossed his hands in a signal for time out. "Wait." He turned his head to Cord. "A few ground rules. This is *my* home. She's *my* wife—"

"We've already established—"

"Shut up and listen. I'm doing everyone a favor by overstating the facts, because we have to tread lightly, for *everyone's* sake. Ember likes being the passive one, so you're gonna accept that I hold the upper hand. It's what she needs and wants and that's why we're here. We clear?"

"Crystal."

"Good." He glanced at her and smiled tenderly, swelling her heart with the level of support he provided. A sense of calm settled over her. "Ember, you with us, baby?"

Her attention focused on her husband. "Yes."

He nodded, stepping in front of her. His head lowered slowly, his lips brushing softly to hers and taking her mouth in a slow, soul-penetrating kiss. "I love you. I love us."

"I love you too."

Austin stepped back, his gaze lingering for an extended moment before he turned to Cord. They appeared to communicate silently.

Cord's brow tightened as he stared at her husband. "Austin…"

"I trust you, Cord."

There seemed an internal struggle taking place within Cord, something she didn't quite understand. The way he looked at Austin… it reminded her so much of herself and the way she saw her husband. And in the next moment, she felt it. Cord let go, the tension leaving his face as though an incredible weight fell free.

He came to her. "I love you, kiddo. I wish... I wish I could make it easier for you and take back everything I feel, but...it's pretty much the most my heart has ever felt."

She laced her fingers with his and squeezed. "I love you too."

He glanced over his shoulder and back to her. "Are you positive this is what you want? Last chance to change your mind..."

She smiled. "I'm sure."

He lowered his mouth to hers. Her body soared at the first press of his tongue, her arms wreathing around his broad shoulders as she lifted to the tips of her toes.

Austin had always been an incredible lover, her only lover—until Cord. Despite her state of mind that night, she remembered how Cord had taken charge, as if he recognized this need in her. How he'd met it so adroitly.

His fingers tugged softly at her hair, angling her head back and exposing her throat as his hands gently mapped out the topography of her curves. As his fingers curled around her hips, his hold became greedy, needy, and he pressed forward, nudging her backward. She fell into his mastery.

Although Austin was challenging, intense and strong willed, Cord was the more demanding lover. Austin took on the dominant role because it was something she required, but he always executed it with a gentle and romantic touch.

Cord, on the other hand, was gentle on the outside, always ready with an easy joke. Yet he harbored a demanding streak that spoke to her. It was in direct contrast to the detectable restraint he showed every time he kissed her. Perhaps that restraint was beginning to slip.

"Fuck, Ember." His hands curled around her waist, pulling her tight as he buried his face in her shoulder. "How far are we taking this? If we go any further, I'm not sure I'll be able to stop."

She licked her lips. "Austin?"

"I'm here."

Breathing fast, she kept her eyes on Cord. What should she ask? Was it really up to anyone but her? Reaching out her hand, she held it open until her husband's fingers closed around hers. She slid her other hand into Cord's. Her boys.

"We're all in this together, right?" she asked. "All of us."

"I'm in," Austin rasped.

"I'm in," Cord echoed.

Her smile couldn't express the level of happiness she felt in that moment. "I'm in too. This is it."

"Wait." Cord's grip tightened as she moved to kiss Austin. "What about... tomorrow, and the next day? When I said I don't know if I'll be able to stop, I meant... ever."

Chills chased up her spine as she considered the future significance of what they were doing once more, the fact that it affected all three of them. Without a clear understanding of each other's feelings, this would never work. Unsure how to respond, she glanced at Austin.

"Let's get through tonight and see how we feel tomorrow. We aren't going to let you just disappear again, Cord. She needs you in her life. *We* need you."

Cord's hands balanced on his hips as he tipped his face toward the ceiling and seemed to silently count to ten. "This...this is fucking hard. It's a lot." Visibly collecting himself, he glanced at both of them and Ember saw the way his eyes were shot with pink.

"Oh, Cord." Releasing Austin's hands, she hugged Cord tight. "It *is* a lot. It's okay to get emotional."

His arms closed around her and squeezed. "I just... I don't want to ruin—"

"You aren't ruining anything," Austin said, taking the words right out of her mouth. His voice rang with conviction.

Cord shuddered and turned toward her husband. "Austin...I...Jesus, I'm..."

"I know, man." Her husband sent him a strained grin. "Me too."

Unable to interpret, Ember accepted the fact something significant had just been communicated and gone a long way toward repairing the rift in a priceless relationship.

Eighteen

Cord

CORD'S HEART was going to explode out of his chest. However he expected his day to go, this was not it. This moment was so surreal, he'd almost laid it all on the line, actually thought of divulging *everything* that was locked inside.

Austin stared at him, his whiskey brown eyes conveying trust and faith Cord wasn't sure he deserved. And Ember... well, Ember was naked, except for that scrap of white lace...waiting for him.

His friend gave another nod and he swallowed. He wanted to yank Austin into his arms and lock him in a hold so tight nothing could ever break them apart again. But that was asking too much when he was already being offered more than he ever expected.

Taking a deep breath, he turned to Ember. Jesus, she knocked the breath out of him. "Come here, beautiful."

When she stepped forward, actually came when he reached for her, he shook his head. "I've waited so long..." he started, his throat closing around his words as emotion choked him.

"I've waited too."

It was so much. Maybe enough talking for now. His fingers feathered through her hair, which was already growing into a fringed mess around her ears. So pretty. So delicately feminine.

Tipping up her chin, he brushed his lips softly against her mouth and groaned. This was the most intense moment of his life.

"Don't hold back this time," she whispered.

He stilled, and studied her. "What?"

The corner of her full lips pulled into a knowing smile, but she said nothing. She wanted to accuse him of something like holding back and then clam up? *I don't think so.*

He scooped her into his arms and she gasped. But as he turned his steps faltered when he caught Austin's strange smile.

Focus.

He made it to the couch in two strides and deposited her on the cushions, following her down. "Give me those sexy lips." His mouth closed over hers, his tongue stealing deep and holding nothing back.

Fuck, she tasted incredible. Her hips lifted against his as his hands roamed down the tapered side of her thighs. Her skin was burning hot, her scent everywhere. He ground his cock against her soft curves, wanting to rip his pants off but resisting so he could take it slow.

His palm dragged up her ribs and cupped her breast, massaging her firm flesh. He needed to get his mouth there. Moving to her jaw, he nibbled, sucked, and kissed. She was so damn petite, so delicately feminine. Memories of the night they'd shared flowed through his mind, cast into sharp relief by the real thing beneath his questing touch.

Easing back, he cupped her breasts, molding them in his hands. She stared at him through thick lashes and when she lifted her arms in complete surrender, folding them gracefully over her head, he was undone.

His mouth descended, pulling one beckoning tip between his lips and sucking hard. Her back arched as she sighed breathily, pressing into him as he worked to her other nipple. The harder he pulled the more responsive she became, offering more little pleading sounds.

His fingers trailed down her soft belly, detouring at her hip and teasing her side. She giggled and twisted. Slowly, he made a show of dragging his tongue down the front of her as she watched him through her lashes.

She panted quietly as he slipped his hand beneath the waistband of her panties and brushed a knuckle over her slit, teasing some more.

"Cord..."

The side of his mouth kicked up in a satisfied smirk. When she said his name it was like finding home. He dispensed with the underwear, lifting first one slender leg, then the other, to slide them off.

The tremble of his fingertips revealed how epic this moment was for them. She wanted all of him? No holding back? She was going to get it.

Wrenching her legs apart, drawing a quick gasp from her lips, he dropped his knees to the carpet. His gaze lowered and his progress dwindled to a halt. Fuck. It was the first time, without darkness or shadows that he'd ever really looked at her there.

His ass dropped to his heels. "You're so beautiful."

"Isn't she?"

Startled by Austin's voice, he remembered they weren't alone. His friend, her husband, had moved closer to the couch and lowered himself to sit next to her, watching *him*.

Damn it. He wasn't done, wanted to keep looking at her. But how could he with Austin staring at him, missing nothing? His gaze shot to

Austin's erection. The man was solid as a fucking rock. Cord's focus jerked over his right shoulder, which seemed the only safe place to look.

Out of his peripheral vision he saw Ember drag her knees together, but then Austin's hand curled around her thigh. "Wait. I don't think he's finished."

Lowering his lashes, Cord followed the way Austin's work roughened fingertip slowly dragged up her thigh and toward the crease where her legs pressed together.

"Let him see you," his friend whispered, and her knees gradually parted again. "Go ahead, Cord."

He couldn't bring himself to look at Austin, but he did look at Ember. Her smile was unsure, but trusting.

Cord swallowed. "You good, sweetheart?"

The corner of her eyes creased with what appeared to be relief. "I'm good. I'm waiting for the Cord who takes charge."

Okay. This was happening. Enough second-guessing.

His mouth dropped to her knee, working slowly up her leg. Austin kept his touch on her other thigh, gently teasing her smooth skin. Cord's hand slid between her legs and accidentally brushed Austin's. "Sorry."

"It's okay."

How was his friend so calm? He didn't really

care once the heat of her pussy touched his fingers. Watching her face, he slipped his middle finger inside and drove it slowly forward until she was stretching from the intrusion and he was three knuckles deep.

His attention snagged as Austin's thumb brushed over her smooth skin, revealing her clit. Cord's lungs struggled to accommodate the shallowest breath as Ember pressed into their touch and Austin rolled that little knot of nerves.

Arousal coated Cord's fingers. He'd never been in any sort of threesome before, was positive Austin hadn't either. No way Ember had. She'd been a virgin when they met her.

Thinking of how this was a first for all of them sort of evened out the playing field and stoked his arousal. He slid his finger out and gently glided back in.

"You like that, baby?" Each time Austin spoke it was a little less jarring than the last. Like they were experiencing pleasure together. He'd take it.

"Yes," Ember breathed, her knees falling wide.

Cord watched his finger slip into her again, cream coating his knuckles and turning his cock into granite. The sight of Austin pleasuring her sweet spot had him leaning forward, the instinct to lick over his friend's fingers as they swirled above her clit enough to make him come in his pants. But as his mouth encroached, Austin's touch pulled away.

Cord's tongue swept through her folds, her flavor gathering on his lips as he captured her clit. She jolted forward and Austin hushed her, tugging her back down. As he squinted through his lashes he saw Austin kissing her, his hands cupping her breasts and teasing her tight little nipples.

Cord put his focus between her legs, wanting to be the one to pleasure her most. His ring finger joined his other digit as he pumped faster, fucking her tight little hole until she was so distracted she broke the kiss and let out a breathy moan. His lips tightened around her swollen bud, his tongue flicking and suddenly her body pulsed and gushed around him as her knees trembled.

Licking his lips, he slowly drew back. She was a beautifully carnal image, sprawled over the edge of the couch, thighs glossy, pussy pink, and her lips parted as she caught her breath. Then he saw Austin...stroking his naked dick.

Cord's stare glued on that thick cock, noting the wide flared head, shiny with— *Fuck. Fuck!*

He didn't want to face everything at once, but his body leaned incrementally toward his friend. How easy would it be to just lean over and— *No.*

His breathing unsteady, he eased away and forced himself to get a grip. Ember let out a little hum and twisted to her side. He followed the line of her hip up to her breasts as her arm reached for Austin.

Blinking hard, Cord debated what to do. *Fuck!*

He should go. Too weird. Too dangerous.

"Don't forget Cord." Austin's voice sent a shiver up his spine. That fucking deep baritone, so gruff and direct. *Fuck me.*

Ember slithered off the couch and onto the floor. She knelt in front of Cord, her eyes filled with true seduction as she looked up at him and rose to kiss his lips. He thought about her, her sexy body, all the things he felt for her, how long he'd wanted her, but nothing was enough to distract him from what he'd fantasized about for practically the entirety of his shitty life.

Fuck!

"Cord?"

He opened his eyes, seeing the question in her eyes. Right. Ember wasn't comfortable with being the aggressor and he was fucking frozen. Damn it. He was ruining everything.

He quickly unlatched his belt and yanked down his zipper. Hands trembling, he caught her fingers and folded them around his cock, forcing her to stroke him hard. He shut his eyes, unable to face the questions seething in hers.

Her fingers firmed, tugging at his needy flesh and he let go, stretching back and putting his weight on his arms as he pumped his hips into her touch.

"Keep going." He was being a greedy, demanding prick, but he couldn't slow down. Slowing down meant thinking.

"Harder," he gritted and her hold tightened.

Behind his eyelids, images of Austin flashed and Cord wondered what the other man was doing. Was he watching her? Watching him?

"Your mouth, Ember. I need your mouth."

Her touch stilled and then fell away. He blinked. His gaze shot around the room, but he didn't see him. Austin was gone. Where the fuck did he go?

Wet heat closed around his dick and he groaned—his focus back on Ember. His hand cupped the back of her head and pushed her lower. Fuck. He was in her mouth! He wasn't going to last very long.

The sound of heavy footfalls had his eyes shooting open. Austin—now totally fucking naked and wearing every fucking sit-up he'd done that spring—met his gaze and held up a foil packet, placing it on the end table. Condom. Jesus. They *were* going there.

Ember turned, her lips pulling away as Austin interrupted the quiet by shoving the couch back. He sent his wife a wink and her mouth closed around Cord again.

"Fuck," he rasped, unsure how he should touch her with Austin watching them. Her mouth was so skilled and it was impossible to think when she took him to the root.

"It's the...strangest thing, seeing you with her," Austin said, his eyes on Ember.

Cord panicked and nudged her away. She lifted her head, lips glossy and swollen, a confused look in her eyes.

"I didn't mean stop," Austin quickly said, when Ember looked at him in alarm. "It's fine, baby. I just meant... it's... similar. Seeing you with Cord, it's a lot like you and me."

Cord let out a breath as Ember's shoulders markedly relaxed. How the fuck was her husband not jealous? The Austin he knew had always been territorial as hell, especially when it came to Ember. Christ, Cord couldn't even deny it pissed him off when she paid too much attention to Austin—her husband—so why wasn't Austin feeling the same?

"Should I keep going?"

Cord blinked and realized she wasn't asking Austin, but directing her question at him. A swell of masculine pride rushed through him and he nodded. "Yes."

She bent forward and placed a kiss on the side of his cock and a surge of pleasure lengthened his spine. He covertly watched Austin through his lashes and drew in a deep breath as Ember's hot mouth again engulfed him.

The corner of Austin's lips twitched in what almost seemed the start of a grin, but then he turned and moved behind Ember. His attention was solely devoted to his wife, so Cord focused the same.

Cord's fingers trembled through her hair as he kept his voice low. "That feels incredible, Ember. Suck harder."

She hummed and glanced up at him through thick lashes. His heart stuttered. This was really happening and nothing would ever be the same.

He stripped off his shirt and brushed a finger down her shoulder, "Let me take my pants off, sweetheart. Don't go far."

She pulled back and he stood, stripping quickly. Austin's groan rumbled and she kissed him. Cord's nostrils flared as he stared at them, finding something incredibly erotic about the other man taking her lips in a passionate kiss, considering where her mouth had just been.

They pulled apart and she crawled back to Cord, unrefined temptation. Jesus. He sank into the carpet, stretching out his legs, and braced his weight on his arms. She smiled as she fit between his knees.

"I'm back."

"So you are..." Nothing about the day came without shock.

"Did you want me to..."

So shy. So submissive. He loved it. "Damn right. Nice and deep, like you were doing."

Her cheeks flushed as she returned to his cock, his eyes going wide as she did something extraordinary with her tongue. Austin moved in closer behind her. His friend didn't pay him any mind as he stroked a gentle hand over Ember's ass.

She moaned over his cock and Cord realized Austin was pleasuring her. Unsure where to focus, he eased his back to the carpet and worked his fingers through the fine strands of her hair as she gave him the best blow job of his fucking life.

Everything was going incredibly well until he felt her concentration slip. Cord angled his shoulders off the floor and stilled. Austin's torso stretched as the muscles in his toned arms bunched and his hips thrust against hers, his face contorted in undeniable ecstasy as he filled her.

She moaned, the sound vibrating up Cord's cock and pulling back with a tight suction. Holy shit. They were both inside of her. Another thrust and she rocked over him, his cock going deeper in her throat.

Fuck. It was as if he could feel Austin's every advance, catch the reverberation of his strength through her. The connection was indescribable.

Another hard thrust of his friend's cock and Ember gasped, her lips opening around Cord's flesh as she panted and Austin doubled his pace. The sound of his friend's balls slapping against her little ass teased his senses and her breath beat against his dick. She could hardly get her mouth around him, being jostled as she was, but fuck, he was about to blow.

"Ember..." He brushed a finger down her

cheek, trying to give her some sort of warning, but Austin was fucking her so hard she'd given up blowing him, simply hanging on. Her tits slid over his cock, rubbing, grinding.

Fuck this. He grabbed her by the arms and hauled her up his body.

Austin drew back as Cord pulled December to him, sealing his mouth on hers. He wanted inside, but there wasn't time. The simple brush of her wet pussy over his thigh and he trembled like an inexperienced first timer and came on his own belly.

Before he had a chance to cover the mess, her body pressed into him and the strange sensation of wiry hair abraded his leg. His head jerked back, breaking the kiss and she cried out as Austin shoved back inside of her. His eyes widened as his friend dropped his weight over them, catching his balance as he landed on his palms, setting them on either side of Cord's head.

Cord didn't know what to do, so he simply held her, his lips against her hair, cradling her to his shoulder, as she moaned with everything Austin gave. He couldn't look away, couldn't stop staring at the muscles cording his friend's neck, and the sinew twisting his arms as he pounded into the woman they loved. Such ownership, such dominance. So. Fucking. Sexy.

His body jerked as more come pulsed in a rapid surge from his cock, caught between his and

Ember's sweaty bodies. He was fucking coming on himself—*again*. What. The. Fuck?

Austin grunted as Ember let out a long cry, her nails digging into Cord's shoulders as her head tipped back. A hard thrust and Austin collapsed. He rolled to the side and lay panting.

Ember slid off of him, their skin sticky, and fit her body into the narrow space between him and Austin. She kissed her husband then turned back to him, her lips pressing to his cheek. "You'll stay, won't you?" she murmured.

Stay? He debated if giving them some breathing room might be wiser. "I don't know."

Austin levered up on an elbow, the ease he'd worn all night suddenly replaced with a scowl. "You have a room here."

"Austin—"

"She invited you to stay."

Looks like I'm staying.

Nineteen

Cord

YOU HAVE A ROOM HERE.

What the hell was he doing? Cord shut the guest room door behind him and squeezed his eyes shut. This was so fucked up.

His hand closed around the knob. He couldn't do this. This wasn't what he wanted when he prayed for a way to be with December again. He should get the fuck out.

Glancing down at his body, he winced. He couldn't go anywhere like this. With a growl, he dropped his clothes on the bed and yanked a towel off the rack as he entered the bathroom. Evidence of Ember's return was everywhere, because he and

Austin sure as fuck never folded the towels, nor were they ever this soft after they washed them.

He was under the water before it had a chance to warm, rethinking his sanity and wondering what they were doing on the other end of the house. He experienced none of the emotions he had the last time he and Ember were together. Except that wasn't true. The love was there, and the passion, but now they were muddled with other desires he couldn't face and nothing about his body felt remotely relaxed.

He couldn't get his memory off Austin's cock shuttling in and out of Ember's sweet pussy. He groaned and rubbed his belly. He couldn't let either of them know he thought about such things.

Recalling Austin's naked proximity with the woman they both loved between them... How she didn't keep them apart but joined somehow... He shook his head. It should be twisted and wrong yet he couldn't think of it that way.

All the years of denying the truth about how much he felt for Austin... So many years. Best friends, best everything. Ember hadn't come between them because Cord wouldn't let anything separate them. It hadn't taken long before he loved her too. Shit, he'd loved her from the start. What they did tonight, it ripped off too many carefully guarded layers of denial he'd built over the years.

The temptation of having a place with them—always—was like offering a cold glass of water to a man dying in the desert sun. He could have Ember, be with her, but he'd never have them both. So while one thirst would be quenched, he'd still feel like he was dying.

It didn't matter how many times they shared her. He'd already jumped to the pathetically hopeful conclusion that it would inevitably happen again, but he'd never have Austin.

Cord frowned. Had he even had *her*? Everything had been so intense, so pivotal, it just occurred to him *they* hadn't had sex. Shit. His entire perception took a turn, minimizing what seemed colossal only moments ago.

Disjointed thoughts paraded through his mind and he leaned his head against the wall. Ember's trusting eyes. Austin's hard cock, his muscles flexing as he fucked his wife...he'd never forget the sight.

He desired both of them. Passionately. As much as he wanted to pleasure Ember, he also wanted to suck Austin's dick. Shit, actually thinking those words... This was a dangerous place to visit, even if only in his head.

Would he be able to take it up the ass? His mind screamed *no*, that wasn't him, but then his dick twitched, saying something very different. Cord shut off the water, nearly snapping the valve off the wall. He roughly buffed his skin dry and untangled his clothes. When had he ever gotten ahead of himself like this? Never fucking ever. Because this was a one-off. Despite his assertions the day before.

I gotta get the hell out of here.

The uncensored fantasies kept coming. Heat flushed through his body and blood thickened his cock as it struggled to rise against the fabric of his jeans.

A bitter laugh scalded his throat. Austin might be some kind of pervert for starting this, but Cord could only imagine the look on his face if he found out about *his* inclinations. But it had to mean something that he'd never felt such things for other men. Only for Austin.

Or maybe that was worse, because of all the women he'd been with, he'd never cared for anyone the way he did December. What if his affection for her had taken root because of his love for her husband? Except... God he was fucked up. Of all the people in the world, he was in love with the two most unavailable ones.

But wait... Hadn't December said it was only Cord she wanted, besides Austin of course, and that her husband wouldn't consent to anyone else? Maybe this was like that, selective. What a fine fucking trio they were.

He palmed his cock through his jeans, trying to soothe the ache, seeing as he couldn't ease his mind. What next?

Heavy footfalls rapidly climbed the stairs and he took a step back from the door just as it flung open. Austin's face was determined and Cord frowned, unsure if this was the part when he got his ass beat.

"What?" he asked, defensively, as Austin backed him toward the corner. "What the fuck—"

When his friend's mouth closed over his, grip tightening around Cord's neck, his entire body tensed. He shoved at Austin's chest and ripped his mouth free.

"What the fuck are you doing?" Jesus, was he that obvious?

Austin's nostrils flared as he stared at him. "Checking something."

Cord dragged his arm across his mouth. "What the fuck were you trying to check? My tonsils?"

Austin panted, glared at the wall, and then turned back to Cord. "Kiss me."

"No! What the fuck, man?" *I want to so badly.* This had to be a trap.

Austin glared at him. "I saw you watching me."

His insides froze. "I was looking at December." *Liar. Tell him. Take the fucking chance. Nothing can get any worse.*

"Liar!"

"Austin, fuck, I wasn't looking at you. And even if I was, it wasn't in that way." Jesus, he was such a fucking coward.

His friend's lips pressed tight as he glared at

the wall again. This was why he couldn't tell the truth. Austin was practically seething, his brow tight with suspicion and his body braced with tension. Admitting anything would be a huge mistake.

"You felt nothing?" his friend growled, eyes narrow and observant.

"Not...for you." Cord caught his breath, already trying to recall where he'd left his keys so he could get the hell out of there. The lies never stopped hurting. "We cool?"

Austin swallowed and shook his head as though still not trusting his words. "I..." His turbulent gaze lifted, whiskey brown eyes troubled, as he looked Cord right in the eye. "I can't say the same," he quietly confessed.

Cord stopped breathing. Couldn't move or even blink.

Austin's broad body dropped to the edge of the bed as if his knees had given out. "This makes no sense."

Cord frowned, terrified that he'd just misheard. "You...felt something? For me?" His heart pounded so hard against his chest he could feel each solid thud down to his fingertips.

Austin shook his head. "When you were touching her, when she was sucking you off, I wanted to touch you right along with her. I never felt anything like that before."

"Maybe you misread—"

"No. I know what I felt."

He had to fend him off. This could devastate December. They had to think about her first. "Austin... I'm not gay."

He laughed. "Neither am I. Or so I thought. I'm not sure there's a label for this." His eyes met Cord's and Cord fought the urge to look away. "Let me kiss you. I'll be gentle."

"Jesus!" he snapped, turning away from him and kneading the back of his neck. The heat of his friend's body encroached on his back and he stilled. "Austin. You need to step the fuck back— right now." *Before all hell breaks loose and we ruin everything.*

Hands, large and masculine, closed over his biceps. "I love you for what you did for us. For me. For her," he whispered and Cord closed his eyes.

His breath became an audible beat between them as it sawed out of him. "I love you too, man, but not that way." *Liar. Pants on fire.*

Austin shifted closer and Cord froze at the foreign feeling of a man's body pressing against him. It was too fucking strange. He stepped forward, but Austin's arm banded over his chest, halting his escape. Cord shoved his arms and spun out of his grip.

"Seriously, get a fucking hold of yourself!" The more he felt exposed the higher his defenses climbed.

Austin's palm flattened over his thundering

heart, his fingers curling toward his pec. "Imagine if the three of us could figure out how to be one. Think of how easy that would make all this. How it could fix everything."

He batted his touch away and jerked back. The wall met his shoulders. "I'm not into—"

His words caught at the dejected look in Austin's eyes. Would December accept that? Him and Austin?

"I've always loved you, Cord. After everything...you did... Everything tonight... You can't call it simple friendship. It's more than that. She knows it. I know it. Don't tell me you can't see it. There's something...more. I feel it." He swallowed and glanced down and Cord so badly wanted to soothe him, but couldn't seem to move or even admit he loved him too—*more*—no *maybe* about it. His friend had the courage of a lion and he was the one with the straw brain. "I don't want to lose you," Austin whispered.

His resolve faltered. "Austin, we can't put her through any more than she's—"

"I think you should kiss him."

His attention jerked to the door where Ember stood. Fucking great. Just. Fucking. Great. Now *she* knew. "Ember, this isn't me—"

"Are you sure?" She drifted further into the room. "Maybe it could be you, Cord. Maybe it's in both of you. Look how long your past is. Consider how much you two have been through."

He searched her face for upset, but saw only warmth and acceptance "We're not gay. Neither of us."

She shrugged. "No harm in being one way or the other. And no harm in kissing if you're secure in who you are. If you feel nothing, then you feel nothing. But…"

He was in a parallel universe, or maybe in a blindingly erotic dream. He didn't give a shit about anyone's sexual orientation and neither did Austin. He did, however, care about their relationship and feared gambling with it once more.

But maybe it was time he quit making excuses. Because everything he wanted was suddenly within reach and nothing was stopping him except for his… What? The room suddenly seemed claustrophobic.

He rubbed his forehead and mumbled. "This is not fucking happening."

She stepped closer and he edged back, afraid to fall under her spell. She arched a brow, and ran her hands over his chest, the cotton sleeves of the robe she'd donned falling away to reveal her slender forearms. Cord had always been fascinated by that part of a woman's anatomy, so sleek, not defined like a man's strength, yet so capable.

"He's a good kisser, Cord."

God, the simplest touch from her felt incredible. "I think we have enough issues without adding to the pile."

"Does it repulse you?"

No. The total opposite. "We're just friends." He was starting to sound like a broken record. What lame excuse would he give next?

She bit her lip. "What if I told you I wanted to see you two kiss?"

He glanced at Austin. He might be curious, but Cord *knew*, had known for almost twenty years.

He didn't want to be some lab rat for them to experiment on. It would hurt too much when Austin realized everything he felt was some displaced emotion for Ember. It was too dangerous. His heart seriously couldn't take one more crack.

"Please," she whispered and he shut his eyes. She pulled his hand and led him toward the bed. "Just try. Sit down."

Letting her take the lead, he dropped to the mattress and kept his eyes closed, the heat from Austin's thigh burning through the seam of his jeans. Slowly, Ember crawled onto his lap, straddling him.

"Start by kissing me," she whispered as her lips hesitantly teased his.

Cord's hands slid over the robe, landing on her soft ass as his mouth slanted over hers and his tongue probed deep. He couldn't resist her, couldn't resist either of them, though he tried. His ship was going down.

She rode the ridge in his pants and his hands

undid the belt of her robe, shoving the covering away. If this was where it ended, he needed to have her one last time. He would not be led, and needed to regain some semblance of control.

"Put me inside you, Ember."

She stilled, his head leaning against hers as he waited, needing her to do what he asked without looking to Austin. She must have recognized something in his eyes and realized how important this was. Her hand slid between them and the button of his jeans popped loose.

He wanted to look at Austin. He wanted...

She tugged at his jeans and he hitched up so she could shove them down. Her heated flesh teased his aching cock. "Condom?"

A crackle of foil rent the air and Austin was there, package in hand. She opened it and pinched the end, working to sheath Cord's straining erection. She rolled it downward with tantalizing brushes of her hand.

Glancing at Austin who was watching his wife's sheathe him, Cord's cock pulsed and he suppressed a shudder of need. That sly little look almost had him coming before anything started. What the hell was wrong with his stamina today? He needed to control himself.

Ember released him and he jerked his attention back to her face, catching the shy smile pursing her lips. His grip guided her down, his eyes rolling back in his head as her wet heat tightened around his cock.

"Fuck. Ride me, Ember," he whispered, leaning forward to kiss her passionately.

Her body rocked over his, all her soft spots dragging against his harder points. His spine tingled as his senses came alive. She fit him so well, perfectly.

Her breasts brushed against his chest and he struggled to remove his shirt, wanting to feel her skin to skin. Austin was suddenly there, helping, his big hands pulling Cord's shirt off the rest of the way. He felt himself twitch as Austin's touch lingered, stroking his back.

Cord shuddered and nearly came. Ember leaned back and Austin's fingers curled around Cord's neck, urging him forward, into her chest. Dipping his head, he captured her sharp nipple in his mouth, distracted by the feel of his friend's fingers caressing his nape. She moaned as he sucked the tip tight between his teeth and flicked the edge with his tongue.

His free hand reached for her other breast and he froze. His eyes flicked open at the feel of Austin's hand already holding her there. He deliberately set his hand over Austin's and their gazes locked.

Ember moaned and Cord was torn by the need to fuck her or face everything he might lose.

His friend removed his choice, leaning in to press his mouth against Cord's.

So much at stake, he instinctively pulled back, but Austin's hard grip held the back of his neck, not allowing him an escape.

"Austin, don't..." he begged without conviction, his words muffled by that mouth he'd craved for years.

"Just try," his friend whispered, his firm lips pressing Cord's. Austin's tongue forced its way in and Cord whimpered, actually whimpered.

Awash with the sensation of clever lips working his own, he gasped as Ember's pussy tightened around his cock. Austin's tongue teased deeper and Cord couldn't manage all the overwrought emotions assaulting him.

It was too much. Ember tightened her muscles, her snug channel sucking at his begging cock. Austin shoved his fingers through Cord's hair, getting a good hold on the tangled curls. The loss of control shook him, and he took it right the fuck back.

With Ember on his lap, impaled on his cock, he devoured Austin, taking what he'd wanted for more than a decade. The taste of him was like coming home, dark and earthy, and he reveled in it.

Austin sighed against the onslaught and pressed closer. Ember shuddered and wreathed her arms around their shoulders. Her climax triggered his own, and he emptied himself into her with painful intensity, dragging his mouth away. Austin drew back, and Cord might have laughed at the shock on his face.

"Well?" Austin rasped.

Throat constricted by too many unrecognizable emotions, Cord tightly nodded.

Ember rested her cheek on his shoulder and sighed.

Austin's startled features smoothed over and a smile curved the corners of his swollen mouth. "Me too," he whispered.

Ember's hand reached for her husband's, and Cord's attention snagged on their wedding bands. He tried not to think too hard about what such symbols represented. Her other hand reached for his fingers and squeezed. "I love you both."

He looked into her eyes and she smiled—it was the first time in a very long time that he saw genuine joy on her face. It was how she used to look, before...

And just like her husband, Cord would do anything to keep her happy. He'd do anything to make *either* of them happy. "I love you too...both of you," he rasped.

Austin's smile curved against his shoulder as his gusty laugh, full of satisfaction, heated Cord's skin. "Me too."

Maybe they were still a little lost, but they were together. There might come a time to atone, but right now, in this moment, they were all together.

TO BE CONTINUED...
Read THROB (Addicted to You 3) Now!

Are you follow Lydia Michaels?
Stalk her on <u>TikTok</u>, <u>Instagram</u>, <u>Facebook</u>, <u>Goodreads</u>, and <u>BookBub</u>!
<u>TikTok @LydiaMichaels</u>
<u>Instagram @lydia_michaels_books</u>
<u>Facebook @LydiaMichaels</u>
<u>Goodreads</u>
<u>BookBub</u>

JASPER FALLS

Wake My Heart *

The Best Man

Love Me Nots

Pining For You

My Funny Valentine

Side Squeeze

CALAMITY RAYNE

Calamity Rayne Gets a Life *

Calamity Rayne Back Again

Calamity Rayne Gets Hitched

BONUS: Calamity Rayne Veiled & Railed

Calamity Rayne Over the Moon

Calamity Rayne Knocked Up

THE SURRENDER TRILOGY

Falling In

BreakingOut

Coming Home

Ruthless Billionaires

One Billion Secrets *

Two Billion Enemies

MASTERMIND

Blind

Untied

NEW CASTLE

First Comes Love *

If I Fall

Shattered Vows

ADDICTED TO YOU

Crush *

Bang

Throb

THE ORDER OF VAMPIRES

Original Sin *

Dark Exodus

Prodigal Son

Immortal Bastard

Primal Kill

Blood Moon

STAND ALONES

La Vie en Rose

Simple Man

Sugar

Breaking Perfect

Hurt

Protege

anteed to leave readers with many book hangovers.

Lydia is the consecutive winner of the *2018 & 2019 Author of the Year Award* from *Happenings Media* and the recipient of the *2014 Best Author Award* from the Courier Times. She has been featured by *USA Today, Romantic Times Magazine,* the *Women in Publishing Summit,* and more.

Michaels started her author career in 2007, becoming a recognized presence and advocate within the publishing industry. She is the CEO of LMC Consulting, a certified author coach specializing in character and plot development, and the founder of the *East Coast Author Convention,* the *Behind the Keys Author Retreat,* and www.LydiaMichaelsBooks.com.

She is happily married to her childhood sweetheart. Her favorite things include cooking Italian cuisine, hosting extravagant dinner parties, sipping espresso martinis, listening to her husband play piano, and escaping to her coastal home on the Jersey Shore. She's an LGBTQ ally, a BLM supporter, a firm believer that the patriarchy must end (women's rights are human rights), and an advocate for pediatric cancer research.

LYDIA

Follow Lydia Michaels on social media!
Facebook | Instagram | TikTok

Thank you for your review!

Reviews help authors so much! If you left a review for this book, I greatly appreciate it!
Thank you,
Lydia

Click here to leave your review!